SECOND CHANCE BRIDE

This Large Print Book carries the
Seal of Approval of N.A.V.H.

SECOND CHANCE BRIDE

JANE MYERS PERRINE

THORNDIKE PRESS
A part of Gale, Cengage Learning

Detroit • New York • San Francisco • New Haven, Conn • Waterville, Maine • London

GALE
CENGAGE Learning

LIBRARY OF CONGRESS CATALOGING-IN-PUBLICATION DATA

Perrine, Jane Myers.
    Second chance bride / by Jane Myers Perrine. — Large print ed.
        p. cm.
    Originally published: New York : Steeple Hill, c2009.
    ISBN-13: 978-1-4104-1871-5 (alk. paper)
    ISBN-10: 1-4104-1871-5 (alk. paper)
    1. False personation—Fiction. 2. Texas—Fiction. 3. Large type books. I. Title.
PS3616.E79S43 2009
813'.6—dc22   2009018633

Published in 2009 by arrangement with Harlequin Books S.A.

Brethren, I count not myself to have apprehended: but this one thing I do, forgetting those things which are behind, and reaching forth unto those things which are before, I press toward the mark for the prize of the high calling of God in Christ Jesus.

— *Philippians* 3:13–14

This book is dedicated to
Betty Davis Lynn,
who has been a friend for longer than I
can remember. Thank you for all these
years of friendship and your Christian
example.

Also to two friends and
critique partners:
Ellen Watkins and Linda Kearney,
who keep me headed in the right
direction.

And, as always, to my husband George
for his love and support, even when he
hated hearing those three little words —
I'm on deadline.

PROLOGUE

Central Texas, 1885

Annie MacAllister's father had always told her she'd never amount to anything because she never thought anything through. Maybe he was right. Maybe that's how she'd ended up in this swaying stagecoach while a disapproving woman glared at her in disgust and a dumpy man across from Annie leered.

Only an hour after the stagecoach left Weaver City, she tried to disappear, to shrink back into the hard bench of the stagecoach. She heard the elderly woman mutter, "Common."

Annie knew why the woman said that. Annie wore a cheap dress, tight across the bodice and fraying at the cuffs. Her long hair curled over her shoulders, and she wore paint on her lips and cheeks.

The expression on the man's face showed that he knew exactly what Annie was — an immoral woman who'd worked in a brothel.

What he didn't know was how much she'd hated every minute of it — how she'd been forced into it.

Next to Annie sat a young woman who wore an undecorated black straw hat and a plain, gray cotton skirt. Her matching basque was trimmed with what had been a crisp white collar when she got on the coach but was now limp and soiled from the dust of the trip.

"Is this your first trip in a stagecoach?" the young woman asked Annie in a soft, educated voice.

Well, if that wasn't a surprise. The woman actually spoke to her in a friendly way. "Yes," Annie answered, then added, "ma'am."

"Mine, too." She smiled. "My name is Matilda Susan Cunningham." Miss Cunningham spoke clearly, just like Annie's mother had, although that was so long ago it was hard for Annie to remember.

"Miss Cunningham." Annie nodded. "I'm Annie MacAllister."

"Where are you going, Miss MacAllister?" Miss Cunningham asked.

"Trail's End."

"I'm going there, too." Miss Cunningham nodded. "Will your family meet you?"

Annie shook her head.

"My employer will meet me," Miss Cunningham said.

"Not your family, Miss Cunningham?" Annie almost bit her tongue. She should know not to pry.

"Please, do call me Matilda, won't you?"

Annie nodded, delighted by the attention of this kind woman.

"No, my family won't meet me." Matilda sighed. "My parents died when I was thirteen. My brother, only two months ago. That's why I had to find employment."

As Matilda looked out the window, Annie realized that they looked a little alike. They both had dark hair and dark eyes, and were tall and thin, although she'd noticed when they'd waited for the stage that Matilda carried herself proudly while Annie hunched over.

When the coach stopped at a home station, all the passengers got off and entered the small frame building. Annie gazed yearningly at the beans and greasy meat the cook stirred and slapped on a tin plate.

"One dollar," said the station agent.

She only had three dollars and fifty-one cents to last her until she found work. She was hungry but not hungry enough to spend a penny yet. She went out to the

11

porch and washed her hands in the pewter basin.

"Would you share some of this meal with me?" Matilda stood on the porch with her plate. "I don't believe I can eat all of it. If you don't mind helping me, I would appreciate that."

Wasn't she the nicest lady? To make charity sound as if Annie were doing a good deed for her. "Thank you, Matilda."

"Let's say a prayer first." Matilda bowed her head. "Dear Lord, we thank You for Your bounty. We thank You for leading us into new lives and know You will be with us wherever our paths take us. Amen."

Annie had been so startled she hadn't had time to bow her head before Matilda began to pray. She hadn't heard a prayer since her mother's funeral. Matilda's prayers were probably answered. God hadn't bothered to grant any of Annie's.

As the afternoon wore on, the pitching and jolting of the coach changed to a rocking motion, and everyone slept. At a stop in Rotain, the leering man left. An hour after that, the disapproving woman got off with one more glare at Annie. Oh, how Annie wished people could see her for the person she was, not for the deeds she'd been forced to commit to survive.

Well, that was the very reason she was on this coach. When she couldn't stand her life for one more day, she'd pulled together every penny she'd saved. Most of it had gone to buy the ticket to Trail's End, a town the ticket agent said no one ever visited. Once there, she'd get a new job, maybe cleaning houses or even working in a shop. She'd live an upright and respectable life and wouldn't have to put up with slurs and lecherous glances.

Matilda and Annie were alone on the last leg of the journey. They chatted for a while until the warmth of the coach caused Annie to fall asleep. She dozed until the lurching of the vehicle woke her with a start.

The motion flung her against Matilda, then tossed them both against the door on the other side of the coach. Annie grabbed the leather curtain and held it tightly, but Matilda's flailing hands couldn't grasp anything to keep her from ricocheting around the interior. She was thrown hard against a window. Then she smashed into the door on the right side and it made a loud crack and opened wide. The young woman flew from the carriage, screaming in pain and terror.

For a few seconds, Matilda's screams continued.

Then the cries stopped. Completely.

The coach finally came down on the right side with a terrible crash. Annie's ankles twisted beneath her, and her head hit the door frame.

Dust billowed up and engulfed her. Tears ran down her face, mixing with Matilda's blood, as well as her own, as it streamed from a cut on her head. Silence shrouded the coach until a man shouted from above her, "Are you all right in there?"

"I'm —" Annie croaked. She swallowed and said in a shaking voice, "I'm alive but the other woman —" She sobbed, the words catching in her throat.

The driver opened the door above her, reached down and pulled her up. The pain in her arm was sharp.

Once she stood on the road, Annie looked at herself. She was covered in blood and grime, her pink dress smeared with splatters and splotches of red while blood stained her sleeve as it dripped from a gash on her arm.

"What happened?" she asked.

"Wheel came off. Spooked the horses," the driver said. "I'm going to have to ride to town to get a new one." He looked inside the coach again. "Where's the other passenger?"

"Back there," Annie said, and pointed fifty yards behind. Fresh tears rolled down her dirty, scraped cheeks. "She fell out."

In spite of the pain, Annie ran toward Matilda, who lay absolutely still. "Matilda," she whispered as she took one of her friend's limp hands.

"No use." The driver shook his head. "She's dead, ma'am. Looks like a broken neck."

Annie sobbed. Matilda had been nicer to Annie than anyone in years. *She'd* had a future. Someone would meet her in Trail's End and help her get settled. Someone expected her. She'd been on the way to a place where she'd begin a new position, where she'd be respected and admired.

How sad that a decent, upright woman with a future had died and left the woman who'd worked in a brothel behind. It should have been Annie. She had no future. No one would miss her. No one cared about her. No one even knew where she was.

Annie should have been the one to die.

"Do you know her name, ma'am?"

As she stood there, Annie remembered the words of that haughty passenger, how people had called her terrible names for years, how men always tried to take advantage of her. Memories of all the slurs and beatings and sins that were her life assailed her. Annie would never be able to get away from that. Never. No matter what jobs she found or how far she traveled, people would always recognize Annie as the woman from the brothel, cheap and sinful and beneath them. Women would judge and men would leer.

She didn't want that following her for the rest of her life.

She took a deep breath and held it for a few seconds before she said, "Her name was Annie MacAllister."

CHAPTER ONE

"I am Matilda Susan Cunningham." Annie said clearly as she stood on the deserted street — the *only* street — of Trail's End and considered her words. Matilda had spoken like a woman of education, exactly the way Annie wished she spoke. Oh, not that she hadn't tried to improve her speech. She was a natural mimic. Her father used to say she put on airs. Then he'd hit her.

"*I* am Matilda Susan Cunningham," Annie repeated, enunciating clearly.

The wind blew dust in Annie's face, then swirled down the street and around the dry goods and grocer's store on her left. Behind her was a rickety building, maybe a hotel. It looked as if the wind could knock it over.

Across the street, the dust blew through the doors of a saloon flanked by a bank and a small building that looked like an office. The sheriff's, perhaps. Further down the street huddled a few more little white build-

17

ings, all nearly hidden in the approaching dusk of early evening.

At the end of town stood a church. At least she thought the small white building with a squat tower was a church, but it might be a school or a home.

That was all.

If she lived here long enough, she'd learn what all the buildings were, but now she wanted nothing more than to go wherever that unknown employer was supposed to take her. Every part of her body ached. The scrapes on her legs and the bump on her head throbbed while the wound on her arm continued to bleed.

And she was afraid, deathly afraid. What would happen if no one came? If her masquerade were discovered? So many ifs and so few certainties.

In her hand, Annie carried Matilda's purse. Inside, she found two letters, a clean handkerchief, a comb, seven dollar bills, a few coins and some pennies. Including Matilda's meager savings, Annie now had a total of ten dollars and eighty-six cents. How long would that last?

The wind continued to blow down the rutted main street, pulling Annie's hair from its tight bun. It swirled around the prim blue skirt she'd taken from Matilda's satchel and tried to lift it above her now properly shod feet.

Trail's End really was the end of the trail.

As she searched the street for signs of her employer, Annie thought about the accident. After the driver left for the new wheel, she'd checked on the injured guard who lay unconscious by the coach. Then she'd changed into Matilda's clothing and picked up the woman's new valise. When the men returned, they loaded Annie and the guard into a wagon.

"What about . . . about Miss MacAllister?" Annie had asked.

"We'll come back and bury the woman out here. No room in the wagon," said the driver.

With that, the wagon took off. During the ride to town, the poor guard moaned with every bump in the rough road. Annie had tried to calm him, but her experience with men had been of an entirely different nature. She used to sing to her father before his drinking got bad, so she tried singing to the guard, softly, songs she had learned as a child from her beautiful but fragile mother. The guard quieted.

After leaving the injured man at the doctor's farm, the driver had brought Annie into town and abandoned her in the middle

of the street. At her feet sat the small valise
that contained everything Annie now
owned. She'd stood clutching her purse and
looking around for at least an hour, attempting to decide what to do.

While she waited, the sun dropped behind
the horizon and the breeze grew cool. Had
Matilda been mistaken when she said someone would meet her in Trail's End? Annie
looked up and down the street, but it was
still deserted. No sign of anyone.

When a light went on above the saloon,
Annie glanced up where she saw shadows
moving behind the windows. She knew who
they belonged to and knew that the women
in those rooms were looking down at her,
wondering who she was. Annie straightened
her back and lifted her chin.

"I *am* Matilda Susan Cunningham," she
said.

She considered sitting in one of the chairs
on the porch of the hotel but feared they
were reserved for guests. If no one showed
up, would her money buy her a bed for the
night? Probably. However, with no idea of
what her future held, she couldn't afford to
spend even one penny.

But someone was coming for her. Matilda
had said that.

Annie picked up her right foot to ease the

pinching caused by the oxfords she'd taken from Matilda's body. She'd hated doing it, but she figured a generous woman like Matilda would have wanted her to. At least, she hoped so. The wind blew down the street again, colder after sunset.

When it was dark, a few men rode into Trail's End, tied their horses and entered the saloon. Without hesitation, Annie turned away from them and picked up her valise. She hurried as fast as her aching legs would take her toward the hotel and the comforting light that spilled out from the open door.

She decided she didn't care if someone from the hotel tried to run her off. She was staying. She dropped the valise and lowered herself onto a chair. Perhaps she would have to spend the night here. She shivered again.

"Miss Cunningham?"

She'd fallen asleep, she realized. With a shake of her head, Annie attempted to wake up. Who was this Miss Cunningham? She quickly realized that she was Miss Cunningham and she jumped to her feet, every joint in her body complaining.

"Yes, sir," she said, ignoring the pain.

In the light streaming through the open door of the hotel, she could see the man. Handsome but serious, tall and strong, clean shaven with thick black hair and a square chin. Concern showed in his blue eyes. Solemnly, he studied her face for a moment, which made her want to turn away, to escape his perusal. Then she remembered who she was and stood up, tall and proud.

"I'm sorry you have had such a wait," he said in a deep, commanding voice. "The stage was supposed to bring you to my ranch. I didn't hear about the accident until I arrived in town to look for you. I hope you haven't been too uncomfortable."

He reached for her, and she started to leap away out of habit until she realized that he was reacting to the blood on her sleeve.

"You've been hurt, Miss Cunningham."

"A few bruises and scrapes. This," she said, looking at her arm, "and a cut on my head." She leaned against the chair to steady herself.

He surveyed her, his eyes moving from what she thought must be a bruise on her cheek and to the blood on her sleeve and skirt. "Let's get you back to the ranch."

She started again when he leaned forward, but he'd only picked up her valise. Of course.

"Is this all your luggage?"

"Yes, sir." She looked at his back as he strode away toward a trim little surrey, then hurried after him. He carried nearly every-thing she had, and she didn't even know who he was or the location of the ranch where he was taking her.

"And you are?" She lifted her head and spoke in the tone that she thought Matilda would use in this situation, strong and certain, despite the hunger, exhaustion, fear and pain competing for her attention.

"I'm sorry." He turned back toward her. "I'm John Matthew Sullivan, a member of the school board and president of the bank. Certainly you know that from my letters."

He smiled at her, an expression that showed both confusion and concern, a smile that so changed his stern visage that it might have warmed her except that she knew how easily men's smiles could come and go. Instead she said, "Oh, yes. Your letters." She put her hand on her forehead. "It has been a difficult day."

"It must have been." He placed the valise on the floor of the vehicle. "Do you feel well enough to start school tomorrow?"

She stopped, one foot inside the surrey, the other on the ground. She couldn't move as she struggled to make sense of his words. "Start school tomorrow?" she repeated.

She didn't want to go to school. What kind of school would there be in such a tiny place? What would they expect her to study and why?

"I know it's soon, but the students are so glad you're here. Because it was so difficult to find a qualified teacher, they've been out since the term ended last April. They're eager to get started again."

Teacher? I'm a teacher?

Oh, dear. Annie bit her lip. Matilda had been a teacher.

"Are you all right, Miss Cunningham?" he said, studying her closely.

She placed her hand on her aching head. No, she was not all right, but she was not going to tell Mr. Sullivan that and destroy her chance to sleep in a bed tonight.

"It's obvious you're exhausted. We'll postpone class until Wednesday so you may rest."

"That would be nice."

He handed her into the surrey, touching her arm for a moment to steady her. Then, as she settled herself in the carriage, he smiled at her, a flash of warmth lighting his eyes. Annie quickly looked away. She did not like it when men smiled at her that way. It made her want to run.

"You may have noticed that Trail's End is not a large town, but the people are friendly." He got in on the other side of the

24

surrey and snapped the reins over the horses. "This area is beautiful in the spring."

The carriage was splendid, new and shiny with leather seats. The matched bays trotted in time with each other. Obviously Mr. Sullivan was a wealthy man.

"Where are we going?" Here she sat, in a vehicle with a man she'd never met, heading off to who-knew-where. Curious and frightened, she wished she could have read those letters Matilda had carried in her purse. "Is the ranch far?"

He looked at her again with a puzzled glance. "As I told you in my letter, you'll live in a room that adjoins the schoolhouse. It's located just a few minutes from my home and about as far from town."

The bays frisked along the road. After only a few minutes, he slowed and turned between stone pillars. "This is my ranch, the J bar M." He pointed at a sign over the drive.

J bar M. Annie carefully studied the sign. "The J bar M," she said.

In silence, they rode down a smooth dirt drive and turned onto a rougher trace. They traveled only a minute or two before Mr. Sullivan halted the surrey.

"Here we are." He jumped from the vehicle.

Annie searched both sides of the road

until she spotted a stone building on the edge of the clearing, partially hidden by trees.

"Miss Cunningham?"

His voice startled her, as did the way he addressed her. She must get used to her new name as quickly as possible. With a jerk, she looked to her right where he stood ready to hand her down from the carriage. What would Matilda do in this situation? No one had ever helped Annie from a surrey. In fact, she'd never been in a surrey, but she'd seen enough to know she shouldn't leap out on her own.

She suddenly remembered the mayor's wife in Weaver City getting out of their wagon. She'd put her hand in her husband's and let him steady her as she descended. So that's what Annie did. As soon as she was on the ground, he dropped her hand and stepped away, smiling at her again with that look in his eye.

She'd seen that expression flicker in men's eyes before, but those were rude men, men who frequented saloons or tried to take advantage of young women in the stage-coach. Mr. Sullivan seemed different, up-right. She must have misunderstood his smile, his warm gaze.

Scolding herself, she lifted her gaze to

study the building for a few seconds. "It's very pretty."

"Yes, it's made of gray limestone, quarried only a few miles from here." He picked up her valise. "My wife chose the material shortly before her death," he said matter-of-factly.

Along the side of the building were three windows with clear glass that reflected the light of a bright moonrise.

"I'll go inside and light a lamp." He headed toward the building, going up two steps before disappearing through a door. In no time, a glow from an oil lamp shone softly through the windows.

As Annie entered, she saw six rough benches, each with a narrow table in front of it, and a desk — oh, my, *her* desk — in the front of the room, on a little platform. Stacked on the desk were a pile of slates and another stack of books of various sizes. The sight alarmed her.

"This is the schoolroom," Mr. Sullivan said, "as, I am sure, you must have surmised."

Surmised. Annie rolled the word around in her mind. It had such a weighty feeling. "Yes, I'd surmised that." She nodded.

He motioned toward a narrow room at the other end of the building. "That's the kitchen. You'll warm the students' lunches there and may use it to prepare your own meals."

So that's how schools did things. "How many students are there?"

Even in the faint glow of the lamp, Annie could see his puzzled expression. He must have written Matilda about that, too. "Twelve. Not a terribly large group to teach, but they are in all the grades from one through seven."

"I'd forgotten." She nodded again, precisely, a gesture that seemed to belong to her new character.

"Your bed and drawers for your personal accoutrements are through this door," he said as he put the bag on the floor in front of it.

Accoutrements. Another word to remember. "I have few accoutrements."

"There is a door to the outside in your room." He pointed. "The facility is behind the building."

She nodded again.

"Several of the mothers cleaned the building to prepare for your arrival. You have a new mattress, several towels and clean bedclothes."

"How nice of them. I must thank them."

"I'll leave you now to settle in. The children will arrive at seven-thirty on Wednesday. I trust you will be ready for them?"

"Yes, Mr. Sullivan."

"A lamp is on your desk with a box of matches next to it." For a moment, he studied the bruise on her cheek and her arm. "Miss Cunningham, may I send our cook, a fine woman, to help you with your wounds?"

"Thank you, but I'll take care of them myself. I'm very tired."

He nodded. "Then I'll wish you goodnight."

"Good night, Mr. Sullivan."

His hand brushed her arm as he moved to the door. At the contact, he stopped and glanced at her as if trying to decide whether he should apologize, and then he turned away quickly, opened the door and closed it behind him.

A woman could fall in love with a handsome, caring man like that without trying, but not Annie. No, she'd learned a great deal about handsome men and ugly ones, and she didn't trust either. With a shake of her head, she told herself to forget her past. It was over, and she was ready to start her new life, preferably without any men, handsome or ugly.

She surveyed the amazing place to which

her deception had led her. For a moment, being in a schoolroom made her feel an utter lack of confidence until she reminded herself she was no longer Annie MacAllister and straightened her posture. She was Miss Matilda Cunningham, the composed and educated schoolteacher of Trail's End.

Well, she would be for at least a few days, until someone discovered she was *not* Miss Matilda Cunningham. During that time, she'd be warm and fed and safe, which was enough for now. With that bit of comfort, she picked up the lamp in her left hand, pushed the valise ahead of her with her foot and entered her bedroom.

It was tiny, but it belonged to her, at least temporarily. Even as her muscles protested, she turned slowly around the small space and smiled. It was hers alone! The narrow bed had been pushed against the rough, wooden inside wall. Two hooks hung beside the window, and a dresser stood next to the door out to the privy. When she placed the oil lamp on the dresser, the light wavered. Was it low on oil? Slipping her shoes off, she thought a sensible young woman would go to bed before it got so dark she would *need* a lamp.

But a sensible young woman would not find herself in a position like this. Annie lowered herself onto the bed and contemplated the fix she'd landed herself in when she'd assumed Matilda's identity.

No, a sensible young woman would not find herself teaching school when she didn't know how to read or write.

CHAPTER TWO

John Matthew Sullivan snapped the reins over the heads of his horses as they trotted down the short road between the school-house and his home. He'd chosen the pair carefully — they had exactly the right stride to pull the surrey he'd had built to his specifications. Painstaking and cautious described him well, characteristics passed on to him by his father.

But for him, the value of the animals lay in their magnificence and spirit, the sheer beauty of their matched paces and movement.

Beauty. His thoughts came back to the new teacher. Although he'd investigated her references carefully and heartily recommended Miss Cunningham to the school board, tonight he hadn't felt completely confident about the young woman who was to teach his daughter and the children of the community. She'd written fine letters, had exceptional recommendations and excellent grades from the teachers' college. However, this evening she'd behaved oddly, seeming uncertain and confused.

Of course, she'd just been in an accident, one in which another young woman had died. She had a wound on her arm. Bruises, cuts and blood covered her.

Small wonder she was distressed and flustered. She was understandably upset from her experience. So what flaw could she possess that now nagged at him?

He slowed to allow an armadillo to saunter across the road and considered the question.

She was too young and too pretty to be a teacher. Under the grime — in spite of it, actually — she was very attractive with thick, dark hair and what he thought to be rich, brown eyes. As a respectable widower and pillar of the community, he shouldn't have noticed that. As a man, how could he not?

Of course, Miss Cunningham wasn't as lovely as his dear wife, Celeste, had been, but even with the dark bruise on her cheek, he could see her features were regular and, well, appealing. But definitely not as fine as Celeste's had been. His wife, alas, had been a fragile woman. Miss Cunningham appeared to be the opposite.

Even with the stains on it, her dress had been modest and ladylike. Her speech had been clear and precise, the tone well modulated. Neat and clean and a good example for the girls in her class. That was strictly all that mattered about the exterior of a teacher.

But she seemed so very young. Although Miss Cunningham had written she was twenty-three, she didn't look over twenty. Of course, there are people like that, who look younger than they are in actual years.

Miss Cunningham seemed like a moral young woman, not the kind of young woman who flirted with men like the previous teacher. Twice when he'd approached Miss Cunningham, she'd pulled away. She'd seemed almost afraid of him, but that was to be expected from an honorable young woman.

And yet something bothered him, something besides her looks and age. He couldn't nail down what it was. It had something to do with her reaction when he mentioned that the students were eager to start class. Surprise, almost shock. Even her confusion after the accident couldn't explain that to his satisfaction.

He'd visit with her tomorrow and see if

he could discover what troubled him. He'd allow her to teach for a few weeks. If she didn't measure up to the standards of the school board, well, actually, they could do nothing. It had taken months to find a teacher of quality like Miss Cunningham. No one wanted to come to Trail's End. The school board had been fortunate to find someone who needed a position as much as they needed a teacher. It would be impossible to find another this year.

"*Buenas noches,* Señor Sullivan," Ramon said as his boss drove into the stable.

"Ramon, what are you doing out here so late?" He stepped out of the surrey and tossed the reins to the man. "You should be home with your family."

"*Gracias, señor. El viejo* fell today. I made the old man rest."

"Duffy fell?" What was he going to do about Duffy? After he was thrown from a horse last year, John had given him the easiest job on the ranch to keep him safe. He might need to hire another man to take the load off Ramon and keep an eye on Duffy.

"Tried to put a bridle up on a hook. Lost his balance and fell off the bench he was standing on."

"I'll check on him," John said. "I still don't expect you to work these long hours.

Understand?"

"Sí, señor."

"After you finish with the horses, go home to your family."

As he spoke, John started toward the small room in the back of the stable where Duffy Smith lived. He preferred the room in the stable to sharing the bunkhouse with the younger, rowdier hands.

The elderly man had taught him everything he knew about caring for animals. He'd always worked hard. Too proud to rest at seventy, he still expected to do his share. That caused John no end of trouble and worry, but also made him proud. He'd probably be exactly the same in thirty-five years.

The room was barely large enough for a narrow bed, small table and a dresser. A lamp glowed in the corner. Duffy's skinny body could barely be seen under the colorful quilt Celeste had made for him,

"All right, Duffy. What's this I hear about you?" John held up his hand as the older man struggled to get up. "Don't try to get out of bed. Stay there."

Duffy's expression was sheepish behind his full beard and thick mustache, both streaked with gray. "I'm fine." He shook his head. "Stupid bench threw me, boss."

Just like Duffy to blame it on the bench. He hated getting old as much as John hated watching it happen. "Do you have everything you need?"

"The boys took real good care of me. I'm going to have a good night's sleep, and then I'll be back to work in the morning."

John shook his head. "You are the most stubborn man I know. Would it hurt you to rest for a few more days?"

Duffy glared at him. "Yes, boss, it would. I'm tough."

"Stubborn old coot." John shook his head. "I give up." He turned toward the door and said over his shoulder, "Take care of yourself."

"Always do, boss," Duffy retorted.

Once out of the building, John headed across the stable yard to enter the house. He climbed the stairs and with a few strides down the hall, he entered his daughter's room. He knew that with the trip to town and helping the new teacher to settle in, he'd be home too late to see Elizabeth before bedtime, to tuck her in and hear her prayers. But he wanted to see her anyway.

Silently, he moved across the floor until he stood next to the bed and watched her sleep, the moonlight illuminating her innocent face. With a smile, he leaned down, kissed her cheek and smoothed the blanket over her shoulders.

Elizabeth had always been more his daughter than Celeste's. With her endless energy and constant chatter, she'd worn her mother out, but he'd loved riding with the child, reading to her and caring for her as she grew up.

How have I been so blessed to have this beautiful child?

As he readied himself for bed, he thought again of the new schoolteacher, unable to rid himself of the nagging doubt. How to handle the situation, to assure the community — and himself — that Miss Cunningham had been the correct choice, even though she'd also been the only choice?

He'd keep an eye on her until he felt comfortable. For his daughter's sake, for the sake of all the children in the community, he would make sure all was right with the new schoolteacher. After all, he'd accepted the challenge to find a teacher. He'd hired her. He was responsible.

He was a Sullivan.

Pain — excruciating pain — and the sensation of turning and twisting, of lurching and rocking racked Annie. She grabbed the side of the coach and reached out for Matilda.

But the young woman wasn't there. With a sob, Annie woke up and attempted to sort out where she was and what had happened, why her right arm, her head and both legs — in fact, her entire body — hurt so much.

It was early morning. She knew that by the tendril of sunlight breaking through darkness to illuminate a narrow strip of ceiling. In the distance, a rooster crowed. In the dim light, she could make out something dark that stiffened her right sleeve. When she rubbed the cloth between her fingers, it crinkled. Blood, she realized.

Her arm throbbed. The blue skirt had wrapped itself around her legs. She shrieked in pain as she tried to untangle herself.

Most amazingly, she was alone on a clean bed in a room with white walls, spotless white walls. No sound of raucous celebration came from the other side of the wall.

"Oh, Lord," she whispered when she realized where she was and why. If this wasn't a moment to pray, even if she didn't expect any response, she didn't know what was. "What should I do, Lord?"

Her stomach growled — not surprising since she'd last eaten with Matilda almost a day ago.

How could life change so quickly and completely? It felt peculiar to know that the driver of the coach had buried Annie MacAllister out there, but here Annie sat in Matilda's clothes, on her bed, in her schoolhouse and with her name. Annie couldn't change any of that.

She looked around and realized she'd slept exactly where she had fallen across the bed last night, fully clothed, not even pulling the sheet over her. Her stomach reminded her again that she hadn't eaten anything before she'd dropped into bed.

Shivering in the cool morning air, she stood and stretched before she padded into the kitchen barefoot. She hated the thought of having to shove her feet into those sturdy little shoes. Why couldn't Matilda's feet have been just a bit larger?

That thought sounded so ungrateful. "I truly am appreciative, Matilda," she whispered. "Thank you." Then she shuddered. Taking the shoes off the feet of a dead woman had been one of the worst things she'd ever had to do.

In the cupboard above the stove, she found a can of tomatoes and an empty cracker tin. The other cupboard was bare except for several dead crickets and a shriveled piece of something Annie couldn't identify but wasn't hungry enough to try.

She'd eaten less than tomatoes for breakfast before, but at least she'd had a can opener then. Now she didn't. Certainly no one expected her to go without food, although never having been a teacher before, she didn't know. She thought Matilda would have brought food with her if that had been a requirement. Perhaps she could find Mr. Sullivan's house and ask him.

She picked up the bucket by the door of her bedroom, carried it outside and filled it from the pump in the yard, moving carefully. She saw no firewood so went back inside, took off her clothing and washed in cold water. Nothing unusual there. When she finished scrubbing off the grime and carefully cleaning the wounds on her arm and head, she put her bloodstained clothing in the water to soak.

Then she turned toward the valise. She hadn't had time the previous day to do more than pull a skirt and basque from the suitcase. Today she needed to see what else was inside. She took a deep breath. She did not look forward to exploring Matilda's personal effects. Taking on the identity of a dead woman had been more difficult, complicated and emotional than she'd ever considered.

Inside were two dark skirts, simple and austere with a pleat down the back, like the

41

one she wore. One was brown and the other black. She pulled out two matching basques, each with new white collars and worn but spotless cuffs, and hung them next to the skirts. Under them, Annie found a lovely white jersey with a short braided front and jet beads around the high neck. For special events, Annie decided as she stroked and savored the softness.

Then came a black shawl, a pair of knitted slippers, several pairs of black cotton stockings, five handkerchiefs, a few more hairpins, a sewing kit and a small box. Reluctantly, she opened the little package. Inside she found a silver watch to pin on the front of her basque. When Annie ran her finger over the engraved vines, tears began to slide down her cheeks. This must have been the teacher's prized possession.

She set the watch down and forced herself to continue. In the bottom of the bag were two books, a notebook filled with writing and many little pictures and another letter. Annie was completely overwhelmed. She'd never had so many nice things. She'd never owned cotton stockings or a cashmere jersey or any jewelry.

Annie put on the black skirt, buttoned the basque up the front and then pulled on the slippers. With no mirror in the little room, she smoothed her hair back into a bun as best she could.

Then she wandered into the empty school-room. She didn't want to be there — and yet she did, very much. She was curious and excited and more than a little afraid with absolutely no idea how she would teach twelve children what she herself did not know. But she felt safe here. She would soon have wood and coal and perhaps something to eat.

She touched the books on her desk and opened one. What did those black marks stand for? She ran her hand down the page as if she could absorb their meaning. The paper felt rough and cold. The circles and lines and odd curlicues printed there fasci-nated and confounded her. Here and there she recognized a *J* and an *M*.

A yearning filled Annie. She'd always wanted to go to school. She remembered her mother telling her she was smart when she was just a child.

But after her mother died, her father said educating a woman was a waste. After all, he'd said, what more does a woman need to know than how to clean and cook and sew? She didn't need to be able to read to take care of a man.

That was about all Annie needed to know.

As her father drank and gambled more, she'd had to work to support them. Only seven years old, she started cleaning houses. If she didn't earn enough for his whiskey, he beat her until she learned to leave the money on the porch and sleep outside.

Then he'd killed a man in a drunken rage, was hanged and the house was sold to satisfy his debts. When no one would hire George MacAllister's daughter, she realized she had two choices: starve to death or become a prostitute. She chose to work at Ruby's, a brothel.

She brought her attention back to the book. Wouldn't it be marvelous to learn? To read books about distant places and exciting people and thrilling adventures, to be able to read aloud to children or silently to herself, to write letters or a story?

Oh, it sounded more wonderful than any fantasy . . . but that was all it was. Soon, very soon, the school board would find out she couldn't read or write and nothing would save her. From what she'd seen, she didn't believe Mr. Sullivan would be kind or forgiving when he found out about her deception.

"Excuse me," came a sweet voice from outside as the door opened.

"Yes?" Annie turned to look down on a

tiny, fairylike creature with a heavy basket. Behind the child stood a Mexican man. She straightened and walked toward the little girl.

Light hair curled from beneath the hood of the child's green plaid coat. She looked up at Annie with enormous, intelligent blue eyes and a smile that sparkled with humor.

"Good morning, Miss Cunningham. I'm Elizabeth Sullivan. This is Ramon Ortiz."

The child struggled across the threshold, carrying an enormous basket. Annie would have taken it from her, but Mr. Ortiz caught her eye and shook his head, smiling.

Elizabeth dropped her burden by the door to the kitchen. "My father sent us with some things for you. He thought you might be hungry. And we brought you a blanket because the nights are cold."

Annie hadn't noticed the cold the night before because she'd been exhausted. How lovely to have a blanket. "Thank you."

Mr. Ortiz followed Elizabeth and placed a bundle on one of the narrow tables.

"How old are you, Elizabeth?" Annie settled on a bench so she and Elizabeth would be face-to-face.

"I'm almost eight, Miss Cunningham."

"What do you like most about school?"

"Reading. I love to read. And to write."

Of course the daughter of the man who hired her would love to do the things Annie couldn't. "Do you like to do sums?"

Elizabeth grimaced. "No, ma'am, but I will try. My father says women should be able to add and subtract."

"Of course we should." That was one thing she could do, thanks to keeping track of how much the men who frequented the brothel owed. That and her piano playing had made her popular with the other women there.

The little girl marched into Annie's bedroom to spread the blanket on her bed, tugging on it to make sure it hung squarely. She stopped to brush a little dust from the dresser and pushed the outside door more firmly shut. The child acted with such grace and helpfulness, as if she were an adult, that Annie smiled.

"I asked Ramon to place the food in your cupboard." Elizabeth frowned as she looked around the tiny bedroom. "I don't know why you couldn't have curtains or a pretty quilt."

"Thank you, but please don't worry about it, Elizabeth. This is the nicest room I've ever had."

Elizabeth's eyes grew round, but she was too polite to ask Annie how that could be.

"My father and I hope you'll enjoy Trail's End. All the students are excited to meet you tomorrow. Most of us like school a great deal."

"Thank you, Elizabeth. I look forward to meeting them." Annie walked into the classroom. "Would you tell me something about each student?" She congratulated herself on sounding so much like a teacher — or at least like her concept of a teacher.

The child stopped to think a moment before she started counting off the students on her fingers. "There are the Sundholm twins, Bertha and Clara. They're only six so just babies. This is their first year in school. Tommy Tripp and I are in the second grade. We can both read and are learning cursive. Do you have a nice hand, Miss Cunningham?"

Annie looked down at her fingers. They were long and thin but covered with calluses from hard work and cuts from the accident. Her palms were red and rough. Why had the child asked if she had a nice hand? And what was cursive? What did it have to do with her hands?

When Annie didn't answer, Elizabeth continued, "Rose Tripp and Samuel Johnson and Frederick Meyer are in fourth grade. The Bryan brothers are all much older but

47

still in the fifth reader because they miss a lot of school to help their father on the farm. There are three of them, but you won't see much of Wilber because he's almost sixteen and really strong. Martha Norton and Ida Johnson are in seventh grade. They know everything." She stopped and thought, her head tilted. "I could make you a list if that would help."

"I can tell you'll be a great help to me."

"Doña Elizabeth, I've finished putting the food away." Mr. Ortiz came into the schoolroom, carrying the empty basket. His voice was soft and respectful with a lovely lilt to it.

"Thank you, Mr. Ortiz," Annie said.

"I'm Ramon, Señorita Cunningham." He bowed his head. "Mr. Sullivan said he told you in his letters that each family contributes a wagonload of wood once each term. They stack it in the shed behind the schoolhouse." He nodded his head in that direction. "Mr. Sullivan sent me with a load so you'll have some when you need it. And I put a small pile next to the stove."

"Thank you, again."

"The shed's where students who ride put their saddles. They tie their horses on the rail outside it," Elizabeth explained as she moved toward the door. "Please excuse me.

48

My father expects me home right away."
She started out before she turned to say,
"Oh, and we'll bring you a loaf of bread
every week from our cook." She smiled.
"I'm so excited about school tomorrow. It's
been a long time since we had a teacher."

"Thank you, Elizabeth. See you tomorrow."

When they left, Annie entered the kitchen,
ravenous. On the table lay a can opener.
She opened one cupboard to discover it
filled with tins, dried meat and a loaf of
bread. A lower cabinet held a sack of oat-
meal and another of potatoes. In the other
cabinet were two plates, three glasses, a cup,
knife, fork and spoon plus some bowls.
What luxury!

The crickets and dried fruit were gone.

She felt incredibly fortunate, blessed with
an abundance of belongings and a feeling of
freedom, even though she knew it would
last only a short while — a few days at most.

For the first time in years, she possessed
enough food to last for nearly a week. More,
if she rationed it carefully.

She considered lighting the stove but doing it with only one arm would be difficult.
Besides, she didn't want to waste any more
time when she had so much to learn. With
a tug, she opened the drawer, took out a

knife and sliced a piece of bread. She was about to take a bite when she remembered Matilda's prayer at the coach stop. If she were to be Miss Matilda Cunningham, she should say grace, even though it didn't come easily. "Thank You, Lord, for this food and for this place. Amen." She nodded, pleased with her first effort.

Her meal finished, she pulled her desk over to the window and studied each book. Hours passed as she copied the letters from a primer. She had to use her left hand because her right was nearly useless. However, she covered the slate with crooked lines and uneven circles that improved as the afternoon advanced. She pressed hard on the pieces of soapstone, writing each letter again and again until the soapstone shattered and her hand cramped. After she finished copying all the letters over and over, she scrutinized them and wondered what she had written.

One of the books showed the letters attached together in a beautiful, flowing wave. Wouldn't it be wonderful to make such lovely lines? Well, she wasn't ready yet. She returned to her straight lines and circles, wondering how on earth she would get through her first day as a schoolteacher.

■ ■ ■ ■

That evening as she fixed her dinner — her third meal in a row of bread and cold canned tomatoes — she heard a knock at the door. She looked down at her food. The knock came again, louder and more insistent.

"Miss Cunningham," Mr. Sullivan shouted, and knocked again.

"Yes, sir." She abandoned her meal and went to the door. There stood Mr. Sullivan and a beautiful young woman.

Annie had never seen anyone as lovely. She had golden curls that fell from a knot on the top of her head, her eyes were a deep blue and sparkled with fun and her smile showed dimples in both cheeks. She wore a blue robe that matched her eyes and, Annie could tell, was beautifully made and very expensive. She was someone's pampered darling, Annie guessed.

"Good evening, Miss Cunningham." He nodded as Annie motioned them in. "I came by in case you have questions before school begins." He turned toward the young woman who was wandering through the classroom. "May I introduce you to Miss

Hanson? She's the daughter of our neigh-
bor."

The young woman turned and gave Annie
such a warm smile that she couldn't help
but return it.

"Won't you call me Amanda? I shall call
you Matilda, and I believe we will be great
friends! You must forgive our rudeness for
dropping in on you unannounced." Amanda
took Annie's hand. Annie hardly knew how
to respond to the beautiful whirlwind. "I
accompanied John because he's very proper.
I'm acting as his chaperone tonight."

"Amanda, I don't believe —" Mr. Sullivan
started to protest.

"But I wanted to come," Amanda continued. "I admire you so much. I've always
believed education is important, but I'm
afraid my poor brain is barely able to hold a
single thought for any length of time."

"Do not allow Amanda to mislead you."
He nodded as the beautiful young woman
floated toward him and placed her hand on
his arm. "She is an intelligent and sensible
young woman."

"Sensible? Oh, John, you certainly know
better than that." She patted his hand before
turning toward Annie. "I truly do respect
your education and your ability to work with
children, Matilda. I wish I had some talent,

any talent."

"Oh, I feel sure —"

"Alas, I fear I'm but a useless butterfly." Her sweet smile turned her statement into a shared joke. "But John said he needed to stop by here before we join my father for dinner. I will excuse myself so the two of you may discuss education and such." Her curls bounced as she flitted toward the teacher's desk.

"How are you feeling, Miss Cunningham?" Worry showed in his eyes. "I hope you've recovered from the accident."

"Yes, thank you. I'm much better." His sympathy warmed her a bit. "Although I fear I will not be able to write for a few days," she said, glancing at her right arm.

"I'm sure the children will understand." He cleared his throat and appeared slightly uncomfortable. Annie suddenly felt nervous. "Miss Cunningham, when we spoke upon your arrival, I felt that we may not have communicated well."

"Oh?" What did that mean? Surely he couldn't have found out what she'd done already, could he?

"When I found you at the hotel, you didn't seem to remember much of the information I had sent you."

"I am sorry I seemed confused. With the

53

accident . . ." She motioned toward the bruise on her face.

"Of course, but I want to make sure you have no misunderstandings about the expectations of the school board. May I sit down?" He settled himself on a bench, leaning on the table before him. Annie had little choice but to sit with him, though it was the last thing she wanted to do. He pulled a paper from the leather case he carried.

"Do you remember all the requirements stated in your contract?" He handed it to her. "This is the agreement you signed last month."

As he leaned forward she could feel the warmth of his breath on her cheek and smell the scent of bay rum cologne. She took a deep breath as an unknown and confusing emotion filled her.

She swallowed, closing her eyes in an effort to regain her balance. When she opened them, the gaze that met hers was icy cold and hard. Chiding herself for allowing her thoughts to roam, she took the sheet from his hand and looked at it. She recognized that there were different sections and a signature at the bottom. Feeling that Mr. Sullivan wouldn't lie to her and having no recourse if he did, Annie nodded and handed the paper back.

"I would like to review the points with you, Mr. Sullivan. Would you read them one by one?" she asked. "So we can discuss them if necessary? Just to make sure I understand them all."

He glanced at her, puzzled, but began to read. "The agreement says that you will receive the sum of thirty-two dollars per month and lodging during the school term."

Thirty-two dollars a month! Oh, my, it's a fortune! She could save it to live on when she had to leave, if she lasted a month. She could buy a ticket to another destination, she could buy a good dinner and . . . oh, she could buy shoes that fit!

He continued. "You will teach for six months per year for three years, with four holidays each year. If you wish," he said, glancing up at her, as if gauging her understanding, "you may sponsor an extra term in the spring. When school is not in session, you may live in the building for the sum of three dollars a month if you clean the schoolhouse."

"All right."

"You agree to arrive by the fifteenth of October — well, you're already here, so that point is moot. Next, you will not associate with people of low degree, who drink alcohol, use tobacco or play cards."

She nodded again. She didn't plan to do any of those things or associate with anyone who did.

"You agree to go to meetings of the school committee when you are needed."

"Of course."

"You are not to marry while you are in the employ of the school."

"I have no intention of marrying." She had no need for a man, gentle or not.

"You are expected to be a member of and contribute your knowledge to the Trail's End Literary Society."

Oh, dear, what did that mean? Well, it was too late to balk now. "Yes, sir."

"You will attend church every Sunday, and prayer meetings, as well."

She couldn't do that. Although Matilda would go to church, Annie wasn't good enough — not nearly good enough — to frequent God's house.

"Miss Cunningham?"

She looked up to see him scrutinizing her, eyebrow raised. "Of course."

"Fine." He smiled. "You have met my daughter, Elizabeth?"

"Yes, she's a lovely child."

"She and I will pick you up Sunday morning." He glanced back at the papers he held. "Finally, the contract lists your duties. You will start the stove on cold mornings, you will help students with their lunches and have them clean up afterward, you will sweep and mop the classroom every evening and you will teach all classes to a level deemed acceptable to the school board at the end of each term."

"Yes, sir. Thank you." She nodded. "I'm glad you reminded me of those duties. Lighting the stove will be difficult with the injury to my arm. Could someone help me?"

"I'm sorry I didn't consider that. I'll send Ramon down in the morning to light it until you are able."

"What time does school start?"

"As I told you yesterday, at seven-thirty. Out at two-thirty. Many students help with chores on the farms in the morning and after school. They may arrive late or have to leave early."

"Of course." She nodded as if she remembered that.

He placed the paper back in his case as he stood, contemplating her solemnly. "You have come to us highly recommended. Your references state you are a woman of high moral character."

She nodded again and vowed to be exactly that kind of a woman, if God would just teach her to read and write overnight.

"We hope you will do better than the previous teacher. She was an incurably giddy young woman who ran off to marry a young farmer after teaching for only three months. I hope you don't anticipate doing that."

"No, sir. I'm not the least bit giddy," she answered truthfully.

"I'm sorry Amanda and I bothered you." His eyes rested on her face for a moment before he glanced away. "As I said, I feared you might have forgotten some of these points and wished to make sure that we were in agreement before school began."

"Thank you. That accident —" She pressed her hand against her temple, which still throbbed.

"John." Amanda approached them. "It's getting late. I'm sure my father's getting hungry. You know what a bear he can be when he doesn't eat on time."

Annie smiled at Amanda's description of her father.

"You are quite beautiful when you smile," Amanda said. "Oh, my, I've done it again." She lifted her shoulders and bit her lip. "It sounds as if I think you are not beautiful when you don't smile. I didn't mean that at all. Just that you are even prettier then." A dimple appeared in Amanda's lovely ivory cheek. "It was wonderful to meet you, Matilda. I shall see you again very soon, I'm sure." She moved toward the door with a rustling swirl of her skirt. "Come, John. I have no desire to face my father when he's hungry."

He glanced at Amanda with affection, then looked back at Annie. "I believe everything is in order for tomorrow. Ramon will come down to light the stove, and I'll ask his wife, Lucia, to help with the lunches until you are used to the routine and your wounds have healed."

"Thank you, Mr. Sullivan." She rose as he took the other woman's arm and turned to leave.

But Amanda hadn't finished. She pulled on Mr. Sullivan's arm. "John, I cannot agree with this 'Mr. Sullivan' and 'Miss Cunningham' nonsense. You're going to be working so closely together and the three of us are going to be such good friends." She turned to Annie. "You must call him John and he should call you Matilda." She nodded decisively, as if she had taken care of the entire problem.

"But that wouldn't be proper," Annie said.

Mr. Sullivan turned toward Annie with an amused smile. "You'll learn that Amanda is not at all proper."

"John!" Amanda protested.

"But she is headstrong and stubborn and won't let this go until we agree with her decision."

"Well, yes, *that* is true." Amanda nodded. "You might both as well do what I've asked."

"But I feel most uncomfortable . . ." Annie objected.

"Miss Cunningham," John began, then paused as he mentally changed her name. "Matilda, you might as well give in. Amanda will push until she gets her way. And she always gets her way."

Amanda smiled smugly.

"Yes, sir," Annie said, then forced herself to add, "John." Although the use of his first name seemed much too familiar, it didn't feel as odd as she'd thought.

"There." Amanda clapped her pretty little hands. "Now we are all friends." She waved and pulled John toward the door. "Excuse us. We must hurry or my father will have started to eat the furniture."

Annie stood in the doorway, watching through the rapidly falling dusk as John assisted Amanda into the surrey, holding her elbow as if she were precious porcelain. Amanda accepted his care as her due, then waved at Annie as the vehicle moved toward the ranch house.

Amanda was a lovely woman. Oh, Annie wished they could be friends, as Amanda seemed to think they could. She easily pictured Amanda having a friendship with Matilda, but not with Annie. Annie felt stuck between her two identities as she closed the door and walked between the tables in the schoolroom. She was no longer just Annie MacAllister, and she wasn't entirely Matilda Cunningham, either.

John had seemed solemn and judgmental — just a little — but he'd been concerned for her. An odd combination, but she hoped it meant he would give her a chance.

"Tomorrow," she murmured. Tomorrow evening, would she still be here? Would the children find out their teacher couldn't read or write? Would she be on a stagecoach out of Trail's End by evening?

Or would she have another day — perhaps another week — of food and warmth and safety?

Oh, please God. She offered up another prayer, still fairly sure it would make no difference. *Please grant me at least a month, just long enough to get one check and find another place to live.*

CHAPTER THREE

Nine faces turned toward Annie, smiles on their lips, their eyes sparkling with excitement.

She'd never felt so guilty before. Had she known her deception would rebound on the nine eager students before her, she wouldn't have . . . Yes, she would have because she had to escape, to find a place to live. But she regretted the consequences and was sorry she didn't have the ability to give these children what they expected and needed.

She glanced down at the silver watch she'd pinned to the front of her basque. It made her feel like a teacher. Seven-thirty. Time to begin.

"Hello, class. My name is Miss Cunningham. I'm your new teacher." Annie stood on the platform and looked at each student. Every child's face glowed with happiness and anticipation.

Hers was the only one in the room that

didn't. For a moment, she considered confessing her deficiencies and running from the schoolhouse. But where would she go?

The children kept their eyes on her, probably expecting her to do more than just stand on the platform in front of the classroom. Annie forced herself to say something. "Why don't you introduce yourselves?"

A slender girl with dark, tightly braided hair stood in the front row to Annie's left. Like all the girls, she wore a long-waisted dress with a lace flounce and black boots. A few covered their dresses with Mother Hubbard aprons.

"I'm Martha Norton. I'm in the seventh grade." Martha nodded at a plump young woman with her dark hair pulled into braids with far less perfection. "This is Ida Johnson. She's in the seventh grade also. We help the younger children," she added proudly with a lift of her chin.

"Thank you, Martha and Ida." In her mind, Annie repeated the names as she smiled at both girls.

Two boys stood in the second row on Annie's right. Boys on the right, girls on the left — they had arranged themselves that way as soon as they entered the classroom.

"I'm Frederick Meyer," said a boy with short blond hair. He wore what seemed to be the boys' uniform: a round-necked shirt in plaid or stripes with trousers that stopped just past the knees and boots. "This is Samuel Johnson," he said, introducing the boy next to him. "And that's Rose Tripp." He pointed at the redheaded girl.

After the other children introduced themselves, Annie said, "We're short three students this morning."

"The Bryan Brothers," Martha said. "You won't see much of them, Miss Cunningham. They have to help on the farm. When they come, they're usually late. Wilber misses a lot. He's almost sixteen and his father doesn't see any reason why —"

"Thank you for all that information, Martha. We'll welcome them back when they are able to return." She paused and looked around the class. "I need to tell you something else." Annie pointed at her right arm. "Children, you may have heard I was in an accident on the way here."

They all nodded.

"Because I hurt my arm, I'll be unable to write for several days. I've been practicing with my left hand and am not very good, so you'll all have to help me."

They nodded again.

An hour later, Annie was enjoying listening to the buzz of activity in the classroom as the students worked together.

"A, B, C, D," chanted the first and second graders while Martha and Ida held up slates with those letters written in strong, firm strokes.

Annie stood behind the group and studied the lesson with much more interest than any of the students, willing herself to pick up everything the older students taught the younger ones. She traced the letters on the palm of her hand, attaching sounds to the memory of the letters she'd practiced, hoping she would remember them that evening.

She looked over Martha's shoulder as the girl gave math problems to the fourth graders and watched the students write the numbers, studying how they formed them on their slates. She'd practice them that evening, as well. By the time Lucia came to help with lunch at noon, Annie had learned a great deal.

The children had brought their lunches to school in pails, and they sat outside in the warm October sun to eat with their friends.

Lucia brought plates for both Elizabeth and Annie. "I'll bring you lunch every day," she said. "And I'll wash your clothing as I have for all the teachers. I noticed when I put another blanket in your room that there is a dress soaking. Is that the one you were wearing when you were injured?"

Annie nodded.

"Then I'll clean and launder it, as well."

"Thank you." Annie felt so spoiled. To show her appreciation, she'd buy Lucia something when she was paid. If she was still here. If she got paid at all.

After lunch, the boys kicked a ball around while the girls tossed hoops to each other, laughing and shouting. Fascinated by their energy and joyful abandon, Annie watched from a bench by the clearing.

When the children came back into school at one o'clock, she glanced at the watch and wondered what she would do with them for another ninety minutes. How would she fill the time? She'd already taught them everything she knew. Almost everything.

"Children, do you want to sing?"

The girls nodded; the boys shook their heads. Annie laughed. She closed her eyes and tried to remember the songs her mother had taught her, deciding which ones the children would enjoy.

"White wings, they never grow weary," she began. When she finished the chorus, she opened her eyes to see rapt expressions on the students' faces — even the boys.

Elizabeth and Ida smiled and clapped, and Martha said, "Oh, Miss Cunningham, that was so beautiful. Please sing more."

"I'll sing again, but this time, you have to sing with me."

Although the boys grumbled, they joined in. She taught them all to sing the chorus and had begun to teach some harmony on the verses when she looked up to see John Sullivan at the door. He wore an odd expression, a mixture of admiration and surprise.

"Miss Cunningham." He nodded at her. "Children." They nodded back at him.

"I came by to pick up Elizabeth and to ask how your first day of teaching went. When I approached the school, I heard your wonderful music." He nodded. "I wasn't aware singing was one of your talents."

"Thank you. The children seemed to enjoy it."

"You didn't mention your musical ability in your letter of application."

"I didn't realize it would be of interest." She smiled and turned toward the students. "Children, you may go now. I'll see you tomorrow."

Eight of the students grabbed their lunch pails and dashed from the building while Elizabeth ran to her father and held her arms out. He reached down to pick her up and envelop her in a hug, his expression softening.

Annie titled her head to watch the two, the love between the often stern banker and his daughter obvious.

"Miss Cunningham is a wonderful teacher. She's really good at math," Elizabeth said, and grimaced, her lips turned down.

"Not your favorite subject," he said.

"No, but it was all right. And we helped her write because of her arm, you know."

"Yes, sweetheart, we're sorry about her arm." John gently placed her back on the ground. "Would you please go read for a few minutes? I need to talk with Miss Cunningham."

Oh, dear.

"Thank you for coming by," Annie said. "The day went well, I believe. We got to know each other, and I began to measure the levels of each child in mathematics and reading."

"After I heard you singing, I couldn't help but wonder — do you play the piano or organ?"

Annie looked around the schoolroom, in case she'd missed such an instrument in her post-accident fog, but there was none. "I play the piano and have played the organ, but I don't read music. If someone sings the melody for me, I can play anything."

"A most talented young woman. I'm sure Reverend Thompson would like to talk to . you. We're in need of an organist at church."

At church? Annie playing the organ in a church? Oh, no. She didn't think so. She shouldn't even be inside a church let alone to help in the service. No, she wasn't fit for that.

"I don't think I should. Thank you, but I'd need to practice and wouldn't like to take time away from the children or from preparing their lessons."

"We have both a piano and a fine organ in our house. You may practice there. Perhaps you could even teach Elizabeth a few tunes. Of course, the church pays only a pittance. It may not be worth your time."

She glanced up at John. She wanted to tell him that money was not the problem, but she could hardly explain the real reason for her reluctance. "It's not the money at all. I just thought — the children. I'm so new, and I do have responsibilities here."

"I don't mean to push you, but you'll be at church every Sunday. And if you're there already . . ."

He smiled. The expression softened his

69

features and distracted her. Might have even attracted her . . . if she were a different woman with a different past.

"You have no idea how much we need a musician." He shook his head.

"Well, yes, of course." She gave in. "I'll discuss this with Reverend Thompson on Sunday, but my arm —"

"Aah, yes. Perhaps not immediately."

After she'd completed cleaning the schoolhouse, Annie heated a can of vegetables and added jerky and cubed potatoes. With a slice of bread, it made a delicious meal. After she washed the dishes and wiped the small table, she took the lamp into the schoolroom and began her work.

How clever, she reflected as she studied the readers, for the publisher of the first level to have a letter next to a picture of something that starts with that letter "*A, apple,*" she read, tracing the letters in the word as she said it. "*B, bug.*" Soon she knew the entire alphabet and had practiced all her letters and many of the short words. Although the round letters she wrote slanted to the left and were a little oddly shaped, an unaccustomed pride filled her because she'd accomplished so much in one night.

Then exhaustion hit her. Tired and chilled

but exhilarated at all she had learned, she carried the lamp into her bedroom, washed and got ready for bed.

If she worked all weekend, perhaps she could learn to read an easy story. Of course, putting the letters together into words was difficult. Would it be possible to have the older girls read a story? She could listen and learn, too.

Yes, tomorrow she'd have Martha do just that, Annie decided as she slipped into bed. She wrapped herself in the blanket and fell asleep, feeling warm and safe — and proud to be doing something important.

John sat up in his bed, unable to sleep. He threw the covers off, stood and moved to the window. Often the sight of the land that had belonged to his family for eighty years soothed him and he could fall asleep again. As he watched, poplar trees swayed, their branches teased by a gentle breeze while the light of the rising moon bathed their leaves in silver.

To his surprise, he could see a light coming from the schoolhouse. It had to be long after midnight — why would Matilda still have the lamp on? What could she being doing up so late? Working? She'd told him she wanted to prepare well.

But even knowing that she spent extra time in preparation didn't calm his concern about her. Several times over the past few days she'd seemed puzzled and uncertain when he talked to her. Had she been injured more seriously than he'd thought? Was she sick? Or had the people who'd written her references exaggerated her competency?

She'd blamed her confusion on the accident. What a terrible ordeal she'd gone through. After the death of her only relative, she'd set off to an unknown future only to suffer an awful accident and watch another person die. In addition, he'd seen the bump and bruises on her forehead, the cuts on her hands and the blood on her clothes from the wounds.

Yes, a most unfortunate incident, but that changed nothing. He was still responsible for the education of the Trail's End children. That was the Sullivan way. Whether her actions were due to the accident or mistakes or illness made no difference — if she wasn't teaching well, he'd have to take action. He'd keep an eye on her to assure himself that his daughter and the other children received a proper education.

Keeping an eye on her would not be a burden, given how pretty she was.

As he watched, the light in the schoolhouse moved from the schoolroom toward the room in the back. Then it was extinguished.

With a yawn, he returned to his bed and pulled the covers up. This time, he slept.

Saturday morning, after surviving three days as a teacher, Annie woke up early. She stretched and discovered she had fewer aches. She checked the wound on her arm and found it was healing quite well.

She felt much better. Although she'd slept only a few hours, she was ready to get up and get back to work, to start learning more. At least until she looked out the window.

The sun had barely begun to rise. The morning appeared only as a fiery glow across the horizon, just beginning to sketch pink rays across the dark sky. This was too beautiful a morning to spend at her desk. For a few hours, she'd reward herself for all the time she'd spent at work. She'd take a walk and enjoy the birds and the sun and whatever else she found. After washing and dressing quickly, she forced her feet into her shoes and raced to the door and outside.

Which way should she go? Straight ahead lay the Sullivan ranch, and she didn't feel comfortable heading that way. She might look as if she assumed a friendship that didn't exist, and she certainly didn't want to trespass on their privacy. Behind her lay the road and, on the other side, another ranch. To her left and right lay land that probably belonged to the Sullivans but surely they wouldn't mind if she explored a bit on the acres farther from their home. She'd walk toward the sun and enjoy the marvels revealed in its expanding light.

As more birds joined the morning chorus, she was surrounded by music. She followed a faint path — barely a trace, really — with tall prairie grass on each side. What might be hiding in there? Mice? Possibly snakes, but this morning she didn't care. She merely wanted to revel in the daylight, to feel the cool air on her face and the sun on her cheeks, to experience the solid crunch of the ground beneath her feet.

She moved through a thicket, dodging the branches that attempted to snag her skirt, touching the rough bark of the trees and noting the bare branches. She knew the sunlight would color her face, but that didn't matter. Real ladies would protect their complexions by wearing bonnets or never coming outside in the sunshine, but she'd always loved her walks, even as a sad child and, later, as a woman escaping the heat and terror of the brothel for a few minutes. She held out her arms to feel the joy around her, to draw it in and allow it to warm those cold places inside.

Once through the grove, she found a very inviting tree stump, seemingly placed there just for her. She sat on it and breathed in the beauty surrounding her.

Within moments, she heard hoofbeats coming hard and fast. Her first reaction was to leap to her feet and hide in the trees, but the rider came into view before she could move. He didn't seem to notice her. He rode with such joy, such abandon, as if this were what he'd been created to do. He and the horse moved together, a picture of effortless perfection and absolute happiness.

The rider wore no hat, his short dark hair blowing a bit. She could hear the sound of deep laughter, and she almost laughed herself, enjoying the sight of this man and his horse, the pure splendor of the two together with the sunlight behind them. A shiver of delight filled her.

Her slight movement alerted the rider that he wasn't alone. He turned the horse and pulled it to a stop, facing her from nearly fifty yards away. Who was he? Putting her hand above her eyes to fight the glare, she still couldn't see his face. He snapped the reins and moved toward her.

Why was she sitting out here alone with an unknown man closing in? Immediately instinct took over. She leaped to her feet and ran toward the trees.

"Matilda?"

The voice belonged to John Sullivan. She stopped and turned, her heart pounding. He galloped up to her, and she realized that he looked like a completely different man out here at dawn, riding as if nothing else existed in the world.

"Hello. You're up early this morning." When he reached her, he dismounted with a fluid motion and smiled.

He wore denim trousers, scuffed boots and plaid shirt, which was quite a contrast to his usual attire. She sensed an ease she hadn't noticed when he wore his proper suit and polished shoes. He was, without a doubt, the handsomest man she'd ever seen. But, of course, handsome men could be the meanest, the roughest and most demanding —

She stopped her train of thought. John was not a customer, and she was no longer in a brothel. She studied his face, his usually stern features softer somehow, more open.

"I like to walk in the morning. And I love to be outdoors," she explained.

Holding the reins of his horse with one

hand, he nodded his head. "I do, too. I don't get out nearly as much as I'd like."

"Why don't you spend more time riding?"

"I'm the town banker. Telling my depositors that I'd rather be with Orion —" he rubbed the horse's nose with one hand "— they're not going to be happy with me."

With a sliver of a smile that charmed Annie against her will, he added, "That's why I get up early and ride for an hour. The pleasure lasts me all day."

"It looks so easy for you. When did you start riding?"

"Since I could stay on a saddle. Anyone who lives on a ranch has to." After a moment he said, "If I remember correctly, you ride also."

Annie gulped and wished she could read the letters Matilda had written so she'd at least know what she *should* be able to do. "Oh, no. I hardly —"

"Surely you're too modest. You listed some competitions you'd participated in."

Before she could reply, the rising sun caught his eye, and he glanced up before turning away to put his foot in the stirrup. "Excuse me. It's time for me to go home for breakfast with Elizabeth. She expects me to be on time."

He mounted, then looked down at her.

For a moment, his gaze met hers and stayed there. Again, that trace of a smile emerged and delighted her, making her want to smile back, although she could not interpret the meaning hidden in his expression.

After a few seconds, she realized who and where she was and lowered her eyes to break their connection.

"Matilda, if you will excuse me?" He nodded at her and turned his horse, riding back down into the valley.

As soon as he was gone, she felt a little cooler in the morning breeze. Well, if that wasn't absolutely ridiculous. She shook her head and reminded herself she was the schoolteacher, not a foolish ninny. John was the banker, the member of the school board who supervised her, and the father of one of her students. If she were to let her barriers down, if she could truly believe that a man wouldn't hurt her — if, if, if. That would never happen. She couldn't allow it.

Nonetheless, she'd watched him ride toward his ranch until he'd disappeared into the trees. Still she stood there, long after he'd disappeared, stunned at how glorious the sight of him had been.

CHAPTER FOUR

"Good morning, Miss Cunningham!" Elizabeth shouted, and waved when her father stopped his surrey in front of the schoolhouse Sunday morning, a clear, slightly chilly day. Annie waved back as she walked toward them.

"Good morning," John said with a slight bow as he got out to help her into the backseat next to Elizabeth.

A perfectly normal action for a gentleman, Annie told herself. No reason to feel awkward when he was only steadying her to get in the surrey. On the one hand, she still fought the urge to pull away from him when he reached for her. On the other, she could not stop admiring him. She wanted to believe he wasn't like the men who'd taken advantage of her for years, many of whom were leaders in Weaver City, men of high standing. Was John different?

Forcing herself to relax, Annie said, "Good

morning to you both. What a lovely morning. Such lovely sunshine." She settled on the soft leather seat and ran her hand across the smooth, cool surface, watching John's back as he clicked the reins. Although looking like a pillar of the community in his black suit and hat, Annie remembered the man she'd met on the meadow, the one who rode so hard and so fast, she thought no one in the county could beat him. Here now, he acted somber and upright. But she knew what he was like on his horse early in the morning. She'd wanted to laugh with that man, entranced by the joy that emanated from him, by the excitement that lit up his eyes.

It was his eyes that gave him away. When they were chilly and grayish, he was Mr. John Matthew Sullivan, banker and father. When they were blue and sparkled with laughter, he was John, a man who seemed to love life.

"It's nice today, Miss Cunningham, but it will get cold shortly. November is not a warm month here. Oh, have you seen the lazy *S*?" Elizabeth pointed to a gate on the south side of the road. "That's the Hanson Ranch. You've met Miss Hanson, haven't you?"

Annie nodded as she looked at the sign.

How odd. The readers she'd studied showed the letter S standing straight up, but on the sign over the gate, the S lay on its side. Perhaps that was the way an S was made in Texas. Yes, that must be the reason. Did all states have slightly different alphabets? She'd have to practice the Texas S on its side this evening.

"That's why Mr. Hanson wants my father to marry his daughter."

Annie's head jerked up, and she looked at John's back. His shoulders became rigid. "Because Mr. Hanson owns the lazy S?" she asked.

"Yes, because their land and our land are so close that it could be just one big ranch," Elizabeth explained.

"I believe you have said enough about private matters, Elizabeth." His voice held a chilly note.

"But, Father, this isn't private. Everyone in Trail's End knows."

"Elizabeth Celeste Sullivan, please do not say anymore."

"Yes, Father. I'm sorry." She sat silently on the seat next to Annie, dejected.

"Why don't you tell me about the church, Elizabeth?" That seemed like a safe topic.

The little girl brightened. "Our minister, Reverend Thompson, rides the circuit, so he's in Trail's End only one Sunday a month. He's here today. The elders lead the service on the other Sundays. My father's an elder," she said proudly. She filled the few minutes it took to get into town with information about the church service and all the members but did not mention Miss Hanson again.

As they approached the small white building, Annie realized she'd correctly identified the church on her first evening in town. Once inside, she noticed five rows of pews on each side with a stove in the middle. A small table with a wooden cross graced the front of the building. Thirty people sat in the church, including her students and their families. They nodded at the Sullivans and Annie when they entered. She didn't recognize a family with three large boys but guessed that they must be the Bryans.

Elizabeth guided Annie to a pew in the front of the sanctuary and then stepped aside so Annie could precede her. John sat on the other side of his daughter. Shortly after their arrival, Amanda and a stout gray-haired man Annie guessed to be her father entered and sat across the aisle.

"Look, there's the sheriff," Elizabeth whispered when the door closed and a thin, dark man slipped into the back pew just as the minister came to the podium in the front.

"Because we have no organist, I will lead the singing this morning. Let us open the hymnal to number fifty-two."

John handed her an open hymnal. There was no music on the page, only words in very small letters. She attempted to read them but the congregation had finished the song — struggling with the pitch and timing — long before Annie could make out the first two or three words.

"Wasn't that terrible?" Elizabeth whispered. "We really do need an organist."

They certainly did. No one had been exactly sure what the tune was. Only Amanda's clear voice sounding above the stumbling efforts of the congregation brought a hint of the melody to the hymn.

When the service was over, Annie rehearsed in her head what she should say as she waited to meet the minister. When she finally reached him, he took her hand and smiled at her with warmth, as if she really were Miss Matilda Cunningham and a member of his flock.

"You must be the new schoolteacher. How happy I am to see you this morning. I've heard about your accident on your way here. I trust you have recovered?"

"Yes, Reverend Thompson. Thank you."

"I know the children are delighted with you. Martha Norton tells me you sing beautifully although I didn't hear you this morning."

"How nice of Martha." As he continued to watch her, Annie added, "I'm not familiar with most of the hymns, Reverend. When I learn them, I promise I'll sing."

"Our new teacher tells me she plays the organ," John said from behind her.

"Miss Cunningham, we are in desperate need of an organist."

What excuse could she give? "I play the organ only a little, but with my arm . . ." Annie held it out. Although it had healed some, she still protected it.

"Oh, but if you would just try for us, Miss Cunningham."

The pleading in his gentle eyes stirred her guilt. "I'd be happy to try, but I don't read music. If someone could sing a tune for me, I might be able to play it."

"Miss Hanson knows all the hymns we use. Perhaps she'd teach you some. The organ's just over there. Why don't you sit down and see if you can play it? I don't know when we last had a musician here."

Annie soon found herself on the hard wooden bench, running her fingers over the cool keys. The intricate carving on the high wooden music holder reminded her of her mother's tiny organ which Annie had played until the sheriff of Weaver City seized it to pay her father's gambling debts.

She spent a moment or two trying to remember the songs she knew. Obviously few of the ones she'd played in her previous life would be acceptable, so she attempted to remember "Amazing Grace." The notes came out a little screechy, and her pumping was uneven mostly due to the pain in her leg and the stiff pedals. But the sound improved the second time.

"Let me sing a hymn for you to try," Amanda suggested. In a pleasant voice, she sang "I Need Thee Every Hour" while Annie pressed the keys and pumped the pedals, attempting to follow along.

"That sounds wonderful," John said. "But we must go. Lucia expects us home for dinner shortly."

Annie looked at her watch, surprised to see it was nearly one o'clock. Time always passed quickly when she sat at the organ. She suddenly realized she was exhausted, and both her arm and legs hurt from the exertion.

"Reverend Thompson, I'll practice and hope to be able to play by the next time you come through."

"Thank you, Miss Cunningham. I will look forward to hearing you again."

"Amanda, I hope you and your father will join us at lunch," John said as Annie ran her fingers over the cool ivory of the keys once more. How lovely to play again, even on this ancient instrument.

"Of course we will, John." Farley Hanson pounded John on the back. "This time we're lucky to have the lovely new schoolteacher dine with us."

"Oh? I didn't realize I was to join you." Annie looked from one man to the other.

"We'd really like to have you. I should have mentioned it earlier." John inclined his head slightly and smiled. "I hope you can join us."

"Please come, Miss Cunningham. I want to show you my room and all my dolls and books."

"Yes, we'd love to have you." Amanda gave her the smile that Annie was sure no one refused. "We can work on some more hymns on the piano in John's parlor."

After accepting the invitation, Annie ended up in the carriage driven by Mr. Hanson after he'd placed his daughter next to John. Amanda had laughed and teased her father about his matchmaking but accepted

John's help into the surrey while Elizabeth hopped in the back.

"Where are you from, Miss Cunningham?" Mr. Hanson asked as they left town.

Annie felt relieved that the ride was short, and therefore, the conversation would be, as well. She was a terrible liar — clearly she hadn't inherited that skill from her father.

"East Texas," she replied. That sounded general enough. "Now tell me about your ranch and this town. How long have you lived here?"

"All my life. This is my family's ranch. I brought my bride here thirty years ago. She died last year." He turned toward Annie with a smile. "I've been a very lonely man since then." His gaze suggested she could alleviate that.

Oh, dear, not a lonely widower. She must not allow herself to drive with him again or he might believe she encouraged him. He launched into a lengthy description of his land, cattle and enormous worth, which lasted until they arrived at the Sullivan home.

The long, two-story stone house had a wraparound porch and large windows with dark green shutters. Green hills towered in the background, creating a magnificent setting for the lovely house that was far grander than any home she'd seen before.

John held the door open for them and Annie entered a front hall that opened to a parlor on each side. Tables filled with lovely bric-a-brac and cabinets displaying a wealth of beautiful possessions covered every inch of the parlor not already occupied by lovely, plump davenports and beautiful chairs upholstered in gold velvet.

"I don't believe I've ever seen such a beautiful home."

"Yes, it is nice," Amanda agreed. "John's wife, Celeste, helped design the house and furnish it."

"A very talented woman." Annie turned to look at John. "And a loving wife and mother," he said with a solemn expression. "Elizabeth, would you please take Amanda and Miss Cunningham to your room to wash their hands?"

As she followed Elizabeth through the house and upstairs across beautiful carpets, Annie became slightly overwhelmed by the Sullivans' wealth.

"John's wife ordered all the furniture in the house from Boston. It's the finest you'll see in the state," Amanda explained as they entered Elizabeth's bedroom.

Indeed, it was. There was a washstand with inlaid patterns on the drawers and a matching armoire. A delicate spread covered the intricately carved bed.

"Belgian lace," Amanda whispered.

The chamber looked more like a museum than a child's bedroom.

Against the wall stood a full-length mirror. Annie approached it hesitantly. She'd never seen her entire body before — only her face in a small, dull mirror the women in the brothel had shared.

The view surprised her. She looked thinner than she'd thought she would. Maybe a little pretty, although it was hard to think that while standing next to Amanda.

Annie turned all the way around, studying herself. The basque fit a little oddly — tight around her arms, which were apparently more muscular than Matilda's had been, and a bit loose around her waist. Nonetheless, it looked plain and neat and clean, all of which suited a teacher very well. She attempted to smooth an escaped curl back into her bun.

"Miss Cunningham, look at my toys." Elizabeth pulled her to the bed. Five beautifully painted china dolls leaned against the pillows, dressed fashionably in pastel dresses with large-brimmed hats.

"Elizabeth, aren't they lovely?" Annie longed to pick one up one but feared she would drop it or muss the lovely gown. "Do you play with them?"

"When I was younger, but now I prefer to read."

After Annie poured water from the china ewer into the matching basin, she washed her hands and dried them on a soft towel embroidered in flowers.

"Miss Cunningham, you may wish to go in here before we go to dinner." Elizabeth opened a door for Annie.

Inside was a porcelain fixture of some kind. The rounded bottom section and the part above were painted with brilliant flowers and gold accents. It was the prettiest piece of furniture Annie had ever seen, but she had no idea of its function.

"Let me talk to Miss Cunningham for a moment," Amanda said, and then explained the water closet to Annie.

Annie had never seen such a thing. She hadn't even known they existed. What luxury never to have to go outside at night or in the cold.

Seated at the dinner table a few minutes later, she studied the silver serving dishes and the lovely ivory china with silver rims. Mr. Sullivan's wealth exceeded anything she could imagine. Never had she felt more out of place than she did here.

During dinner, Mr. Hanson continued to treat Annie with special attention that embarrassed her terribly. He was at least twenty years older than she was and not at all attractive to her. She felt very uncomfortable with his flattery and gallantry. How could she stop him without being rude?

When the embarrassing meal finally ended, John said, "Farley, if you don't mind, I'd like to talk to Matilda about some school business. Also, she has expressed an interest in playing our piano."

"Thank you for the meal, John. I will go attend to some work I need to finish this afternoon. Miss Cunningham, it was a true pleasure."

"Thank you, Mr. Hanson," Annie said, grateful to John for the reprieve from Mr. Hanson's attentions.

When the Hansons left, John sent Elizabeth into the parlor and watched her seat herself at the piano before he turned to Annie. "Farley Hanson's wife died last year. As I'm sure you've guessed, he's looking for a new wife. I feel I must remind you of the terms of your contract."

She frowned, attempting to understand his words.

"If you came to Trail's End to find a rich husband, Matilda, I warn you I will oppose any such effort."

Annie stepped back. "I assure you I have no desire to marry. I only wish to teach school." Shaking, she turned to join Elizabeth in the parlor, unable to comprehend the tone of John's voice and the ice in his eyes.

John was completely baffled by his own behavior. Why had he spoken to Matilda so rudely? He watched her as she approached the piano and sat on the bench next to his daughter. As Elizabeth sang, Matilda followed, playing only with her left hand, which reminded him that she still had not recovered from the accident.

Why had he felt the need to warn her away from Farley, a good man and a friend? Seeing him flirt with Matilda had bothered John. He had to admit she had done nothing but politely discourage the old fool.

Perhaps he himself was the fool, struggling with an odd emotion that was so different from how he'd felt about any woman before. He was confused and uncertain around Matilda, both feelings he was not used to coping with.

What was it about her that drew both him and his friend? Men who had never acted foolish about a woman before?

Well, of course, there was the fact that men outnumbered women greatly out here. He'd gone to St. Louis to find Celeste, who had hated every moment of her life in Texas. A woman as lovely as Matilda with no family to guard her as Farley did his daughter — such a woman was sure to attract attention.

Yet she showed no flighty tendencies. She did not flirt. She had not encouraged Farley, nor had she showed any interest in John himself. He realized with a start that this was what probably bothered him most.

He sighed as he watched Elizabeth and Matilda in the parlor. He'd always found the ranch house stifling, a reminder of his overpowering, controlling father. He often didn't like the man he was in this house, much like his demanding parent. At times like this, he longed to be outside, training horses with Duffy or riding across the prairie or even mucking out a stall.

It was time and past for him to stop allowing his father to dominate his life from the grave. But habits formed over a lifetime bound him like a lasso. The lectures that a Sullivan behaved differently — was not guided by mere feelings — still echoed and shaped his behavior.

He watched the teacher with his daughter.

Matilda played a chord, then placed Elizabeth's hand on the piano keys and told the child to do the same. She smiled up at her teacher, so sweetly, with so much trust, and followed the instructions. When Elizabeth picked out the tune after Matilda had showed her the correct keys, they both smiled.

This was a woman who obviously loved children and who was a good teacher. A woman who attracted him so much that he walked into the parlor to stand next to her, hoping that she would turn that beautiful smile on him.

And he'd done it even before he realized he'd moved an inch.

Annie glanced up to see John next to her. Which man was he now? The stern banker who lectured her? Or the daredevil who raced across the meadow with wild abandon? The banker intimidated her, but she actually feared the other man more. The man with the fleeting smile and the sincere blue eyes was far more dangerous to her because that man attracted her. That man she could fall in love with.

When she stood to leave after practicing a few more pieces, he looked down at her. "I must apologize for my earlier words, Matilda." He shook his head. "I meant them as a mere reminder, but they came out rude and judgmental. I'm sorry."

Yes, this was a man she could care about. But she dared not allow herself to.

CHAPTER FIVE

On Monday morning, Annie called the students to order. "Children, let us go over some of the last letters of the alphabet." Annie picked up a slate to show the Sundholm twins. "Here's a *Q*." Her circle was round and even. "Here's an *R*." Her strokes were strong and clear. "And here's an *S*." She made it just the way she'd seen it on the sign in front of the Hansons' ranch.

To her surprise, the older children became very quiet looking at each other as if they did not know what to do.

She looked at the *S* but could see nothing wrong with it. It lay flat on the line she had drawn below the letter.

"Miss Cunningham," Elizabeth said. "I think you want to tilt your slate like this." She took the slate and turned it so the *S* stood straight up. "The way you held it, the letter looked like a lazy *S*, like the Hanson brand."

"Thank you, Elizabeth. How clever of you to notice that." Annie put the slate down and bit her lip. "Children, why don't you run outside now for just a little bit."

"But, Miss Cunningham, it's not even time for lunch yet," Ida said.

"Yes, children, I know, but it's a lovely day. Run around a little. I'll call you back for arithmetic in a few minutes."

When they left, Annie sat behind her desk and dropped her face into her hands. How could she ever have thought she could fool these children? A lazy *S*. She'd written a lazy *S*. Now they all knew she didn't know a real *S* from a lazy *S*. Eight-year-old children knew the difference, but she didn't. Tears spilled between her fingers.

"Miss Cunningham."

She looked up to see Rose and Samuel.

"We didn't mean to hurt your feelings by laughing. We're sorry," Samuel said. "The other children sent us in because we hurt your feelings."

"Miss Cunningham, you're the best teacher we've ever had. Please don't cry." Tears gathered in Rose's eyes.

"I'm the best teacher you ever had?" She wiped at her face with her hand.

"Oh, yes. You are so nice and so pretty. And you sing so well, and you know your numbers." Rose nodded. "We all really like you."

"The last teacher didn't want to teach us anything. Sometimes she was mean." Samuel looked at her with wide, sad eyes. "Please don't cry. We won't laugh anymore."

"Oh, children, I want you to laugh. I want you to enjoy school." She stood and waved her hand. "Go on outside, and play for a few more minutes. I'm fine. Just a little tired and shaken. From the accident, you know."

"Yes, Miss Cunningham." The two ran toward the door.

The best teacher they've ever had? Annie collapsed in her chair, laughing so hard that tears of joy spilled down her face. For the first time in her life, she felt like the luckiest woman alive.

On Wednesday, Annie sat on a bench in the shade of the twisted post oak trees and watched the children play. The students ran and hopped, laughing with the delight of the young. The sun reflected on Rose's red braids and Frederick's blond hair seemed to set those colors on fire. The last blossom of a blue mist flower that shown purple against its ashy green leaves drew her attention while a goldfinch sang *te-dee-di-de*.

She smiled. She never thought she'd find

herself in such a paradise. She'd lasted for six whole school days. She'd learned to print well and had just begun to work on cursive. Late at night, she'd puzzled through the stories in the first three readers, read several geography lessons and assigned poems for the upper levels to memorize. She was successfully teaching herself as she taught her students.

"Miss Cunningham!" A shout interrupted her reverie.

Annie leaped to her feet and ran in the direction of the voices where little Clara Sundholm lay on the ground. Annie kneeled next to the child.

"What happened, Clara?"

Tears rolled down the child's face. "I fell down." She pointed to a scrape on her knee.

"Oh, sweetheart." Annie wiped the child's face with her handkerchief. Clara held her arms out. Startled, Annie picked up the girl who threw herself against her teacher's neck and sobbed.

"There, there." She patted Clara on the back as the child cuddled against her. Annie had to squeeze back tears herself. The softness of the child and her utter trust opened something inside Annie. The reaction felt like ice melting. She felt a warmth and tenderness she remembered from her own mother's hugs and she allowed the child's affection to curl around her heart and embrace it tightly.

She stood and carried Clara to the bench where she settled down with her. Little by little, the girl calmed down and with one last sob, fell asleep, her head against Annie's shoulder.

Annie looked down at the exhausted child. She gently rubbed Clara's cheek with the back of her hand and softly sang a lullaby as she rocked the little girl.

When the sound of hoofbeats intruded, she looked up to see a stranger approaching on a roan gelding.

"Good afternoon, Miss Cunningham." He pulled up his horse a few feet from her bench.

All she could see was a thin face with a long, jagged scar across his cheek. Startled and a little frightened to be alone in the clearing with this unknown man and her students, she clutched Clara more tightly to her chest and turned to look for the other children.

With slow grace, the man dismounted and stood beside her. "Who are you?" Annie demanded, fear making her forget her manners.

"Didn't mean to alarm you, ma'am. I'm

Cole Bennett." He took off his hat to show dark hair tied back with a strip of leather. "Sheriff Cole Bennett."

Of course. She recognized him from church.

He nodded toward the bench. "May I sit down?"

With a nod, she relaxed — but only a little. Yes, sheriffs were lawmen, but many were retired gunfighters, nothing more than hired hands for crooked ranchers.

"Teacher." Clara squirmed. "You're holding me too tight."

"How are you, Clara?" He smiled at the child who lit up his gaunt face. He was a handsome man, despite the scar.

"Hello, Sheriff." The child looked down at her knee and then at the others playing in the grass. "I'm fine now. I want to play." She jumped from Annie's arms and dashed toward her friends.

"I came by to introduce myself, ma'am." He leaned forward on the bench. "To let you know that if you need anything for yourself or for the children, you only have to come to town or send Ramon to get me."

"Thank you, Sheriff. That's comforting to know. If I need you, where would I find you?" She cautioned herself not to relax too soon. She knew this type of man too well.

Her father had once been handsome and charming, at least for long enough to court her mother.

"Most often I'm in my office in the jail, which is just down the street from the hotel."

"What are you doing here, Bennett?" John's voice interrupted.

Annie looked up in surprise. Although his horse stood only a few feet away, she hadn't heard his approach. Wary of the sheriff, she'd missed his arrival. From his words and glower, she could tell that John obviously did not approve of her conversation with the sheriff.

"I thought I should introduce myself to the new schoolteacher." He stood, nodded at her and put his hat back on. "A pleasure to meet you, ma'am."

"For me also, Sheriff." She got to her feet and watched as he mounted his horse and rode off.

"Matilda, I know you are innocent in the ways of the world, but you should not associate with that man." John shifted in the saddle as his black horse danced sideways.

"He merely stopped to introduce himself. He seemed nice."

"He's anything but nice. Bennett's a retired gunfighter. He's not the type of man a schoolteacher should associate with."

Although Annie was glad John considered her innocent in the ways of the world and hoped he would never find out differently, she wondered why he spoke so strongly. She did not plan to keep company with the sheriff. He'd only paid a polite call on a newcomer to town.

John wasn't jealous, was he? How absurd. He was just a man very concerned with appearance. She'd noticed that before. It was important to him that the teacher *he'd* hired would avoid anything that could be considered immoral.

"Please remember you agreed not to associate with people of low degree. That describes Sheriff Bennett exactly." He tugged on the reins to control the restless horse.

"I have no plan to associate with anyone of low degree," she said, irritated by his repeated lack of trust in her.

He nodded. "I only wished to clarify the matter."

"You need not clarify this issue. Be assured I understand my contract. If you remember, we went over it together." Afraid she would lose her temper, Annie turned toward where the students were playing. She kept an eye on Clara, telling herself she did that not because she didn't want to meet Mr. Sullivan's eyes but to assure herself the child had recovered.

After nearly a minute, she heard, "I've done it again, Matilda."

She turned back to see him shaking his head.

He smiled ruefully. "I jump to conclusions about you. Again, I apologize."

"Thank you." What else should she say?

"I came here to tell Lucia to return home. Her son is sick."

"Oh, dear. How ill is he?" Annie stood.

"I don't believe it's serious. Ramon just requested that Lucia come home to care for him."

"I didn't know she and Ramon had a son. How old is he?"

"Miguel must be almost eight by now."

"Eight? Why isn't he at school?"

"He works at the ranch."

"But he should be in school. Certainly Miguel will do much better in life if he can read and write."

"Unfortunately many young people in this area don't attend school because they are needed by their families. Others cannot afford school, even with the low tuition rate."

"How sad," she said, recognizing that he could have been talking about her as a child.

What would John think of her if he knew her story? What would he say? More importantly, what would he do? Annie never wanted to find out.

"I also came to give you a message," he said. As Annie took a few steps toward him, he frowned in concern. "Are you limping?"

She looked down at her feet. Although she'd laced her shoes loosely, they pinched so much that she hobbled toward him. "I hurt my foot in the accident. My shoes rub, but I'm sure I'll be fine shortly."

"We cannot have you in pain, Matilda. Not even for a short time. Do you need new shoes?"

"I would like a new pair, but I don't have the money to buy them yet." And she had no idea when she would be paid — or if she would be paid when the children told their parents about the incident of the lazy *S*.

"Then I'll advance you part of your salary." He reached in his pocket, took out a bill and handed it to her. "You have, after all, taught for a week. Do you need anything else?"

Annie, astounded, almost couldn't think clearly. "A brush. I lost my brush in the wreck, and some soap."

"I'll have Lucia bring you soap tomorrow. Also I'll put some money on account for you at the general store, as well as the bank. You can draw it from either place for your necessities."

"Thank you, John." She smiled, delighted by the feel of money in her hand and the thought of wearing shoes that fit properly. "You said you had a message for me?"

He simply watched her for a moment, his eyes filled with an admiration that made her self-conscious. She shifted, ill at ease under his scrutiny.

He finally cleared his throat and said, "I've been asked to bring you to a meeting of the school board on Tuesday of next week in my office at the bank. We'll leave here shortly before seven." He turned, got into the surrey and had driven off before she could say anything or ask for more information.

What would they expect of her at such a meeting? Would they test her? Would they expect her to read for them? Or to recite a poem?

She sighed. Well, there was nothing she could do about it now. She'd have to wait until Tuesday and hope she could show herself to be competent.

"Thank you, Mr. Sullivan. That sounds fine. I'll be ready," Annie yelled.

Two o'clock Friday, at almost the end of the school day, Elizabeth waved her hand, trying to get Annie's attention. "Miss Cunningham, Miss Cunningham."

Annie looked up from Clara's arithmetic. "Yes, Elizabeth?"

"Guess what I'm getting for my birthday?"

"When is your birthday, Elizabeth?"

"Today, today!" Her face glowed with excitement, then changed quickly to dismay. "I was supposed to tell you. Lucia is bringing a cake today, just before the end of school. So everyone can celebrate with me. I'm sorry. I forgot to tell you."

"That's all right." Annie smiled at the rest of the class. "Do you mind that Elizabeth forgot to tell us, or can we all agree to eat the cake Lucia brings to help Elizabeth celebrate?"

Everyone shouted their approval. "I think we'll all enjoy celebrating with you."

"Good." Elizabeth smiled again. "But can you guess what I'm getting for my birthday?"

"A new doll?" Clara asked. The boys made sounds of disgust about such a feminine gift, but Elizabeth shook her head.

The guessing continued: an apple, a hairbrush set, new shoes, a dress. No one found the correct answer.

"A pony!" Elizabeth finally said. "My father is giving me a pony. I'll ride it to school on Monday."

"A pony," Martha said. "What color?"

"I don't know yet. He'll have it for me when I get home."

Everyone told Elizabeth how excited they were about her present and wished her happy birthday. After they shared the delicious torte Lucia brought down, the other students left for the day.

With an impatient Elizabeth dancing around, anxious to get home to see her pony, Annie helped Lucia clean up and then saw them off, waving as the two headed to the ranch house in the wagon.

Finally alone, Annie went back into the schoolhouse and twirled around the room. She'd lasted another day. "Thank you, Lord," she whispered, the prayer feeling more natural.

The students had sung a lot and done sums orally, but she seemed to have them convinced she was a real teacher. Over the weekend, she'd have two days to work, to learn, to attempt to read several stories in the upper-level readers and understand them. Two days minus time for Sunday services, but that still left her plenty of time. Annie pulled a desk over to a window again and began to work.

The wind picked up at sundown, whipping around the corners of the sturdy schoolhouse. Surely, Annie thought as she looked out the window, a storm was coming to break the drought. But no sound of rain pattered on the roof.

Annie had finished reading several stories and sat up to stretch. Her shoulders hurt constantly from leaning over the desk, but the persistent work helped her feel more confident. As she leaned her head on her hands in an effort to relieve a headache that plagued her, she heard a persistent sound from the back of the building, loud enough to be audible above the roar of the wind. What in the world was it?

She shook her head and picked up the book again, but the odd sound continued, just loud enough to distract her. A glance at her watch told her it was only ten o'clock, which meant she had several more hours of work ahead.

But the noise didn't stop. It interrupted her concentration as she read the moral story about a little girl named Minnie who always complained. The author of the story held Minnie up as a good child who attempted to teach everyone to behave as perfectly as she did by her constant nagging. She seemed like a whiner to Annie. Happy to have a reason to stop reading this particular story, she stood and headed toward the sound.

When she walked past the kitchen, the sound grew louder. Entering the bedroom, she realized it came from outside her back door.

She stopped. Should she open it? If there were anyone outside who wished to do her harm, it would be easy enough for him to break in. Slowly she approached the door, opened it and peeked out through a narrow slit.

No one was there, but the sound continued. She looked down. On the top step stood a tiny ball of fur. In an instant, it tore past her feet and into the building as the wind grabbed the door and slammed it behind the creature.

Annie turned. In the middle of the room stood a small bit of black fluff with four white feet and a dot of white on its nose. From its mouth came the loudest caterwauling Annie had ever heard. And it didn't stop.

"Come here, kitty." Annie reached out her

110

hand, but the little animal backed up and growled. Annie put her hands on her hips and looked at the cat. What should she do?

"Are you hungry?" It did not, of course, answer, but strutted out of the bedroom with its little black tail standing straight up like a scorpion's. And it kept up the loud, demanding meowing. How could such a small creature make so much noise?

Annie had no other choice but to follow it. She was, after all, in charge of the schoolhouse, responsible for its good order and cleanliness. Allowing the kitten to wander through didn't seem responsible. Of course, what harm could something so small do?

More than she would've thought. By the time Annie found the cat, it had pounced on a piece of soapstone and knocked it to the floor causing it to break and scatter dust and fragments all over; discovered a piece of paper that it tore up into small scraps with great delight; and scratched on the door jamb, leaving deep marks with its sharp little claws.

"No, kitty." When it didn't pay any attention to her, Annie took advantage of the animal's inspection of a bug to pick up the kitten.

"Meooooow," the tiny creature complained in a voice loud enough for one of the cougars Annie'd been told lurked in Texas, then wiggled away.

Annie went into the kitchen and opened a can of milk, poured it in a bowl and added a little water. She found the kitten exploring her desk and put the bowl next to it. In no time, the cat had lapped the bowl clean and began washing her face with her tiny white foot. Before it finished, the cat blinked a few times, then curled up on the desk and fell asleep.

What was she going to do with it? She watched for a few minutes while it slept, its sides rising and falling. She placed a finger under the animal's chin and scratched. Loud purrs sounded through the school-room.

What *was* she going to do with it? Annie picked up the lamp in one hand and the cat in the other. The little creature pressed its soft, furry warmth against her chest and continued to purr. She suspected the schoolhouse wasn't the place for a kitten. Maybe a big mouser who lived outdoors, yes, but not this little speck of fur that was barely the size of a mouse.

Annie put the lamp on the dresser, then opened the door and leaned over to put the kitten back outside. It woke up and looked at her with wide, startled eyes, digging its claws into her basque and refusing to let go.

"All right." Annie stepped back inside and closed the door. "You can stay for tonight — just tonight. Tomorrow, when the wind lets up, you're going back outside." She lifted the kitten's chin and looked into its face. "Is that understood?"

It purred.

Annie folded a towel and placed it in the corner of her bedroom. "That's your bed for tonight." She placed the cat on the towel, then began to undress. Before she slipped on her nightgown, the little animal had scaled the blanket on the bed and curled up in the middle of it.

"All right." Annie laughed. "You can stay up here tonight. But tomorrow you're back outside," she repeated.

"Miss Cunningham, Miss Cunningham!"

Someone was knocking and calling her name at the front door. Annie turned over and attempted to ignore the sounds. It was Saturday morning. Certainly she had the right to sleep late. Or was there something in her contract about getting up early on Saturday mornings?

Then the knocking began at the back door. She opened her eyes slowly and

113

discovered a cat lying on her pillow. Oh, yes, the kitten. The sight reminded her that her exhaustion this morning was due to a small, furry tornado that had raced across the bed all night long.

Sunshine filled her room. What time was it?

"Just a minute!" she shouted with as much courtesy as she could find inside her sleep-deprived body. She slid off the bed, stumbled toward the dresser and picked up her watch. Nine o'clock. She should be up by now.

"Just a minute," she repeated but more politely. She'd glanced at the chemise she slept in and wondered how she could answer the door — she had no robe. When she moved the cat so she could use the blanket, it howled in protest. Annie wrapped the cover around her and opened the door to peek outside. "Oh, good morning, Lucia."

Lucia stood outside with a bundle in her hands. "Good morning, Miss Cunningham. I'm sorry to bother you, but Mr. Sullivan sent me."

Was the board meeting this morning? Annie shook her head. No, Tuesday evening. Had she forgotten an appointment John had scheduled for this morning? She opened the door and allowed Lucia inside.

"It will take me a moment to get dressed."

Lucia took another step inside, put the bundle on the bed and untied the twine. As she did, the kitten jumped across the covers and attacked the string. Lucia jumped back.

"Oh, Miss Cunningham, you have a kitten." She scratched the cat's ears. "It's so cute. Does it have a name?"

Annie thought of the little creature's loud protests and remembered the story she'd been reading about the girl who always complained. "She's Minnie. She wandered in last night when it was so windy, but I'm not keeping her."

As if she understood, the kitten started her loud meowing.

"Miss Cunningham, we have badgers, foxes, armadillos, bobcats and raccoons in this area. If you don't keep the cat, the scavengers will eat her."

Minnie wouldn't even make a mouthful for any of those animals. Perhaps she'd keep her a few more nights, or until she was big enough to defend herself.

"Mr. Sullivan sent me to ask if Elizabeth could come over to show you her new horse."

"Of course."

"I brought you some bacon and a few biscuits, so you wouldn't have to fix your

115

breakfast this morning." She handed Annie the bag. "I reminded Mr. Sullivan you don't work on the weekends, but Miss Elizabeth was so insistent. He can't turn her down."

"I'm glad she wanted to share her excitement with me."

"And he's bringing over a horse for you to ride," Lucia said.

"He shouldn't do that." Annie clasped her hands in front of her. "I really don't ride."

"Well, Mr. Sullivan seems to think you ride and that you'd be happy to have the opportunity."

Matilda probably rode well. She'd looked like the type of woman who did everything capably. Annie was the type of woman who'd never been on a horse and wasn't all that fond of the large animals. They had a tendency to prance and to show their big teeth.

"Maybe he has me confused with one of the other applicants for this position."

Lucia shook her head. "You were the only applicant."

Oh, dear.

"Mr. Sullivan sent me over with a divided skirt, one of his wife's. It should fit you." Lucia held it up. "He didn't know if you had brought your riding clothes with you."

Annie shook her head as she took the garment from Lucia. What had she gotten into? "I didn't bring riding clothes," she said. She did not add "Because I've never ridden a horse, ever."

She'd have to ride. Clearly John expected it. It would make Elizabeth happy, but could she even stay on the horse's back, never mind actually ride it?

She'd have to. Suddenly, teaching herself to read didn't seem so hard after all.

CHAPTER SIX

After Lucia left, Annie pulled on the divided skirt with her brown basque, combed her hair, then settled down to enjoy a biscuit and share the bacon with Minnie. With a few minutes remaining before ten o'clock, she went outside to await the Sullivans.

"Miss Cunningham!"

Annie looked up to see a pretty chestnut pony frisking along with Elizabeth on its back.

"This is my pony, Brownie." The child brought the horse next to Annie and stopped it after a few unsuccessful tugs on the reins.

"Soft hands, Elizabeth," John said from a few yards behind his daughter, astride Orion. He was wearing denim trousers, a plaid cotton shirt and a wide-brimmed hat. He looked quite handsome and approachable — the banker was nowhere to be seen today.

He nodded toward the pretty brown-and-white pinto mare he led. The animal looked calm which made Annie feel just slightly better.

"Good morning, Elizabeth. Good morning, Mr. Sullivan." Annie smiled and put her hand on the new pony's neck. "She's beautiful. Tell me all about her."

"My father bought her for me at an auction in Fredericksburg. They just delivered her yesterday." Elizabeth loosened her hold on the reins a bit, and the pony pranced sideways.

"She has a lot of spirit." Annie watched as the girl attempted again to rein in the pony.

"Maybe a little more than I realized." John moved his horse closer to his daughter with the protective affection he always showed toward her. "But I'm sure that with practice, Elizabeth will be able to control Brownie."

"She's a wonderful present. Thank you for bringing her to show me."

"As I'm sure Lucia told you, Elizabeth and I were hoping you could join us for a ride. We're going over to the high meadow so Elizabeth can spend some time getting used to Brownie there," John said.

"I haven't ridden in so long." She studied Elizabeth, who rode with her elbows in, lightly holding the reins, her feet resting comfortably in the stirrups. Could she do that? If the horse didn't start bucking or doing those other wild things she'd seen the animals do, probably so.

He frowned as if attempting to remember. "I thought you'd written that you rode daily."

"Well, yes, but I've never been a very good rider." Well, didn't that explanation sound foolish? She walked toward the gentle mare. The horse didn't seem intimidating. Annie feared she'd have to get on her back and attempt to ride, but how?

Again, she remembered the mayor's wife in Weaver City. She stood on a step and put one foot — the left foot? — in the stirrup and threw her right leg across the horse.

But even if she could get on the horse, she'd never fool anyone into believing she was an accomplished rider. And, although she'd healed greatly since the accident nearly two weeks earlier, her leg still ached.

"Oh, Miss Cunningham, we're going to have so much fun."

She turned back to see Elizabeth smiling in anticipation. With a sigh, she said to John, "If you could help me, I'd appreciate that," she said. "My leg is still a problem."

John quickly dismounted and tied his horse to a post. "I do apologize. Elizabeth wanted to show you Brownie so much that I didn't even consider that you may still be in pain."

The horse wasn't too big. As long as it stood patiently before Annie, she might as well try to get on. She put her hand on the nose of the mare, which nickered softly.

"She seems like a nice creature."

"Elizabeth learned to ride on Mercy."

If a child could ride this horse, certainly Annie could. She took the reins, stood on the step and placed her foot in the stirrup.

Mercy shuffled her feet and moved away, which almost caused Annie to fall on her face. She'd grabbed the saddle and held on, but it confirmed her belief that horses could not be trusted.

"I'll hold her still." John took the reins.

Reciting the points of mounting a horse to herself, Annie swung her leg over the saddle and found herself on Mercy's back.

"Well done," he said, looking at her closely for a moment. With a much smoother motion, he mounted his horse.

Watching Elizabeth trot off ahead of her, Annie held the reins lightly, sat straight with her elbows in and gently pressed Mercy's sides with her legs. Fortunately, the mare followed Elizabeth's pony toward the meadow. As they broke through the grove of trees, Annie gasped in delight at the view. In the distance, she could see herds of cattle grazing. She pulled on the reins and, amazingly, Mercy stopped.

White-tailed deer — three or four does, several bucks and three fawns, slender, graceful and so fragile looking — grazed on the long grass and clover. When they heard the horses, the deer lifted their heads, then turned and disappeared into a thicket.

Twined around tree stumps were thick trumpet creepers, their orange blooms brilliant against the grass. Hummingbirds and butterflies flew from flower to flower in the warm sunshine.

"This is beautiful," she said, her voice conveying amazement. "You must love this place." She took in the beauty for a few more minutes before she asked, "How long have you lived here?"

"Forever, it seems." He smiled as he looked across the meadow. "My great-grandfather came to the area from Boston. He joined with Stephen F. Austin in 1823, when Mexico opened the area up to Americans. We have letters he wrote to my great-grandmother before she joined him. He said that hundreds of bison covered the land as far as a man could see." He stretched his arm out and waved it across the area ahead of them.

His pride in his family glowed on his face, and Annie was torn. On one hand, she felt drawn to him, in awe of his passion about the place of his family in history; on the other, she wondered what she was doing next to him, looking out over this land that had belonged to his family for generations when she didn't even know where her parents had come from.

"In 1835, my grandfather was at Gonzales. He stood by the canyon and waved the 'Come and Take It' flag with the 'Old Eighteen.' My great-uncle fought and died at the Alamo with Davy Crockett and Jim Bowie, and my father fought at San Jacinto."

"Your family has been part of Texas from the beginning."

He nodded. "The Sullivans have been on this land for over sixty years. I can't tell you how proud I am of my family and my name. We are Texans.

"But enough about me, Matilda." He turned and smiled at her. "Why don't we sit over there." He dismounted, tied his horse up and turned to her, his closeness warming the chilly morning. Holding his hand out, he waited for her to dismount.

Well, she had little choice. Reversing her method of mounting the horse, she attempted to turn in the saddle; but her aching right leg made her clumsy. Her foot slipped in the stirrup at the same time the mare took a step. If he hadn't caught her, she would've fallen in a heap at his feet.

Awareness of him shot through her. Embarrassed of both that odd feeling and her clumsiness, she shrugged from his grasp and turned toward him. "Thank you."

"We should have been more considerate about your injuries." He took her arm again and helped her sit down on a log. "Now we can talk about you."

Not what Annie wanted. She needed to change the subject but couldn't think of a way to distract him. They were surrounded by the sounds of nature, held gently by the splendor of the high meadow, serenaded by the birds and all the melodies of God's world.

"Are you comfortable?" he asked once they were both settled, watching Elizabeth ride her pony around the meadow.

"Why don't you tell me about your background and interest in education?" Annie replied before he could ask any questions. "Did you attend Trail's End school?"

"Until sixth grade. At that time, my father decided I needed a better education, and he sent me to boarding school in Dallas."

"How old were you?"

"Ten or eleven." He shrugged. "It was expected."

He must have been lonely. She felt sad for the little boy he'd been.

"That's the reason I'm determined to raise the educational standards here." He rested his elbows on his thighs and clasped his hands together as he watched his daughter, love and pride evident on his face. "Her grandparents want her to go to St. Louis for school. I want to keep Elizabeth here with me as long as possible, but I also want her to have a good education."

As if Annie were the one to do that. A stab of guilt shot through her.

She thought he was about to ask her a question, so she hurried on. "What did you do after boarding school?"

The scent of flowers along with the occasional buzz of bees was hypnotic, so much so that Annie was worried she might slip up and say something she shouldn't to this man who believed she was who she said she was.

"I attended Waco College and studied business and finance."

As she watched him, she saw his expression change from his excitement about the school in Trail's End to a distinct lack of interest. Noting the change in his voice, as well, she asked, "Didn't you like it?"

"When I was young, I wanted to be a veterinarian." He gave a deprecating laugh. "I've always loved animals. I wanted to attend Iowa State College."

"Why didn't you?"

"My father expected me to be a banker and rancher, to take over his businesses." He turned toward her. "As you may know, ranchers don't respect the new science of veterinary medicine."

"They don't? Why not?"

"Ranchers have been caring for their animals for years, probably centuries. They won't put up with some new college graduate telling them what to do."

Thinking of the ranchers she'd known, she said, "I see your point."

"And Iowa, as you know from geography, is a long way from Texas. I probably would have hated Iowa. It gets cold there, and it isn't Texas."

Then he laughed, a true laugh. Annie joined him, even though she didn't know why they were laughing. But hearing the sound of their amusement soaring over the meadow felt wonderful and freeing.

"Someday," he said, "I'll tell you a few interesting stories about how we take care of animals on the ranch. Even better, I'll show you our veterinarian's office. Duffy, one of the ranch hands, taught me everything he knows. He's the one who made me want to be a veterinarian."

His gaze held hers. All she could think was how blue his eyes were, not cold at all as she'd thought earlier. His smile, even the tiny sliver he showed her, made her breathless. She didn't feel at all like Annie or Matilda but instead, like a new, very happy and slightly unsure young woman.

"Matilda, you have a wonderful laugh," he said in a soft voice that made Annie believe he'd felt the same way about their shared moment.

What was happening between the two of them? She was overcome by a feeling of breathlessness and wonder, and a need to know more about the man. He slowly reached out and took her hand, looking at her as if she were the most beautiful woman in the world.

Elizabeth's voice shattered the enchanting moment. "Father, I'm tired now, and Brownie wants to go home."

In an instant, he let go of her hand, stood and turned toward his daughter while Annie put her hands to her cheeks, certain they were pink with embarrassment. How could she have dared to look at John like that?

And yet, he'd returned her gaze and held her hand, filling her with pleasure and feelings she didn't recognize.

If she weren't so happy, she'd be completely terrified.

As he drove to pick up Matilda for the school board meeting, John thought about the conversation they'd had Saturday morning. He'd wanted to know her better and had attempted to learn about her life, but she had been reticent. No, more than reticent. She'd avoided talking about herself by asking him questions. Not that he didn't enjoy telling her about himself, but he'd wanted to see if she seemed less disoriented. Or perhaps he had just wanted to know the lovely young woman better.

The conversation had convinced him she'd suffered no ill effects from the accident, but his own state of mind confused him. Something had passed between them three days earlier that had turned his life inside out. Although she was his daughter's virtuous young teacher, he wanted more — more than he should. And now he had no idea of how to treat Matilda. Should he act like the school board member or the man who found her to be beautiful, charming and everything he desired in a woman?

There was no doubt what his father would say, if he were alive: act like a Sullivan and forget this absurd folly. But John no longer had to answer to his father, and he enjoyed this feeling of attraction too much to deny it.

He found her waiting for him when he arrived at the schoolhouse. He stopped the surrey and stepped out to help her, behaving like the man he was, the man he'd spent most of his life becoming: upright and honest and never foolish. But he feared his smile showed how he really felt.

"Good evening," he said as he took her hand to help her into the vehicle. "Do you have any questions about the meeting tonight?"

For an instant, her lovely skin went pale and her beautiful dark brown eyes opened wide, enormous in her face. He suddenly felt protective. What could be frightening her? "Don't worry. The school board is happy with your first two weeks. You won't have to do more than answer a few questions." He got into the surrey next to her.

"Thank you," she said. "I have worried."

The quiver in her voice helped him understand how much she had worried about the upcoming meeting, but he had no idea how to calm her. With a snap of the whip, the

129

horses took off.

"Miss Cunningham, we are delighted to have you meet with the board," Mr. Johnson, the grocer, said. "The children seem very happy with your teaching. Ida and Samuel have expressed this often."

"Thank you, sir." She looked around at the members of the school board in the bank office. She knew Mr. Hanson, of course. She thought the tall woman with pale blond hair in the corner must be the grandmother of the Sundholm twins. In the corner sat Mr. Tripp, the carriage maker and the father of Tommy and Rose. John looked very much in charge, certain and sure in conducting the meeting. This was Mr. Sullivan she was seeing — he was no longer John, the man she'd spent time with Saturday morning.

"Miss Cunningham." He spoke in a serious but reassuring voice. "Some of the members would like to ask you questions."

Annie nodded.

"I wonder if you could tell us what techniques you use to teach," Mr. Hanson said. "I have heard that you use the older children to teach the younger ones to read."

Annie calmed the flutter in her stomach. "Well, yes, I do." What other choice did she have when she knew so little? "I believe that the older children review what they've learned when they teach the younger ones, and it allows me to work with another group on arithmetic."

"An interesting concept," Mr. Johnson said. "But don't you find that the older ones need additional help with their reading and writing?"

"Of course, but right now we are reviewing. The children have been out of school for almost six months. I want to make sure they remember what they learned last year before we move on to new material." Oh, she spoke as if she knew what she was doing. She sounded like a real teacher. Confidence began to spread through her.

"How long will that take?" the elderly woman asked.

"A month, perhaps." Until she learned to read much better. "Although I expect to do this occasionally during the school year. I've seen how working with the younger children helps the older children retain information."

"Perhaps you can tell us some other methods you use." John opened the leather folder and inspected a paper inside. "How have you used what they taught you in school?"

She paused to give herself time to gather

her thoughts to make something up. "I learned to use two subjects together, one to teach the other," she blurted out with no idea where the words had come from. In the back of her mind she could remember someone — had it been her mother? — teaching Annie her numbers while reading her stories. It had been so long ago, and she'd been so young.

"Could you give us an example?" the elderly woman asked.

"I use a song to teach the alphabet," she said, surprised at her own words.

"Would you sing it for us?" Mr. Johnson asked.

"Oh, yes," Mr. Johnson said. "We'd like to hear that, wouldn't we?"

All the members agreed.

Floundering, Annie wondered what to do. Everyone on the board sat in silence, waiting for her. She cleared her throat, then opened her mouth to sing the multiplication table, which she knew very well now, to a tune. She had no idea if the numbers would fit the tune, but she had to do something. Fortunately, the numbers and the notes came out almost even, with just a little flourish at the end. When she finished, Annie looked around the room. All the members looked at her with pleasure, even admiration.

"As I said before, you have a lovely voice, Miss Cunningham," John said. She glimpsed that half smile briefly, before he became serious again. "The children are fortunate to have you as their teacher."

"Thank you, sir." She lowered her eyes, pleased to have survived that question.

"If there is nothing more," John said, looking at each board member, "some of the mothers have prepared a small party to welcome you, Miss Cunningham."

Once the other members of the school board began to leave, John could think of no reason to put off the short drive to the ranch. After he'd helped Matilda into the surrey and started the horses toward the ranch, he reminded himself that, although there was clearly something between them, she was alone in a strange place with no male relatives to protect her.

He wasn't the kind of man who would take advantage of a vulnerable woman. Of any woman. But neither did he have any idea how to behave toward her in their situation.

"You did very well at the meeting tonight," he said.

"Thank you."

After that, conversation languished. He sensed that she was as uncomfortable and uncertain as he was.

When they reached the schoolhouse, he stopped the vehicle, walked around it and held out his hand to steady her. When their hands touched, he felt the attraction again, stronger now. Standing close to her as she turned to walk toward the schoolhouse, still steadying her with his hand under hers, he was drawn by her scent. He guessed it was only the soap Lucia had given her, but on Matilda it smelled like every marvelous fragrance in the world.

When she reached the steps of the schoolhouse, Annie looked up at him and removed her hand from his. "Thank you, John. I enjoyed meeting the other members of the school board. I believe the evening went well. Don't you?"

But his thoughts were elsewhere. Under the bright light of the moon, he could only think of how lovely she was: her oval face, her beautiful dark eyes, her long lashes, lovely arched brows and the thick, dark hair he longed to feel loose and curling through his fingers. "Matilda, you are very beautiful," he whispered, reaching for her hand again.

Her eyes opened wide in fear. She pushed his hand away as she attempted to escape from his touch, almost in a panic.

As soon as he realized his actions and words scared her, he stepped back. "I apologize. I don't know what I did, but I'm deeply sorry my words and actions frightened you."

How had he alarmed her? He had no idea. He hadn't thought he'd spoken or acted disrespectfully; yet she was terrified. What had he done?

Her shoulders shook and tears ran down her face. He reached out a hand in an effort to comfort her, but she moved away. With the steps behind her, there was little space for her to flee. He quickly took another step backward.

"Are you all right?" He looked into her terrified eyes as he attempted to hand her a handkerchief. She didn't take it. She didn't answer.

"What can I do?"

She shook her head. Without a word or a glance toward him, she stumbled up the steps, entered the schoolhouse and closed the door behind her.

"Good night, Matilda," he said to the door. He stood in the clearing for a moment and watched, wondering what to do.

After several minutes, the lamp went on in the schoolroom and then moved toward her quarters. He strode to the surrey.

He had no idea how he'd upset her. He'd been raised to be a model of moral rectitude, to be a dutiful son with the added burden of living up to not just one but two biblical names. He'd been faithful to his wife and had never looked at another woman during their marriage or since — not until now.

Yet somehow he'd frightened Matilda beyond all understanding when he told her she was beautiful. Didn't women like that? Or was it holding her hand that scared her? Or both?

Had something happened in her life that made her skittish around men, or was her reaction due to her virtue? And what should he do about it?

He leaped onto the seat and clicked the reins. He had no idea what he should do, but knew better than to go back to the schoolhouse and ask her tonight.

Shaking, Annie closed the door to the schoolhouse and leaned against it.

Was it so obvious what she was? Was *trash* written across her face? Why did men believe they could touch her whenever they wanted? How did they know that she wasn't a lady? She'd tried to become one. The futility of all that effort caused tears to pour down her cheeks while loud sobs racked her.

"Meow?"

The cat was still inside. She hadn't been able to put the tiny thing back outside. It had become such good company in spite of its constant noise. Or perhaps because of it.

She took off her shoes and padded slowly across the classroom, lit the lamp and carried it to her bedroom with the kitten trotting behind her.

She noted the narrow bed where Minnie sat, the unsteady dresser where she'd placed the lamp and the dresses hanging on the nails. A shabby little place by the standards of some but beautiful to her. She'd felt safe here.

For a moment, she closed her eyes. Those times from the past, the terrible experiences that she'd tried so hard to forget, were shoving their way past the barricades she'd built, plunging into her thoughts. The terror and pain of the first time, the raised hands, the beatings, the brutality. The fear that caused her to shrink back still, to try to hide from men by escaping into herself.

With his touch and his whispered words, John had opened the doors, and the horror of all those years had come swirling out to overwhelm her. She fell onto the bed, longing to be free of memories. But of course that was impossible.

Back when she worked in the brothel, she spent most of her nights playing the piano, but every now and then, a man would buy her time. It was always the customers who knew she didn't want to be bought. Usually they were rough. She touched her lips and remembered they'd been cut and bleeding in the past.

Some part of her knew that John would not abuse her this way. And the whispered words and handholding was nothing compared to what she'd suffered before she arrived in Trail's End. But those actions had often been the beginning of the process. They announced what a man had on his mind. The forwardness made it clear that a man knew what kind of woman she was back in Weaver City. Back when she was Annie MacAllister, a woman who'd worked in a brothel.

But she wasn't Annie MacAllister anymore. She was Matilda Cunningham. At least that's who she was to John.

She sat up. Had she completely overreacted? Had standing alone in the darkness with a man awakened those nightmares? Perhaps her reaction wasn't his fault at all.

"He held my hand and whispered that I was beautiful," Annie said aloud. What was so bad about that?

Annie wiped her tears away. Yes, she'd overreacted. She'd leaped ahead in her mind to what had happened when she was a prostitute. John wasn't one of those men. He'd held her hand to help her across the ground, like a gentleman, and he'd told her she was beautiful, perhaps because he actually meant it. He hadn't forced her in any way. He'd moved away when she'd become frightened. Could it be John wasn't like the men from her past? Perhaps he'd only acted like a man attracted to a woman and she'd overreacted.

If that was the truth — and she now thought it was — how could she face him again?

The following afternoon, Rose approached the teacher's desk. "Miss Cunningham, I'd like to read a story to the twins. Would you listen to make sure I don't make any mistakes?"

Although she didn't know if she could read fast enough to tell if Rose made mistakes, Annie nodded. Rose sat on the bench with Bertha and Clara while Annie stood behind them and leaned over so she could see the book.

As Rose read, she put her finger under each word. How nice. Annie could easily follow the printed words as Rose read them, and she recognized almost all of them.

After Rose finished, Samuel asked if she would listen to him read a story. He read a more difficult story but in the same way, pointing at every word.

Annie was suddenly struck by a realization that nearly took her breath away. The students were not practicing their reading. They were teaching her.

She was mortified and moved. So much love for her students filled the slowly warming corners of her heart that she couldn't speak. She'd never tell them she knew but was incredibly happy that she had ended up in Trail's End with these students. *Thank you, Matilda,* she thought. *And thank You, dear God.*

That afternoon, after all the students but Elizabeth had left, Annie picked up one of the books she'd found in Matilda's valise, the one with the drawings. In what Annie guessed was Matilda's clear writing, she found plans and activities to use in class, but she didn't have any of the supplies to make a thaumatrope, or decorations for the holidays or a game of anagrams. She sighed. Perhaps she could ask the school board for supplies when they met next.

Several minutes later, she checked the watch on her collar. It was almost four o'clock.

"Perhaps I should walk home, Miss Cunningham."

"Your father wouldn't want you to walk home alone."

"Could you walk with me? Then Ramon could bring you back." She looked at Annie pleadingly.

"If no one comes within the next few minutes, we'll do that. Let's give them a little more time."

"They might have forgotten me." She stood to look out the window.

"Elizabeth, do you really believe your father would forget you?"

"No, Miss Cunningham." She smiled. "I know he'd never forget me."

"Why don't we go in the woods, to look for flowers and identify trees?" That, at least, was something Annie knew. She held out her hand, and Elizabeth skipped over to take it. "We'll be close to the schoolhouse so we can hear your father when he arrives."

They found a jasmine twined around a

dead tree and listened for the song of a mockingbird and the tapping of a woodpecker. After a few minutes, they heard a surrey stop and a voice call for Elizabeth.

Elizabeth ran through the grove of trees. By the time Annie arrived, she had jumped into her father's arms and he hugged her.

"I'm sorry, Elizabeth," John said. "One of the traces broke and Ramon had to find another. Then, well, many little things happened." He put Elizabeth down and turned toward Annie. "Good afternoon, Miss Cunningham." He nodded at her.

"Good afternoon." She noticed he kept his distance.

"Elizabeth, would you please wait in the surrey? I need to talk to Miss Cunningham privately."

What did he want? Had he found out her background or that she couldn't read? She had so many secrets. It could be anything. She stepped back. They seemed to be playing a child's game with one of them constantly moving away.

"Please, don't be frightened, Matilda." He took off his hat. "I apologize for whatever I did last night that frightened you." He paused. "I don't know what I did exactly that scared you but promise you have nothing to fear from me."

She struggled to consider a response, but he continued.

"I meant no disrespect. I realize that an innocent young woman like you may be uncomfortable with a man expressing his . . ." John seemed to run out of words, and she could not help him. "I'll behave more circumspectly in the future."

He hadn't figured that she was a fallen woman. But while she felt great relief that he still thought she was an innocent, she couldn't help but be embarrassed that she had overreacted and had misunderstood him so completely.

"I'd like to give you this, as a show of my regret for having frightened you." He held out a book to her.

"Oh, no, I cannot take a gift." She shook her head.

"I believe you will like this. Please."

He stood in front of her, tall, strong and determined. But when she noticed the pleading look in his eyes, Annie took the book he held out. She tried to make out the letters on the cover, but the printing was strange and she couldn't understand what they spelled.

"It's a book of poetry. The sonnets of Shakespeare."

The name sounded familiar, but she could

not quite place it. She decided to keep her response simple. "Thank you."

"You're welcome." He smiled down at her, his eyes now filled with relief. She wanted to apologize to him in turn, but she still could not find the words. He stepped back and glanced toward his daughter in the surrey. "Good afternoon, Matilda."

"Good afternoon, John." She enjoyed saying his name almost as much as she enjoyed hearing him say hers.

She watched the surrey drive off. "Thank You again, God," she whispered. "You are truly generous and gracious."

She opened a page of the book and could make out the words *Shall I* and *to a summer's day.* The other words in the first line of the poem stumped her.

Well, she'd just have to keep practicing.

But this time she'd have something better than the children's readers to work on. This time she had a book of beautiful poetry. What had John called them? Sonnets, yes, that was it. She'd have to find out the difference between a poem and a sonnet.

But the best part was that these poems came from John. She rubbed her hand over the tooled cover of the book and smiled as she watched the last bit of dust disappear beyond his horse.

Yes, John had given her this book, and she'd treasure it forever.

CHAPTER SEVEN

"What fun to have your company for the meeting of the Literary Society," Amanda said to Annie as she snapped the reins and the cream-colored mare moved a little faster.

In a pale blue phaeton, Amanda sat up straight and held the reins firmly, obviously enjoying the display of her skill. She wore a fur-trimmed cape over a soft blue robe with a bustle that forced her to sit very straight.

Fingering her black skirt, matching basque and wool shawl, Annie felt a stab of envy before Amanda turned to her, tilted her head and smiled.

"You and I are going to have so much fun together, Matilda. Just the two of us going off on our own, even if it is just to town! I hope you'll forgive my silly chatter, but I'm so pleased to have a friend like you."

"Oh, I do not think you are silly. Being with you is a delight." How could she possibly envy Amanda for having so much when she shared so much with Annie?

They had just entered town when Amanda said, "I'm happy John asked me to take you. He usually attends these meetings and escorts the teacher. I do hope there is no emergency."

"I don't know why John could not attend, but I do thank you for carrying me with you."

"I know you'll have wonderful suggestions for the meetings." As Amanda stopped the phaeton in front of the church, several men approached the vehicle, except for the sheriff, who actually looked as if he were attempting to escape. Amanda stopped him in his tracks. "Sheriff," she called, "would you please help me down?" She tossed him the reins.

"At the first meeting, I will just listen and learn," Annie said.

"Probably wise, but I am so seldom wise." After the sheriff tied the reins to a post, Amanda put her hand on his arm. Annie could not help noticing how uncomfortable the sheriff looked.

Then Mr. Johnson appeared on Annie's side and helped her down. "My wife is the president of the Literary Society, Miss Cunningham," Mr. Johnson said with a proud smile. "As you must know from the other places you've lived and taught, this society is the cultural center of our little town. We're very proud of our group and the example of the women in our community."

"I know this meeting will be an uplifting experience," she said, hoping that nothing was expected of her yet.

When they entered the church, she saw Mrs. Johnson in the front of the room. She was a tall woman with ramrod-straight posture, a flinty glare and a firm command of the meeting.

"First," she said, "I want to introduce our new teacher, Miss Matilda Cunningham." Annie stood and smiled at the several dozen people assembled there. She knew her students and their parents, as well as the people who attended church, but there were some she hadn't met before.

"Miss Cunningham, we welcome your suggestions and hope you will make a presentation for us in the future," Mrs. Johnson said. "Perhaps a patriotic poem?"

Annie smiled and nodded.

After a business meeting, the program began. Ida recited a section of "The Prairie" with lovely hand motions. A very uncomfortable Samuel Johnson stumbled through

"Concord Hymn" under the unyielding stare of his mother. Finally, with Amanda leading them, everyone stood and sang "Hail, Columbia" and "My Country 'Tis of Thee."

When the program was over, the ladies served refreshments. Annie found herself surrounded by the parents of her students, who told her how much their children enjoyed school. After a few minutes, Annie excused herself to look for Amanda. She found her in a quiet corner with the sheriff, one hand on his arm while she flirted, smiling brilliantly.

How could a man resist Amanda's beauty and charm? Well, the sheriff could. He glanced down at Amanda occasionally but kept his face expressionless. His lack of interest, however, did not deter Amanda. Finally, she took his arm and pulled him toward Annie.

"Isn't it delightful?" Amanda said. "The sheriff has consented to follow the phaeton home." She looked back up at the sheriff. "My father will appreciate your making sure I arrive home safely."

"That's what he paid me for, Miss Hanson."

Amanda's face fell. "He paid you? My father paid you to follow me home?"

"Yes, ma'am. He came to my office this morning. You just tell me when you're ready to leave and I'll follow."

"Well, I have to admit I was surprised to see you here. You usually don't attend these meetings."

"No, I don't."

"And you usually don't accede to my requests so readily."

"No, ma'am, I don't." He nodded. "I'll be waiting outside."

Amanda watched him saunter out. "Is he the most bothersome man you have ever met?"

"I think he's a very nice man," Annie said, trying to keep her amusement out of her voice.

"Yes, I imagine he would find you interesting and treat you courteously." Then she shrugged. "But he finds me to be a flibbertigibbet and can barely tolerate me," she said.

"Oh, I'm sure he thinks you're lovely."

Amanda sighed. "Well, I wish he did, but I have to admit that he doesn't. He ignores me or swats me away as if I were of no consequence, although he always does it very politely." She shrugged. "I guess I've lost my touch with men. Or at least with this one." She sighed again before asking,

"Are you ready to go?"

"Yes." Annie said good-night to Mrs. Johnson and the other parents and then followed her friend to the door.

During the short drive between town and the schoolhouse, Amanda teased the sheriff mercilessly as he rode behind the phaeton on his horse. He answered each comment with a courteous, "Yes, ma'am," or "No, ma'am."

"The man is the most frustrating person," Amanda whispered as she stopped the vehicle in front of the schoolhouse. "I'm going to make him miserable on the way to our ranch." She kissed Annie on the cheek before the sheriff helped her down.

As they drove away, Annie put her hand on her cheek. No one had kissed her with affection since her mother had died. That Amanda Hanson was a darling.

She continued to watch the phaeton and the sheriff until they disappeared around a curve. Annie felt very sorry for the man under Amanda's continued assault. If Annie weren't an upright woman who scorned gambling, her money would be on Amanda.

"Miss Cunningham, Mr. Sullivan asked me to bring you these." It was almost three o'clock on Wednesday afternoon and all the

151

children had left when Lucia arrived with a bundle. Annie left her desk where she worked to read a story from the fifth reader — she had fairly well conquered the other levels and their moral little tales — and took the parcel Lucia held out.

What could it be? "I shouldn't accept gifts from Mr. Sullivan."

Lucia lifted an eyebrow. "Don't think of this as a gift. Just open it."

Annie tore the paper from the bundle to find a pair of shoes inside. "Oh, Lucia, I can't. It wouldn't be proper."

"Miss Cunningham, I've watched you hobbling around as long as you've been here. Elizabeth has worried about you, too. Mr. Sullivan told me you injured your foot in that carriage accident. Is that right? Does it still hurt?"

Annie nodded. "I'd planned to buy myself another pair in town but my foot hurt too much to walk that far."

"I apologize if I speak out of turn, Miss Cunningham, but it seems to me that people who are as poor as you and me can hardly turn down something practical like this. They're just shoes, and there's no one else wearing them right now."

Annie looked at them. They were black and not as serviceable as Matilda's, mostly made up of little straps and a small heel. The leather was so soft that Annie could not help but rub it gently.

"I think if he was after your virtue, he'd give you something nicer than a pair of his wife's old shoes."

"His wife's shoes?"

"When he came to breakfast this morning and Elizabeth reminded him about your problem, he asked me to go through his wife's things. He said he had no idea if her shoes would fit you, but it was a waste to let them sit in a closet if you could wear them."

Annie tugged off Matilda's shoes and slipped Mrs. Sullivan's on. They were a little snug also, but the leather was soft enough that she could feel the shoes give. "I think they'll get more comfortable as I wear them."

"They're dusty. I wanted to clean them up but Mr. Sullivan thought you'd want them right away. Mrs. Sullivan died nearly four years ago, and they've just been sitting in her armoire."

"How did she die?" Annie asked as Lucia started to put cans away in the cupboard.

"She got sick and never got better. She wasn't a happy woman, always wanted to go back home. She didn't like the heat or the sun or the wind in Texas. She missed the theater and libraries. She hated the fact that we don't have electricity or telephones."

"How could she not love Texas?"

Lucia laughed. "There are folks who don't." As Lucia closed the cupboard, the schoolhouse door opened and Amanda entered.

"Does Elizabeth look like her?" Annie asked.

"Elizabeth is prettier. She has a sparkle that her mother lacked."

"How delightful." Amanda entered the building with a swirl of her skirt and a laugh. "You're talking about the late Mrs. Sullivan. Or, as my father says, 'the first Mrs. Sullivan.' "

"Hello, Miss Hanson." Lucia picked up her basket. "I'm on my way out. Goodbye, Miss Cunningham." Lucia nodded at Annie and Amanda as she left.

"Goodbye, Lucia. Thank you for the food," Annie called after her. " 'The first Mrs. Sullivan'?" Annie asked Amanda.

"Yes, my father hopes *I* will be the second Mrs. Sullivan. I don't know how to convince him that will never happen."

"Does John want to marry you?" Annie paused, realizing that her words sounded insulting. "Oh, not that any man *wouldn't* want to marry you."

"I used to believe that." She sighed. "It's a depressing thought that John is only lukewarm toward the idea of spending the rest of our lives together. And the sheriff runs whenever he sees me."

"I take that to mean the ride to your ranch did not turn out as you had hoped."

"Did the sheriff take me in his arms and vow his undying love? I fear not." Amanda sighed and looked so downcast that Annie had to smile. "You find that amusing? When I go into decline, you won't laugh."

"You're hardly likely to go into a decline." Annie motioned toward a bench and Amanda sat. "Tell me what happened."

"Well, after we left here, I slowed the phaeton down so Sheriff Bennett would have to ride next to me. Instead, the man sped up and rode ahead of the carriage. He told me that he was making sure I did not ride into an ambush." She laughed and shook her head. "I do not know why I bother with the man."

"Well, I do know why. The sheriff's the only man that does not come whenever you smile. He's a challenge."

"Of course."

"If he paid the slightest bit of attention to you, you'd get bored and have nothing to do with him."

"Well, that does sound like me, but only back when I was much younger."

"And how old are you now?"

"I'm almost twenty, and still not wed." Amanda smiled sadly. "I don't believe your statement about finding the sheriff a challenge is completely true. He's a man I admire and trust, which is unusual for me. I find most men foolish, except for John. And I find *him* boring. Sheriff Cole Bennett is neither."

"This isn't a game you are playing with him?"

"Oh, la, I don't know." She waved her hand. "Now, let's forget all about men. I am going to sing a solo in church Sunday and need to sing it for you so you can play."

"Of course, but first I want to ask you one thing. If 'the first Mrs. Sullivan' disliked Texas so much, why did she marry John?" What a nosy question. She opened her mouth to take it back, but Amanda had begun her answer.

"None of us really knows. But once Elizabeth was born, she just wasted away. It was awful to watch, and nothing could cure her." She slowly turned her gaze to Annie. "You aren't interested in John, are you?"

"Of course not. He's my employer," Annie replied.

"I wish you were." Amanda sighed. "If you were, my life would be so much easier. If John married you, I wouldn't have to marry him."

"Would marriage to John be so terrible?"

"Oh, no." Amanda sighed. "But it would be dull. I want more." She stood and twirled. "I want excitement and fun and — Oh, Annie, I want so very much more!"

"I hope you find it," Annie said.

"Now, listen," Amanda said, returning to the mundane. "Let me sing my solo for you and see if you can finger the melody."

The next day, Annie sat at her desk, correcting the twins' slates during the children's outdoor time when she heard a loud thumping on the roof of the schoolhouse. She leaped from her desk, frightened that one of the children had fallen. She ran outside, but couldn't see them. Where could they have gone?

Then she heard loud laughter and was almost run over as the boys ran around the building toward her.

"Children," she shouted. "What is it? Are you hurt?" Then she looked at their laughing faces and saw a ball in Frederick's hands.

"We're playing alle-over, Miss Cunning-ham."

"Are you going to throw the ball?" Martha asked the boys as she came around the building followed by the rest of the girls.

"Did we disturb you?" Ida asked. "I forgot. The ball bouncing on the roof probably startled you."

Annie nodded, then put her hand on her chest to calm her rapidly beating heart. "The game you're playing made the thump on the roof?"

"Oh, yes! It's so much fun." Elizabeth hopped and skipped. Her face was flushed, and her hair had escaped her big bow. "Have you ever played alle-over, Miss Cunningham?"

"No, I don't believe I have. How is it played?"

"Boys against the girls," Samuel said. "With a team on each side of the building. One team yells 'alle-over' and throws the ball over the building. When the other team gets the ball, they run around the schoolhouse before anyone on the first team can tag them."

"It's our favorite game," Tommy said. "Except most of the girls can't get the ball over the schoolhouse."

Ida studied Annie for a moment. "Are you

158

a good thrower, Miss Cunningham?"

"I don't know. I've never played this game. I'm not sure a teacher should."

"All the other teachers have played," Rose said. "And we really need you."

"Yes, Miss Cunningham, please play," Frederick begged.

"All right. I'll try." From all the cleaning she'd done in Weaver City and now in the schoolhouse, she thought she'd become fairly strong, and the game did look like fun.

The children cheered and returned to their sides of the schoolhouse.

It surprised Annie to discover she was able to throw the ball over the building, an odd talent but useful in this situation. Before long, with the throwing and running and laughing and shouting, her hair had fallen from its bun and perspiration beaded her forehead.

Then, just as she shouted, "All right, boys, here comes the ball. You can't catch us," Annie looked up to see John staring at her.

"Oh, I'm sorry." She attempted in vain to straighten her hair. She did not look in the least bit like the responsible teacher she should, but she was having the most wonderful time.

"I was just admiring your skill," John said. "I didn't realize we'd hired such an excellent athlete to teach here."

Embarrassed at having been caught in such disarray, Annie said, "Children, I think it is time for us to go inside."

"No, no, please continue. It looks as if you had a great game of alle-over going on here."

"You know the game?"

"Of course. One of my favorites when I was a student here. Unfortunately, I never get to play it anymore."

Annie smiled at the image of the town leaders tossing the ball over and running around the bank building.

"Please play," Tommy begged. "Miss Cunningham's too good."

John said, "Why not?" He took his hat and coat off and placed them carefully on a bench. "Gentlemen, let's play."

By the time Annie called an end to the game fifteen minutes later, dirt covered John's expensive clothing, his dark hair curled against his sweat-covered forehead and he was smiling and laughing.

Again Annie was amazed at how handsome and happy John was. The way he looked reminded her of the time she'd seen John on his horse tearing across the prairie. Suddenly she felt a little breathless. Probably because she'd been running so hard.

Probably because the game had worn her out.

More likely because John was here.

"We're so pleased you joined us, especially Elizabeth." She looked down at the child who leaned against her father's leg. "Is there anything you need to discuss with me?"

"No, nothing. I was on my way to the bank after lunch and heard the laughter. I had to track it down."

He gave Annie a smile that caused her stomach to drop out. She felt slightly weak.

"I'm glad I joined you, but now I'll have to go to the ranch and clean up so I can go back to work."

He hugged Elizabeth, then looked at Annie. His glance took in her hair, loose and curling around her face. He looked into her eyes and let his gaze linger for just a moment. "Good day, Miss Cunningham."

"Good day, Mr. Sullivan," she said in the voice of a teacher, trying to disguise her feelings. Little by little, every time she saw him, she trusted him more. And, yes, every time she saw him, she felt more and more attraction.

Yes, something had changed for her, but she didn't know exactly what. And she didn't think she wanted to know. She couldn't face that — not yet.

CHAPTER EIGHT

A month. Annie had lasted almost a month. During that time, she'd taught herself to read and print. Every Saturday, she wrote out assignments for the next week and made sure she knew how to complete every task. While the older children worked on cursive, she practiced with them.

By staying up late every night and working all day Saturday and most of Sunday, she'd become a teacher. Now she felt she earned every penny the school board paid her. Most importantly, the students were learning — all twelve of them.

The Bryan brothers, Philip, Travis and Wilber, had started attending school a week earlier, after their chores on the farm were finished. Although Wilber had immediately moved to the sixth reader, the two younger brothers had trouble with the fifth level.

"Children!" She stood up from her desk. "Attention please." When all the students had put down their slates and books, Annie said, "Thanksgiving is in ten days. We'll take part in the service on Wednesday evening preceding the national holiday."

The students clapped and could barely contain their excitement.

"We're not going to sing, are we?" Philip asked.

"Some of us will sing. Others will recite sections of President Lincoln's proclamation, about Thanksgiving." She held up the American history book in which she'd found the words. "I'll read the entire proclamation to you, then assign parts." She glanced at the class. "Listen carefully." She read, "The year that is drawing towards its close has been filled with the blessings of fruitful fields and healthful skies. To these bounties . . ."

The children listened attentively until the sounds of an approaching horse distracted them.

"Miss Cunningham, the stage brought you a package." John interrupted her reading as he opened the door. In his arms was a large box, almost half the size of her desk.

She took a step toward him as her stomach clenched. Who would send her a package, especially such a large one? No one knew where Annie was or cared about her, and

Matilda said she had no family.

But she'd probably had friends. Of course she had. Why hadn't Annie considered that?

"Miss Cunningham, you have a package." Clara hopped up and down. "It's so big."

"I've never seen a package that came on the stage before," Frederick said.

Annie hadn't, either. She wished she could enjoy it, but it worried her — she could lose the position she loved because someone knew the real Matilda and had sent her a package, a large package.

"Open it!" The twins jumped up and down in excitement.

John placed the box on her desk. The address written on the top said very clearly, "Miss Matilda Susan Cunningham, Teacher, Trail's End, Texas."

There was no mistake. Annie put her hand on her chest and took a deep breath. Someone knew where Matilda was supposed to be and would expect to hear from her and probably wondered why she hadn't yet.

"Children, this box is personal." John's words stilled the excitement of the students. "It's Miss Cunningham's. She'll want to open it in privacy."

Disappointed, the students returned to their seats.

"Thank you, Mr. Sullivan." She turned

toward the class. "Children, I'll open the box tonight. I don't know what my —" she paused to consider her words "— friends may have sent. Tomorrow, I promise I will show you everything that is not personal." She forced herself to smile. "That will give you something to look forward to. Do you want to guess what is in here?"

The students perked up.

"Each one of you can make a guess. Write your guesses up here, on the blackboard. Tomorrow we'll see who is correct." As the students rushed to the front, Annie added, "We'll start with the youngest. Bertha and Clara." When they came forward, she handed them the chalk. "Choose something you know how to spell."

"Very nicely done," John said quietly. "You changed their disappointment into a challenge." John gazed at the board where Clara wrote *book* in her clear printing.

He did not, Annie noted, look at her or step closer. The desk separated them, a comfortable barrier.

"I'll give a prize to those who guess correctly what is in the box." John reached into his pocket and pulled out a handful of coins. "A penny for each." He held one up.

While the students buzzed about the prize, he placed the money on her desk. Before

Annie could move her hand away, his fingers touched hers. A response rushed through her, a feeling of warmth and . . . well, she still didn't know what it was, but the emotion was . . . pleasant. Yes, pleasant and maybe more than that. She pulled her hand away and glanced up to find herself looking into his eyes.

For a moment, his gaze held hers and she could not turn away. The linking of their eyes led to a deeper sharing on a level she couldn't understand. It felt as if, while they stood there, their eyes and fingers and emotions connected. An understanding flickered between them. She took a step closer to him.

"Miss Cunningham, did I spell *pencil* correctly?" Rose asked.

Annie snatched her hand from the desk and turned toward the board, mortified to be caught staring at John in such an oddly intimate manner. Fortunately none of the students seemed to have noticed the private moment the two of them had shared.

"Use a *c* instead of an *s,* Rose. *P-e-n-c-i-l.*"

"I'll leave you with your class, Miss Cunningham." He smiled at her and a velvety warm yearning filled her. "Would you like me to take the package to your quarters?"

She returned his smile before dropping

her gaze. "Please leave it here."

As he left, she watched him go. At the door, he turned and waved.

As difficult as it was, Annie pulled her concentration back to the excited children, each of whom wrote a word on the board. Candy, paper, pens and clothing were among the guesses listed. Annie herself had no idea what could be in there. In fact, she feared opening the box, but whether she did or not wouldn't make a bit of difference. Whoever sent it threatened her future.

After the students finished writing their guesses, Annie continued with President Lincoln's proclamation about Thanksgiving. She passed the book to the students so each could write down their lines to memorize, but the presence of the box distracted the students — and Annie, too.

After lunch, the students practiced singing "We Plow the Fields and Scatter," and worked on memorizing their presentations.

"Remember," Annie said as the students prepared to leave for the day, "everyone must come to the Thanksgiving service. It's one of the times we show the community what you've learned here."

And then she was left alone with the box. With anticipation and intense dread, she approached it and pulled off the string. As soon as the twine hit the floor, Minnie was on it, battling it with all her might. Minnie had grown since she'd catapulted into Annie's life, but she was still just a kitten. Annie was suddenly very grateful for her companionship as she tried to calm herself enough to deal with the box. Finally, she opened the container and looked inside. The contents filled the entire box and on top of it all lay a letter. She picked it up and took it to the window to read. It was written in cursive, the beautifully curved letters strung together in straight lines. She was glad that she had improved at reading cursive even if her efforts to write it were slow.

"Dear Tilda," she read aloud. So that's what her friends called her. Tilda. "We hope you arrived safely in Trail's End and have settled in. Please write and let us know how you are."

How could she do that? Her friend would certainly know Matilda's handwriting. Well, she'd consider that later.

"The church took up a collection for you and the school. Please find enclosed paper, books and other supplies."

How lovely. Weren't church people wonderful?

"My mother's health continues to . . ."

What was that next word? Annie went to

the blackboard and printed the word to sound it out. "De-ter-i-or-ate," she said. "Deteriorate. My mother's health continues to deteriorate. I will not be able to visit you for Christmas as we had planned."

Thank goodness for that.

"I do hope you will come back home for a long visit when the spring term is finished. Your friend, Edith Palfrey."

Annie looked at the address at the top of the letter. The teacher had come from Houston, a long trip for a young woman alone.

Setting the letter aside, Annie began to unpack, placing each layer on a different table. First she pulled out a large jar of hard candy. The children would love that. Next were packages of paper and yards of fabric, as well as lace, beads and other trim. In a large envelope were scraps of material, the type women saved for quilts. Beneath that were embroidery frames with yarn, scissors and a pot of glue. Pencils, pens, a knife and bottles of ink followed and, on the bottom, ten books — a few readers and books on science and history.

Annie stood back and surveyed the bounty that threatened to topple off some of the tables. Where should she put all this? What would she do with such a quantity of supplies?

And how would she use everything? The pens? She'd never used one before and guessed she'd need to practice. But first, she'd practice using a pencil. She held one up, admiring the wood grain.

She put the fabric and trim in the empty drawers of her dresser. Some of the books fit on top. The scissors, pencils and knife went in her desk drawer. The rest she stacked on the bookcase.

"Thank you, Edith Palfrey and everyone at the church," Annie whispered. Matilda certainly had wonderful friends. "Dear Lord, bless them all."

What was she going to do about Matilda's friend Edith?

She looked at the letter. She couldn't answer it, but she could learn from it. For an hour, using a newly sharpened pencil, she copied the letter over and over, now able to use her right hand. Despite her aching arm, her handwriting began to take shape. It flowed. Although it looked a great deal like Miss Palfrey's hand, the writing showed Annie's individual touches.

After her success reading Miss Palfrey's letters, she decided to attempt those from John to Matilda. She took them from her desk drawer. In his clear hand, they were easy to read and spelled out what he had told her before. Relieved that she already understood everything that was expected of her, she slid the letters into the desk and picked up her pencil again.

It wasn't until Annie moved the cat from the middle of the bed and crawled in after midnight that she allowed herself to consider what had happened that day with John. She allowed herself to savor that moment, when his touch hadn't frightened her at all — in fact, it had pleased her. In her mind, she could see the expression in his eyes. Could it have been true affection that had glowed there for an instant? Only a moment, but she'd seen it. At least, she thought she had. How and why would a man so handsome and rich and personable find Annie interesting?

Well, he wasn't exactly interested in Annie. It was the real teacher who attracted him.

And yet, wasn't she Matilda now? She'd become the teacher when she'd left her former life on the road to Trail's End. She'd become the teacher when she'd entered the schoolhouse, when she'd taught herself to read and write. Everything that was Annie, every single bit, had perished out on the prairie a month ago.

She was no longer the same person. No reason existed why John shouldn't find her attractive. Except, of course, that she was only the teacher and he was the banker who lived in a huge house with many beautiful furnishings and silver trays on the dinner table and a water closet so grand it looked as if it belonged in a palace.

And, no matter how much she tried to convince herself, she was not Matilda. She only wished she were. She pondered as she rubbed Minnie, who had curled up against her side, purring.

John had been courteous and respectful — he hadn't allowed himself to be alone with her since that other occasion. That showed esteem for her.

How did she feel about that? John was handsome, a Christian man who loved his daughter. He treated Annie with respect. But she couldn't forget the warmth of his fingers against hers and the longing in his eyes.

If things were different, she could fall in love with him. If she were truly Matilda — if she didn't have Annie's terrible background, if she weren't living a lie — she could fall in love with him.

She had no idea how to behave around a respectable man like John. No knowledge of what the tender glances and affectionate smiles meant to a man, or how a lady — a real lady — responded. She was amazed to discover that she was no longer afraid of John Sullivan. In fact, she'd begun to feel she could she trust him.

The next day, Annie gave a penny to each child who had guessed an item in her package. Then they began to make a cornucopia from a length of yellow fabric Edith Palfrey had sent. They would stuff it with their pictures of the abundance from the land.

As the students worked on the art, Annie had an idea. "Would you please write a note to my friends?" she said to Ida, gesturing toward her arm. "I'd like to send a thank-you note, but my writing is so painful and slow."

She carefully dictated the letter to Ida, who wrote it in her nice hand. Exactly how to get a letter to Miss Palfrey wasn't clear to Annie. But she was certain Amanda would know.

Pumping the pedals of the organ, Annie played "Now That the Daylight Fills the Sky" while the congregation sang. This

Sunday would only be Scripture reading, offering, prayers, and hymns because Reverend Thompson was on the circuit.

After the hymn was complete, John stood to read the Scripture. "This reading is from the Gospel of John, chapter eight," he said.

"And early in the morning he came again into the temple, and all the people came unto him; and he sat down, and taught them. And the scribes and Pharisees brought unto him a woman taken in adultery; and when they had set her in the midst, They say unto him, Master, this woman was taken in adultery, in the very act. Now Moses in the law commanded us, that such should be stoned: but what sayest thou? . . . Jesus . . . said unto them, He that is without sin among you, let him first cast a stone at her. . . . And they which heard it, being convicted by their own conscience, went out one by one, beginning at the eldest, even unto the last: and Jesus was left alone, and the woman standing in the midst. When Jesus had lifted up himself, and saw none but the woman, he said unto her, Woman, where are those thine accusers? hath no man condemned thee? She said, No man, Lord. And Jesus said unto her, Neither do I condemn thee: go, and sin no more.

"May we all remember these words of our Savior. 'Go, and sin no more.' " He bowed his head. "Let us pray."

"Neither do I condemn thee," Annie whispered. Had Jesus *really* said those words? Well, John had read them from the Bible, so Jesus must have.

Jesus had forgiven the woman. Annie struggled to understand that. Jesus forgave the woman taken in adultery.

"Go, and sin no more," Annie whispered the words. Her hands shook so much that she had to fold them together. She'd decided she'd sin no more before she left Weaver City. That resolution had been reinforced when she'd assumed Matilda's identity, but she didn't realize that Jesus could forgive her — or that *anyone* could.

Thank goodness she didn't have to play a hymn right away. John's prayers always lasted so long that she'd have time to recover from her amazing discovery: she'd been forgiven and she wasn't the only sinner.

What wonderful news. There was hope for her. Jesus had spoken to and forgiven a sinful woman. Jesus reached out to her through the scripture, through His words, through His love, through His forgiveness.

In Weaver City, no one could partake of

communion unless the elders and minister believed they were good enough and gave them a communion token. Annie had never been granted one because she was not good enough in their eyes.

But Jesus had decided she was. She couldn't stop smiling. Jesus forgave her. Jesus had given her a second chance.

So wrapped up was she in her joy that she didn't hear the end of the prayer until John cleared his throat and said a very loud, "Amen," which led her to believe she'd already missed several. With a start, she began to play the next hymn.

After that, she turned around on the organ bench and studied the congregation. Tall and solemn, John stood behind the pulpit to receive the offering. Her students and their families watched him, serious and devout.

Would they listen to and believe her? If she got to her feet now and confessed her sins and deception, would they forgive her as Jesus had?

They might, but she didn't think they would. Not all of them. Even though he'd read the words from the gospel, John probably wouldn't like his daughter being taught by a formerly illiterate ex-prostitute. Amanda would turn her back on an im-

moral woman. She could only guess the re-
actions of the others, especially that flinty
stare of Mrs. Johnson. She thought they
wouldn't be as forgiving as Jesus.

Feeling like a coward, she decided not to
risk the life she'd stepped into, the life she
loved so much.

Not yet.

CHAPTER NINE

The evening before Thanksgiving, Annie stood back to admire the cornucopia the students had created as Wilber hung it on the front wall of the church. The pictures of squash and wheat and apples poured from the opening in plentiful, interesting colors and shapes.

"Very lovely, Matilda."

She looked to her right, not surprised to see John there. She'd become aware of his presence in ways most unusual to her: his scent of bay rum, the sound of his confident stride, the feel of his warmth, although he wouldn't stand too close to her.

She was still amazed that his presence no longer frightened her as much as it confused her. He'd kept his word, and yet she still had no idea how to respond to him. How did a woman act around the town banker? Her ignorance made her feel stiff, nervous and uncomfortable.

"Everything is so pretty." Amanda danced into the room, her pale green skirt twirling with her. "You are so very talented." She put her hand on John's. "Aren't you proud you hired such a marvelous teacher?"

"Of course I am." He put his hand over Amanda's and patted it.

Amanda would fit the role of John's wife exactly. She had beauty, manners and charm. She knew how to talk to a man, to allow his hand on her arm without flinching. Of course, Amanda found John boring, but Annie knew marriages had been built on much less.

"And you." Amanda rushed to give Annie a hug. "You must be so proud of your students." She stepped back and smiled at Annie. "You're the best teacher the children have ever had."

"Oh, certainly not," Annie protested. If so, the children had put up with terribly ignorant teachers.

"I agree with Amanda." He stood next to his friend and nodded. "You have done a fine job."

"Thank you."

"And look at your new clothes." Amanda placed her hand on the sleeve of Annie's white jersey. "Cashmere. It's so soft."

"It's actually not new. I just haven't had

179

an opportunity to wear it before."

"Isn't it beautiful, John? Doesn't our teacher look pretty tonight?"

Too embarrassed to listen for his reply, Annie glanced behind her and noticed the pews were filling. Her students stood at the back of the church, looking uncertain. "I need to help the performers. Will you excuse me?" She hurried toward the students, glad to have a reason to escape for a moment.

As people entered the church, Annie inspected the crowd and attempted to estimate the number in attendance. She noticed that the sheriff stood in the doorway. After that, Annie was too busy to notice anything.

The students recited President Lincoln's proclamation with only a few errors. Loud and enthusiastic applause followed. Then the older students staged a tableau of the landing of the Mayflower, followed by the girls singing hymns of thanksgiving. The program ended with Mr. Johnson declaiming about the blessings of Thanksgiving in the home, and a psalm sung by Amanda. After John's benediction, Annie checked the time. After days of work and preparation, the program had taken less than an hour.

"Beautifully done." Mr. and Mrs. Johnson shook her hand.

"I was proud of my boys," Mr. Bryan said, shuffling toward her. He looked so very ill and thin; she could understand why his sons had to help so much. "Didn't know Wilber could learn all those words." He shook his head. "Wish he could spend more time in school —" Before he could complete the sentence, his body was wracked with coughs.

"It's all right, Dad." Wilber led him to a chair. "I'll get you some punch."

In the small back parlor of the building, the church ladies provided refreshments. On this warm November evening, the crowd moved outside to socialize while Annie returned to the sanctuary to take down the decorations.

"Very well done, Miss Cunningham." The sheriff stood in the doorway to the parlor with a glass of punch in each hand. "I thought you might like something to drink after all that work."

"Thank you, Sheriff." She took the punch from him and sipped it.

"And maybe a little help with the decorations. All your students have left you here to clean up while they eat. Some have even headed home."

When he reached to remove the cornucopia from the wall, she realized that it was

181

handy to have someone taller and stronger do part of the work. "I appreciate your assistance, Sheriff, but I suspect you have another reason for not joining the group in the parlor."

"What?" He looked at her, uncertain of her meaning.

"I've seen your attempts to escape from Amanda Hanson."

His expression of surprise and — what else had she seen in his eyes? Sadness? — made Annie wish she could take back her words.

"I'm sorry," she hurried to say. "That was ill-mannered and interfering."

He smiled ruefully for an instant before he assumed his usual impassive expression. "Just startled me. I thought I'd hidden my efforts to stay away from Miss Hanson pretty well."

"Why would you want to do that? She's lovely."

"Yes, she is." He shook his head. "She is also a singularly persistent young woman who gets an idea in her head and won't let go, no matter how impractical and foolish that idea is."

"You believe her interest in you is foolish?" Annie considered his statement for a moment and realized its validity. In her experience with the upper class, they'd always made it obvious Annie wasn't one of them. However, in Trail's End, as the schoolteacher, she hadn't been aware of exactly where the line was drawn, especially not after Amanda's warm welcome and the kindness of the parents and students.

"I can't believe Mr. Hanson would be happy to see a former gunfighter courting his little darling," the sheriff continued.

"But if Amanda wanted that . . . ?"

"I don't have any money." He shrugged. "I didn't hold up stagecoaches or rob banks in my youth. I have a fairly honest streak in me and I live on what I earn. I don't have nearly enough money to keep her in handkerchiefs much less those fancy gowns she loves. And can you imagine her standing over a hot stove to prepare dinner?"

"I can't believe Amanda's going to give up."

"I don't allow myself to yearn for what I can't have." His eyes met Annie's. "The sheriffs and schoolteachers of the world don't get to marry into families like the Sullivans or the Hansons. I don't even think of it."

"Would you like to?" she put her hand over her mouth. "Oh, there I go again. I'm sorry."

"What I'd like doesn't matter. It's what I know. I figure Miss Hanson will get tired of chasing me, and life will be easier for both of us."

Annie saw Amanda glance in the sanctuary from the yard, her smile widening when she saw the sheriff.

The sheriff followed Annie's gaze to see Amanda heading inside. "Have a nice evening," he said to Annie as he grabbed his hat and dashed out the door.

"Drat the man," Amanda said as she entered the sanctuary at the exact moment his boots disappeared. "He seems absolutely determined to get away from me." She threw herself into a pew and sighed. "I do not understand why. Other men enjoy my company."

Annie settled next to her. "Then why don't you flirt with those other men?"

"Oh, la, I do, but I've known them forever. The good ones are married and the others, well, the others are stuffy or ne'er-do-wells or gamblers or just not . . . interesting." She frowned. "Or they want to marry me for my father's money. You know," she sniffed, "it's difficult to be courted because Daddy has money."

"I'm sure."

Amanda waved her hand. "This discussion is much too gloomy. Tell me, where did you get the lovely fabric to make the cornucopia?"

"Didn't I tell you? I received a package from my friend Miss Palfrey. She sent papers and pens and yards of lovely fabric."

Amanda laughed. "Oh, Annie, did you ever think that she sent the material so you could make new clothes for yourself?"

"No, the students —"

"The students can use *some* of it. I'll come by and pick some lengths for Lucia to make you a few new basques." She stood. "Daddy's probably ready to go home. Why don't you come to our house after church Sunday for dinner?"

How should she answer the invitation? Annie didn't want to spend time with Mr. Hanson, concerned that she'd encourage his attentions.

"Don't worry about my father." Amanda laughed. "He's courting a very nice widow in Fredericksburg who's much closer to his age."

When she walked into the Hanson house on Sunday, Annie noticed immediately that it was more expensively furnished and impressive than the Sullivans'. The parlors were larger and more cluttered, the dinner table groaned under the number of dishes and the walls of Amanda's bedroom were covered with pink velvet.

"Let's look at the stereopticon," Amanda said after they'd eaten. "We ordered some new slides I know you'll love. Come over to the sofa and I'll show you."

Amanda pulled a tall metal stand across the table and placed a piece of cardboard on it.

"I've never seen one of these," Annie said, inspecting the object.

"Oh, you'll love it. Look through there." She pointed at an oddly shaped oval opening. "This one is of the pyramids in Egypt."

A wonder took place before Annie's eyes. She felt as if she were there, in this place called Egypt, as if she could reach out and touch the oddly shaped structure even though she knew it was merely a picture on the card Amanda had placed in the stereopticon. Although she felt sure a pyramid was the triangular building in the foreground, she had no idea what it was or where Egypt was or why anyone had built such a thing.

"Here's a picture of an abbey close to Yorkshire."

Amanda continued to put in more slides. Something the French were building called the Panama Canal, the countrysides of

England and France, views of New York and Chicago and San Francisco. As she watched them, Annie realized how ignorant she was. Oh, she'd worked so hard, but she had so much more to learn, so very much more.

She'd come across a few of these places in her reading, but she'd had no idea the cities were so much bigger than Weaver City, which was the largest place she'd ever been. She'd learned from the picture in the stereopticon that New York had lots of tall buildings and crowds of people — more people than Annie had ever seen in one place at one time.

What was the Panama Canal? Where were these other places and why were they important? She suspected she should know most of them in order to teach history, but she didn't.

Her mind in a swirl, she leaned back against the sofa. She'd worked so hard and she still didn't know enough, not nearly enough. Amanda knew all this because she'd lived in an educated household and had gone to school. For years.

How would she ever learn it all? It would take the rest of her life. But she only had a few weeks.

"Matilda, are you all right?" Concern wrinkled Amanda's forehead.

No, she was not all right but she couldn't confess that now. "A little overwhelmed," she said. "I've never imagined these places looked like this." She sat up. "Do you have more slides? I'd like to see them all."

Because Annie had shown so much interest in the stereopticon, Amanda sent it home with her. She spent the rest of the day looking up the places in the history book and making notes. By midnight, she'd learned a great deal about Egypt and Greece, but so much remained for her to study. Tomorrow, she decided, she'd show some of the slides to the class and then assign a place to every child to report on, using the books Miss Palfrey had sent. She would learn as the students did for as long as she could.

With Minnie in her lap, Annie settled on the front step of the schoolhouse and leaned against the door. It was nearly dusk. The students had left hours earlier and she'd been reading the seventh-level history book ever since. Dates and names flitted hither and yon in her brain but refused to organize themselves there. Her head ached as if she'd hit it several times with the book. That probably would have been easier than reading the volume and nearly as effective.

Leaning forward, she dropped her head into her hands and tried hard not to cry. She'd believed she'd made it, that she'd learned enough, that she'd become a teacher. How stupid and pretentious of her. She'd listened and read enough to learn words like *pretentious* but the real facts — what the older students had to know — still eluded her no matter how much time she spent trying to stuff the knowledge in. Each new fact raised more questions which made her realize how much more there was to learn. On top of that, history seemed interconnected. To understand the American Revolution, she had to understand the Magna Carta, the history of England and much more.

As she considered the situation, the wind swept through the grove of trees around the schoolhouse. The branches waved noisily and the leaves shook, whispering secrets to each other.

Weary, she felt so weary and old and . . . foolish. Heedless, as her father had always said. She took a deep breath. She hadn't thought of him for months, not since she'd become Matilda Cunningham. Now he came back to mock her, to tell her that he'd been right, she never planned ahead.

She hated that.

Dear God, please help me. I know I've sinned by telling this lie, but now I want to be the best teacher I can. Please help me. As she prayed, she let her pain pour out wordlessly, knowing that God heard her. Finally she whispered, "Amen," but kept her head bent.

Hearing something in the breeze, Minnie leaped from Annie's lap and ran inside the schoolhouse.

"Matilda?"

She lifted her head from her hands. In the fading light, she could make out John on his flashy black horse, the right mount for a successful rancher.

"Yes," she answered.

He dismounted, and tied the horse to the stair rail, only a few feet from her. "I wanted to check your windows and see if everything's tied down. We're supposed to have a storm tonight, although it may be all wind." He surveyed the sky with a frown while the wind blew and the leaves crackled.

"Do you believe we'll finally get rain?" she asked. They hadn't received a drop since she'd arrived, and everyone discussed the possibility of drought. She turned her eyes away as if studying the darker sky in the east, but she could still feel his presence, the warmth of his closeness.

"I don't know, but I hope so. I'm going to check the schoolhouse."

"Thank you."

She heard him outside the building, checking the windows. Then he entered through the back door and, from the rattling she heard, seemed to be making sure that all the doors and windows fit tightly.

Within five minutes he was back. "Everything seems all right. You should weather the storm with no problem." He placed his hand on the stone wall. "The walls of this building can withstand anything, but the windows and the doors aren't as strong."

For a few seconds, she studied him, then smiled. "John, why are you here? Since I arrived, this building had held up in other windstorms and you didn't come to check on things." She touched the wall. "It's made of stone."

After studying the schoolhouse seriously for a few seconds, he turned toward her and grinned sheepishly. "All right, it was an excuse. I wanted to see you. I want to see more of you, but I don't know how. If I spend time alone with you here, gossip could ruin your reputation. So I decided to come down to check the windows."

She wanted to spend time with him, too, but how? "I'd like to see more of you, too."

191

As they looked at each other, a "meow" came from beneath the steps.

"What do we have here?" John leaned down to peer beneath the steps and picked up Minnie.

"That's Minnie." She glanced up at him. "Is it all right to have her in the schoolhouse?"

He held the tiny animal in the palm of one hand and gently rubbed her ears. A loud purr emerged from the little body. Annie was amazed by how gentle his large hands were. Finally, he gave Minnie to Annie and said, "She seems healthy. I'm sure she'll be a great mouser when she grows several inches."

He continued to watch Annie, the now familiar expression of yearning in his eyes that touched the longing within her. "We haven't solved anything," she whispered.

He took a step toward Annie and she didn't move away. Then he lifted a finger and ran it down her cheek, slowly, tenderly, the warmth of his caress pouring into those cold and barren places within her.

"No," he whispered. "No, but we'll keep trying. If it's all right with you, we'll keep trying. There has to be a way."

She nodded, putting her hand on his for a moment before he stepped away. "Goodbye," he whispered. "You stay inside where it's safe."

As she watched him ride off, she wished she could call him back. She wished he would lean toward her again and run his finger down her cheek.

He cared for her. At least, she thought he did. John was gentle and concerned for her. How would a kiss from him feel?

CHAPTER TEN

"Miss Cunningham, you want to know what I'd really like to do?" Wilber Bryan asked.

She stood outside, watching the children play duck duck goose. The weather had become colder each day in December, but the students still liked to run around outside after a morning of work. Pulling her shawl more tightly around her, she asked, "What is that?"

"I'd like to take the eighth-grade examination."

She turned from the children to study Wilber's face. "The test students take to get into high school?"

He nodded. "I can't go to high school, but it would feel good to know that I'm smart enough, that I know enough, too."

Annie could almost hear the words Wilber hadn't said. His sentence might have ended with, "If I didn't have to take care of the farm." No, with his family situation, he couldn't go beyond eighth grade, but if taking the examination was his dream, Annie would do whatever was possible to help him.

"How are we going to do that, Wilber?"

"I wondered." He dropped his gaze to the bare ground. "Would you teach me? I don't have to do much at the farm right now, not until we start planting. I can stay late after school maybe, if you could teach me then. And maybe I could come on Saturday afternoons?"

"Wilber, you know we can't be alone together in the schoolhouse, don't you?"

He nodded. "I know." With a shrug, he added, "That's okay." Shoulders bent, he began to shuffle back to where the other students were playing.

"But I have an idea, Wilber. Let me check on something. I'll let you know if we can work it out."

He turned to smile at her. "Thank you, ma'am. I could pay you a little for your time. My parents know this is important to me. They'll help."

Annie knew the Bryans had nothing extra — not a penny — and the more she taught, the more she learned. "Don't worry about that."

When Lucia arrived to help with lunch, Annie asked, "Would you like Miguel to be able to read and write and do sums?"

Lucia looked around her quickly. "Shh, Miss Cunningham. There are people here who do not think Mexican children should be in school."

"But would you like him to?" Annie whispered.

"So much. He could have a better life. Mr. Sullivan is very good to us, but who knows what will happen tomorrow? Only God knows where Miguel will end up working in twenty years, but if he could read and write . . . Oh, that would be a wonderful thing. He'd have a future."

"Wilber Bryan asked me to tutor him but I can't do that alone. If you came to the schoolhouse after two-thirty and perhaps on Saturdays to chaperone, you could bring Miguel. I can work with him while he's here. No one would know but the four of us."

Tears gathered in Lucia's eyes. "Oh, Miss, yes. We can come. Thank you."

The next afternoon, Annie explained Lucia's agreement to Wilber and suggested he stay late the next day.

"Thank you." Eagerly, he opened the math book to the section on algebra and started working on his slate.

The next afternoon, Annie said, "Miguel,

I have some books here you may enjoy," Annie said. She put a primary reader on his desk. "You can see pictures of different objects. The letters that make up the objects' names are below the picture." She pointed at the page.

"I see that, Miss Cunningham."

She handed him a slate. "Write the list of words over and over, until your letters look just like the ones in the book."

After an hour with Wilber and Miguel, Lucia had to leave to help with dinner. Annie gave each student a book to study and bring back the next day. When she closed the door behind them, she felt a sense of purpose. The intelligence God had given her might change the lives of these two young people and, if she wasn't mistaken, also of Lucia, who'd carefully watched everything her son was doing and used her finger to copy the letters on the tabletop. Tomorrow Annie would give her a slate to practice with.

Amanda nudged the door of the sheriff's office open, slowly and silently, in the hope of seeing his initial response when she entered. "Hello, Sheriff Bennett."

He glanced up at her, exasperated and not a bit pleased.

Never one to back down in the face of

disappointment, Amanda walked right in, showing a confidence she wasn't quite feeling.

Like a gentleman, he stood.

"Because it's almost Christmas, I've brought you some cookies." She placed a plate of decadent chocolate fudge, several lemon scones and pulled cream candy on his desk. "The lemon ones taste especially good."

"Thank you." He nodded. "And thank your cook, please."

"You don't believe I made them myself?" She smiled at him, showing every dimple.

He didn't respond. Instead, his eyes returned to the paper he'd been reading. His lack of interest was enough to make even the most determined flirt give up. When she didn't leave, he fixed his gaze on her. "Do you wish to report a crime?"

"Sheriff, I swan. You ignore everything I do. Don't you recognize it when a young woman flirts with you?" She glanced up at him and fluttered her lashes.

"Miss Hanson, I've been a lawman for years. I recognize clues. It's not that I can't identify them. Sometimes I'm just not interested in pursuing them."

She almost staggered when the meaning of his words hit her. Not interested. She touched the charming blue bonnet, which brought out the color of her eyes, to make sure it sat correctly on her curls. He hadn't even noticed how stunningly attractive it was. With a sigh, she said, "I made the cookies myself. I hope you enjoy them." Then she hurried out of the office.

As she turned to close the door behind her, she was startled to see the sheriff studying her as if she were one of the tempting delicacies she'd brought him. Almost immediately, his expression became neutral, but she'd seen that bit of . . . of some emotion she hadn't seen in him before. She could read clues, too, and he'd been lying — he *was* interested. In fact, she could say that for a second, she'd seen desire on his face.

"Goodbye, Sheriff," she called. With a smile of determination and delight, Amanda climbed into the phaeton, flicked the reins and started home to prepare a new strategy.

Annie's first Christmas in Trail's End would arrive in a little over a week. If she weren't a mature, professional teacher, she would have skipped down the road in anticipation of the holiday. She forced herself to walk slowly and primly from the schoolhouse toward town. Coins jingled in her purse and a few dollars were folded inside. On this cold, bright Tuesday afternoon, she planned to buy presents. A bottle of soothing balm for Lucia whose hands were raw from washing clothes, something frivolous for Amanda and a bag of candy for the students.

As she walked, she noticed the grass along the verge had died, and dust rose from the road to cover her shoes. The children said this had been the driest year they could remember — no rain for five months. She studied the clear, cloudless sky. No chance of showers today, either.

Only a few feet from the dry-goods door, she paused and opened her purse to count her change. When she'd reached fifty-seven cents, she heard the door of the store open and she glanced up to see a man walk out. She recognized his face. In horror, she turned away, allowing him to see only her back.

Although he'd stopped only a few feet away from her, she didn't think he'd seen her face. Hadn't he been looking down the street in the other direction when he'd left the store? She stood there trembling, her head bent, praying. *Please, Lord, don't let him recognize me.*

After what seemed like forever, she heard him walk away, his boots clomping against the boards of the sidewalk until he mounted a horse and rode off.

When the sound of hoofbeats died away, Annie allowed herself to breathe again, but she couldn't stop shaking.

What had brought Willie Preston from Weaver City to Trail's End?

Had he recognized her? She thought not. Preston had frequented Miss Ruby's enough to recognize Annie, prostitute and daughter of the drunken murderer George MacAllister. But she didn't think he'd seen her well enough to identify her. Besides, she looked very different now.

More than anything, she wanted to go back to the schoolhouse and hide, but she would not allow Willie Preston to change her plans. With a quick glance down the street to make sure he'd left, she turned and entered the store. As she studied a bolt of fabric she couldn't afford, she asked Mr. Johnson, "Was that a newcomer to town? The man who just left?" Her voice quivered a little, but other than that, she sounded fairly normal.

"Him? No, just passing through." Mr. Johnson finished straightening the cans on a shelf. "Had a lot of questions, but said he had to head back to Weaver City."

"Questions?" She realized she was clenching the fabric. She forced herself to let go of it before she set wrinkles in it.

"Wanted to know a few things, like where the Sullivan ranch was."

"Did you tell him?"

"Told him I didn't know anyone named Sullivan," he said. "Can't trust strangers, that's what I think."

Preston had asked about the Sullivan ranch? Did that mean he knew where Annie lived? Had he tracked her down? If he had, why?

Oh, no reason for that. Annie was no one. She'd never done anything important enough for someone to look for her. His being here had nothing to do with her. Must be pure coincidence that she lived in the place he'd asked about.

But why had Willie Preston come to Trail's End? Why had he asked questions about the Sullivans? Preston would work for anyone, doing whatever his employer paid him for. Did his questions mean the Sullivans were in danger? Oh, surely not. What connection could there be between Trail's End and Weaver City? Between Willie Preston and the Sullivans?

After she got home and put the gifts away, she paced through the confines of the schoolhouse. If she weren't so worried, the sight of Minnie racing behind her and attacking her hem would have made Annie smile, but she couldn't find anything amusing at this moment. She went outside and settled on the bench to think. However, she found all of her thoughts in such a jumble, she couldn't stay still. Why was he here? What would he do about her? Would he hurt the Sullivans? Did she need to tell John?

After twenty minutes with no answers, she went back inside. All the worrying in the world wouldn't solve the problem. She'd have to wait until Preston did something. It could have been mere coincidence.

But she didn't think so.

To distract her thoughts, she pulled the fifth-level mathematics book out and opened it. Numbers always calmed her.

When Annie opened the book, she saw something near the back of the book that she'd never seen before: math problems that used letters, as well as numbers. She read, "$25 + x = 39$." What did that mean? A few pages later, she discovered something called an equation, which used brackets and parentheses.

How did those letters and signs end up in arithmetic? What did one do with them?

She turned back a few pages to see the chapter heading: "Algebra." Algebra? What was algebra? Obviously it had something to do with *x* and *y* and other signs.

She hadn't bothered to study mathematics ahead of the children because she was good with numbers. She understood and could teach arithmetic with no trouble.

How could she possibly have guessed there was more to it than numbers? She closed the book and shut her eyes. This was worse than she'd ever considered. With the addition of geography and history, she had to work every night and all weekend to stay ahead of the students now. How could she possibly find time to learn algebra? And she figured there were probably more things she'd never heard of lurking in the book.

But she refused to consider that now.

How could a person possibly learn all this? It seemed as if every time she felt comfortable and confident, she discovered she didn't know a thing.

Perhaps she should leave at Christmas. She'd lasted one semester — far longer than she'd expected to. Now all this new work faced her.

And Willie Preston had come to town.

But she loved this place. She looked around at the snug little schoolroom and the warm stove. She loved the children and they were learning. If she left, there wouldn't be another teacher until the next October. The delay would be worse than having a teacher who didn't know everything.

No, she wouldn't leave. She wouldn't allow Willie Preston to take this from her. She wouldn't allow algebra and the Panama Canal to frighten her. She'd learn it all, even if she never slept again.

"Dear God," she whispered. "Please be with me. Give me the strength and ability to learn everything I must." She paused. "And one other thing, God. I thought I was safe here, but I'm not. I can't ask You to help me with a lie, but please, please, let me finish the school year, and I'll never lie again. I promise." Leaving her thoughts with God for a few minutes, she finally added, "Amen."

Calm filled her as she listened to the sound of the wind swirling around the small building. Even with Miss Cunningham's past coming back in the form of the letter and package and Annie's seeing her own past in Willie Preston's visit to town, she knew God would guide her and grant her strength and courage.

She also knew God would expect her to confess and reveal her identity, but she couldn't do that yet. In a while she would. Sometime, but not with Christmas coming and the children depending on her so much.

Of course she had to tell the truth.

But not yet.

With the exception of taking her to church, John hadn't seen Matilda for three weeks. He had trouble thinking of reasons to stop by the schoolhouse when the students were there and even more trouble when they weren't, especially since he worried about doing something that frightened her.

He wouldn't be here now if his daughter hadn't given him a reason. Matilda had set up a spelling bee for today, part of several events she'd scheduled before the Christmas holiday. He'd promised five shiny pennies to the winner of the bee, and his daughter had decreed he must be there to present it. Not that he minded. He would do almost anything Elizabeth asked.

So there he sat on his horse, watching the students play alle-over. Although it was December, the temperature was mild. He'd arrived early, which left him nothing to do but watch the children — and their teacher.

He tried not to focus on Matilda because he feared his expression gave away his feelings. And yet he could see her well enough to notice the curly wisps of beautiful dark hair that had come loose from her tight bun and curled around her neck.

"Father!"

His daughter was jumping up and down, waving to him. "Hello, Elizabeth."

"Mr. Sullivan, how nice to see you." Matilda smoothed her hair back before she took the ball from one of the Bryan boys. "I'm glad Elizabeth talked you into attending."

"Good afternoon, Miss Cunningham. Have I arrived too early?" He got down from the horse and tied the reins to the rail.

She glanced at the watch she had pinned to her dress. "Oh, no." She smiled, breathless, her cheeks red from playing alle-over. She was truly lovely.

"We're finished here, Mr. Sullivan. Please come into the schoolroom and we'll get settled."

He watched as she effortlessly corralled the students and marched them inside. Each sat quietly and pulled out a few papers to study. Once the teacher reached the platform, she divided the students into teams and had them stand on either side of the room.

"Clara, please spell *ocean,*" she said.

He couldn't take his eyes off Matilda. Her hair would not stay put, continuing to spill from its tight bun and curl around her lovely face. He couldn't think of anything else he'd rather be doing than sitting here at the Trail's End School Spelling Bee and admiring the teacher.

After two rounds, only a few of the students had dropped out. Matilda had comforted each, telling them what a fine job they'd done with difficult words. No wonder they all loved her. When Ida's turn came again, she said, "Miss Cunningham, give me a hard word."

The teacher smiled. Had he ever noticed her pretty smile?

Of course he had.

"Conscience," Matilda said.

When the bee ended six rounds later, Ida had won and accepted the prize with the confidence of one who knew all along she'd receive the pennies. After the award presentation, John nodded to the class and left, though he wanted to stay for the rest of the day. Duffy would laugh if he knew the teacher had John acting like such an idiot.

From the front of the classroom, Annie watched Amanda slip through the door, her arms filled with boxes. Immediately Wilber leaped to his feet to help her.

"Children," Annie said. "The evening of Tuesday, December twenty-second, there will be a holiday presentation here in the schoolroom, and we need to start decorating for that."

The students cheered, knowing her words meant an end to studying for the day.

"Miss Hanson is going to help the girls. Boys, I need you to take the saws from the shed and go out to cut evergreen boughs." She laughed at the speed with which they jumped up, grabbed their coats and ran outside.

Amanda opened a box of sliced apples and oranges that she'd baked for hours. The girls got to work decorating them with ribbons.

"Miss Hanson also brought Christmas cards." Annie held one up. "You can cut out the pictures and the verses and make an ornament for the tree by hanging them from a ribbon."

After an hour, the boys returned, their arms full of branches. After decorating outside, the boys brought boughs inside and hung them on the classroom walls while Amanda and the girls placed ornaments on them.

Annie took a deep breath, inhaling the scent of Christmas. "Doesn't it smell wonderful?" she asked.

After the excited children left, she gave Amanda a hug and thanked her.

Now she had to sit down and learn algebra, and more about geography, history and science. She opened the mathematics book and saw a chapter toward the back with the title "Calculus." She didn't even want to think about how much time that would take to master.

With a sigh, she lifted Minnie off her desk where the kitten had been batting an ornament, placed her on a bench and began to work again.

Never before had she joined a congregation in welcoming the Savior. Never before had she realized what the birth of the Holy Child meant to the world and to her. The fact that He had been born because He loved everyone, even sinful Annie MacAllister, amazed her. She was special. She was a beloved child of God.

She closed her book and stood to walk to the window where the sky darkened and the first stars shone. As she watched, she drew in a deep breath and thought about the shepherds in the field and how they must have felt when the Heavenly Host appeared to them on the plain: fear and glory and wonder.

This evening, joy and wonder filled her.

And a depth of love for her Savior so overwhelmed her that she wrapped her arms around her body as if attempting to hold it tightly within her.

"Thank You, dear Lord," she whispered. "Oh, thank You."

After a few hours of work, anticipation and joy washed over Annie. This was the first Christmas that she would truly welcome the newborn Savior. The feeling of joy was almost too much for her to contain.

Chapter Eleven

"Sheriff Bennett, you're looking very festive tonight." Amanda gripped the poor man's arm with determination and pulled him toward the steps into the schoolroom for the Christmas program. "Is that a new shirt?"

As she stood at the door watching the two, Annie felt sorry for Amanda, who was experiencing her first rejection — and a very decisive one at that. She probably shouldn't have asked both of them to help her prepare, but she'd needed assistance.

She wore a new basque Lucia had made her from the fabric Miss Palfrey had sent. She'd chosen lovely blue cashmere. Earlier, she'd attempted to catch her reflection in the windows, and if she wasn't mistaken, she looked nice.

"Sheriff Bennett, would you please put that big wreath over the desk?"

"Matilda, I pray for patience every day,"

Amanda whispered to Annie as they watched him put the wreath up. "But that man is trying what little I have left."

"Why don't you pray for God to help you win the sheriff?"

"I don't think God works that way. I believe God has given me the tools." She gestured toward her lovely dark green gown. "It is up to me to use them." She sighed. "Perhaps it is just not meant to be."

"How does this look, Miss Cunningham?" the sheriff asked.

"Down a little on the left side."

"Good evening, Miss Cunningham." Elizabeth walked in with Lucia. "Lucia and I felt you needed something to brighten your room because people will walk all over the schoolhouse tonight." She held up a lovely quilt with a lone star design.

"How lovely," Annie said. "Come, help me put this on the bed."

The cover brightened the room and made it look less shabby. "Thank you, Elizabeth. I'll be so warm. It's lovely."

"Elizabeth? Have you arrived yet?" John's voice came from the schoolroom.

"Oh, there he is." Elizabeth skipped toward the door. "My father had to come from town. That's why Lucia and I were early."

Before she left, Annie looked around her small chambers. Little by little, it had become hers. Using a length of fabric, she'd covered the area where she'd hung her clothes, Wilber had placed a piece of wood under the dresser to level its leg and now the new quilt. It felt like home.

Hearing the buzz of conversation in the schoolroom, Annie hurried from her bedroom and began to greet the parents and other guests.

"Grandmother, this is what I made." Bertha pointed to her ornament on the decorated bough behind Annie's desk.

"Miss Hanson helped the children so much with their ornaments," Annie told Bertha's grandmother.

"I didn't realize Miss Hanson taught young children, as well as all her other praiseworthy activities," the sheriff said, shaking his head.

"You have no idea how talented I am." Amanda smiled and took his arm. "Why don't we find a nice place to enjoy the program, and I'll tell you all about it."

The man was doomed, at least for this evening.

"Very nicely done." John stood next to Annie, admiring the decorations. "I look forward to the program."

For a moment, she savored being near John and wished she could lean closer or put her hand on his arm. Then she glanced at her watch. Time to start. With a clap of her hands, she walked toward the front and the crowd quieted. "Welcome to the Christmas program of Trail's End School." First she led the group in Christmas songs interspersed with tableaux: playing in the snow and throwing snowballs, a family singing and reading the Bible and a stable scene. After several students recited and others sang, everyone joined in to sing "Oh, Come, All Ye Faithful."

With the program over, Annie watched the students and their guests as they wandered around the classroom looking at the displays, chatting and enjoying the cookies and lemonade.

"Is Mr. Sullivan courting you?" The sheriff seemed to have escaped from Amanda and stood at Annie's elbow.

"What?" Annie whirled to face him. "Why would you think that?"

"I'm a man."

"And what, exactly, does that mean?"

"I know how a man looks at a woman he's attracted to."

Annie looked around the schoolroom. John stood talking to Mrs. Johnson. As he listened to her, his gaze found Annie. That warmth she'd seen before glowed in his eyes.

"Like that," the sheriff said. "Most teachers would love to be courted by John Matthew Sullivan. He's wealthy. What more could you want?"

"I . . . I'm not interested. At all."

"You plan to be a teacher all your life? Die unmarried?"

"Until they have to drag me out of the schoolroom." She laughed, but it wasn't a joke. She would love to marry and have dozens of children, but beneath the facade lay her real self, and no man would want to marry Annie. And Annie, well, she wasn't sure she could love a man enough to have his children, despite what she'd been feeling for John.

The sheriff studied her face. "I've wondered if you have a secret in your past."

"What do you mean?" Annie asked, startled.

"I've learned to read people pretty well. But don't worry — I won't ask you about it. Maybe you'll tell me one day."

She wouldn't.

"And your secrets?" she asked.

He shrugged. "I have a few. They aren't all bad. It's just better that no one know what they are." He grinned for a moment, then became serious again. "I believe we're two of a kind, Miss Cunningham. We've worked hard to get where we are and might prefer no one investigate very closely how we did it. Maybe we have pasts that are better left hidden." He headed toward the refreshments.

Two of a kind, the sheriff and Annie. Perhaps so, but she refused to let him know how close he'd come to the truth.

By eight-thirty, most of the crowd had cleared out. She'd told the sheriff that Wilber would help clean up the next morning and watched Mr. Hanson assist his daughter into their carriage. Elizabeth and Lucia had left earlier. After everyone had departed, she looked outside and saw one horse remained. Orion. Had John waited for her outside the schoolhouse after everyone else had left?

"Matilda, could you please bring me a lamp?" he called.

That sounded innocent enough. She nodded and went back into the schoolroom.

When she brought the lamp, he said, "Can you hold it for me? Right here?" He pointed close to the horse's front left foot. "Orion's got a rock caught under his hoof and I can't see it. I can feel it, but it's not coming out." He held up a short knife to show her. "I

217

don't want to hurt him." He held the hoof closer to the lamp. "I could walk him home, where I've got a better tool, but I don't want him to be in pain."

She watched him attempt to remove the rock, his hands tender and careful with the big animal. Then a cool breeze hit her and she shivered.

"I'm sorry. I forgot how cold it is. You should go back inside."

"No, this is interesting." And it was, seeing the trust of the animal as John hunted for a way to pull the rock out. "And you need me to hold the light."

With a final pull, the pebble popped out. John placed the animal's foot back on the ground and stood to put his hand on the horse's neck. "Good boy. It's out and you're fine." Then he turned toward her. "Thank you. We're fine to go now."

In the shadowy solitude, Annie felt that familiar breathlessness she experienced when alone with John — only with John. He glanced at her, and in the dim glow of the lamp, she saw a vulnerability in his expression, a fierce longing that amazed her.

Odd that vulnerability and longing should cause her to take a step back. But it did.

"I've frightened you again. I'm sorry." He straightened. "But I don't know how I did that. Matilda, you must know I'd do nothing to hurt you."

She nodded. She did know that.

"Do you know . . ." he began to say, then stopped as if he were reconsidering his words. "I'm very attracted to you."

For a moment the impulse to run came over her but he didn't move toward her or reach in her direction. And, for some reason, she wanted to hear what he had to say.

Because the lamp had grown heavier with each second, she put it on the ground. The light pooled around their feet but left their expressions in shadows.

"Please don't be frightened," he said. "I have thought about this for weeks, about what I want to say to you." He paused and cleared his throat. "This is not easy for me, but I want to tell you how I feel, and I wonder if there is any chance you return my feelings."

"I don't know."

"Do you find me repulsive?"

"Of course not." How could he think such a thing? Had her behavior caused him to think this?

"But I scare you."

"Not much, not anymore." She paused. How to explain it? "Any fear I feel is no longer because of you. I've had . . . some frightening experiences in my life."

"Then I'm willing to wait, but I would like to know if that is a realistic thing for me to do." Suddenly, he laughed. "I'm so relieved to know you don't find me repulsive."

With a courage she didn't know she possessed, Annie took a step forward. She could see his smile.

"I'd like you to consider my words. I know you are a virtuous young woman. I won't push you or alarm you in any way, but I would like to court you."

She stifled a gasp. "But you cannot. I cannot keep company with a man. My contract."

"Your contract states you won't keep company with people of low character. I don't believe that describes me."

She watched him, feeling his intense gaze on her.

"I'm willing to wait until you feel comfortable," he repeated. "I would like to court you."

She could think of nothing more to say but realized he expected an answer. "Thank you." As soon as the words left her mouth, she knew they sounded ridiculous.

He took a step toward her. Annie didn't move away.

She could almost feel the air between them vibrating with emotion. He cared for her, she knew that. Her feelings weren't as easily categorized. He was a handsome man. He behaved carefully with her, which meant he was kind and considerate. And yet there must be more than that or the very air wouldn't be throbbing. Perhaps she couldn't recognize her feelings because they were so buried beneath the experiences of the past years. But there was something very real going on between the two of them.

The fact that she both recognized and accepted the powerful attraction made her wish to flee, but she didn't. He deserved more.

" 'Thank you'?" he repeated. "What does that mean?" When she couldn't answer, he continued, "My request cannot come as a surprise to you. Surely you've noticed the amount of time I've spent at the school just to see you. Can't you read the interest in my face? Can't you tell how I feel when I look at you?"

"Yes, a little, but I didn't . . . I didn't understand. Not completely. I didn't realize . . ." She stopped, unable to think of words to complete her thoughts. She couldn't explain that, as much as he attracted her, in the end she would disappoint

221

him. Who would want to court a former prostitute? And he would leave her when he found out.

He studied her, his expression uncertain. "How do you feel about my wish to court you?"

He was asking about how Annie felt? No, he wondered how Matilda felt. At the moment, neither woman could think of an answer.

"I find you very attractive, but . . ." She shook her head. "My past, those experiences I mentioned . . . they make it hard for me."

"No?" He sounded surprised, obviously not expecting such a response.

"I'm sorry."

He stood very still. She picked up the lamp and could see that his eyes were that flat, icy blue. "Then I shall wish you good evening, Matilda." He bowed stiffly before he turned and mounted his horse.

She watched him ride off. Had she done the right thing? He was handsome and rich and personable. She could easily fall in love with him, if she allowed herself to. If he courted her, if he asked her to marry him, Annie would become Mrs. John Matthew Sullivan, the wife of a rich man who would take care of her. Matilda might have welcomed his question and been able to assume that role, but Annie could not. Annie's life was a lie. She could not compound the lie by hiding it from a husband.

Awkward.

No, that word barely fit the emotions John felt. *Embarrassed? Mortified?* Maybe those fit better. *Humiliated* described the feeling best. He'd hoped he'd found a woman he could care for, a first in his life. He had cared for his wife, but what he felt now was so different.

He'd believed she hadn't been averse to him. He almost laughed when he realized what he meant was that she hadn't run away from him, that she had allowed herself to stand alone with him a few minutes in the dark. Obviously he had misunderstood everything she'd said and done, and had fooled himself into thinking there was or could be something between them.

He gave Orion a gentle nudge with his heels and the horse sped up. What he needed was a long, hard run to clear his head, but it would be too dangerous to do at night.

Her remarks were all that was proper but everything he hadn't wanted to hear. He didn't wish for her to throw herself at him as Amanda flirted so outrageously with the sheriff. He had hoped she'd answer his question with feminine deference, which would indicate she returned his interest and would be flattered to be courted.

He drove into the stable yard and dismounted.

"Good evenin', boss." Duffy held the reins. "You look as sad as a cow that lost her heifer."

Exactly what he wanted — for Duffy to identify his feelings. Now he felt like an old fool, acting as ridiculously about Matilda as Farley Hanson had. He straightened, said, "Evening, Duffy" and headed toward the house.

After he kissed Elizabeth good-night, he went toward his bedroom, took off his coat and hung it on a chair.

At least Hanson had found a woman in Fredericksburg. Maybe John should look for a mature widow.

But he couldn't do that. He felt too strong an emotion for Matilda. He'd always supposed that if he found the right woman, she would return his feelings. He'd never expected to be turned down. The rejection — perhaps lack of enthusiasm was more accurate — had cut him deeply. He leaned his forehead against the glass. He considered praying, but the God he worshipped didn't expect John to come to Him with every little thing. His God expected John to take care of things himself, so he would.

He could not have meant what he said.

In an attempt to turn her thoughts from John, Annie had thrown herself into cleaning the schoolhouse. With the help of Minnie chasing after dust bunnies and scraps of paper, she'd swept the entire floor until not a speck of dirt or the tiniest bit of paper remained. Then she wet a cloth and scrubbed the surfaces of the desks and tables.

By that time, she'd worn herself out. Yet his statement still echoed in her brain. He would like to court her.

No, he would like to court Miss Matilda Cunningham.

No man wanted to court Annie.

What difference did that make? Everyone thought she was Matilda. She had thought of herself as Matilda for two months now and felt very comfortable in the role. She taught the children. She played the organ and attended church. She had discovered her faith and prayed.

And Jesus had forgiven her.

"Dear loving God." She kneeled next to her desk. "Please help me. I know what I did was wrong, but it's turned out so well. The students are learning — Miguel and Wilber are speeding along with their lessons — and people like me. They respect me. Is that wrong? I'm warm and happy and have food and I don't have to —" she shuddered "— do those other things, those terrible things. Please guide me, dear Lord. Amen."

But she received no immediate answer.

CHAPTER TWELVE

Annie had dreaded attending the Christmas Eve service with John. But when Duffy arrived with Elizabeth to drive her to church, she felt a stab of disappointment at John's absence. Elizabeth announced that her father would be riding his horse down later.

"Oh, Miss Cunningham, I hope my father bought me some books for Christmas and maybe pretty new clothes. A large parcel arrived yesterday." The excited child held her arms out to show the dimensions. She chattered on during the short ride to town, speculating about what that package might contain.

The women who decorated the church had placed candles in each window to guide the Christ child. Inside, tapers flickered in the wreaths and evergreen boughs, which decorated the plain pews and the pulpit. Annie had never seen anything so beautiful. She took her place at the organ and, as the congregation entered, she played the favorite songs of the season. She listened to the Christmas story from the Gospel of Matthew — oh, she'd read it herself last week, but to hear it in church, surrounded by the faithful, well, it was all so new, so marvelous. Her heart leaped when the minister proclaimed, "Christ is born," and the congregation answered, "He is born this night."

For a moment she sat on the bench and watched the smiling congregation leaving, chatting and making plans, while she just wanted to take in the glory of this moment. Her Savior had been born. She was so absorbed in this realization that she didn't notice when someone approached her.

"Happy Christmas," John said from a few feet away.

"Oh, it is a very happy Christmas," she agreed.

"You look lovely tonight, Miss Cunningham." He smiled at her. "You seem to be glowing."

"It is Christmas, sir." She smiled. "Has there ever been a more wonderful day?" Then she stood to hug Elizabeth, who was almost asleep on her father's shoulder. "Happy Christmas to you, Elizabeth."

The child gave her a drowsy nod. "Happy Christmas to my favorite teacher," she said.

Oh, yes. What a truly joyous night.

The next day, Annie dressed in her brown skirt with the gold basque. She wore a new black-wool cape she'd bought as a Christmas gift for herself. It was plain with no fur trim, but it kept her warm. Then she put on her new bonnet — black with black and white lace ruffles around her face. She attempted to see herself in the glass but couldn't quite make out her reflection. She could only hope she looked pretty. Oh, the bonnet wasn't as dashing as the leghorn shade hat she'd seen in the catalog, but this one cost less and suited a serious teacher.

She scratched Minnie under the chin, picked up the present she'd made for Amanda and started her walk to the Hansons' ranch for Christmas dinner.

Amanda had told her to ask John for a ride, but Annie hadn't. She felt uncomfortable around him after what had happened between them. She'd tried to imagine a life with John, but she could see no way around telling him the truth. No matter how much she tried to pretend she was someone else, to believe that the good life she'd built here was real and true, she still knew her secret would have to come out. Even as kind as he was with Minnie and his horses and his daughter, he'd never forgive her for her past and her lies.

So she would walk. It wasn't a long distance and she'd be comfortable in her new, warm cape. Besides, with dinner at two, it would still be light and not too cold by the time she started home.

When she arrived, carriages were being taken around to the stable by stable boys. She didn't see John's surrey. After she knocked, a maid opened the door, took her bonnet and cape, and Annie entered the front parlor.

In a corner stood a Christmas tree, at least seven feet tall, covered with candles and a star on top. She moved slowly through the crowd, nodding at the other guests until she arrived at the tree. The ornaments were miniatures of animals, musical instruments and toys — a tiny wooden doll, a small intricately carved cat, a bugle. There were red and green glass balls, metal ornaments and cardboard pictures. Strings of berries wound through the branches.

"Do you like it?" Amanda grasped Annie's hand.

"It is absolutely lovely, Amanda! Did you do this?"

"You know I'm a useless creature." Amanda laughed. "I pointed and told the servants what to do."

"Is the sheriff coming?" Annie whispered.

"No." She shook her head mournfully. "He *said* someone robbed the bank in Derth. He had to investigate it today. And maybe tomorrow. He wasn't at all sure when he'd be back." She frowned. "You don't think he's trying to get away from me, do you?"

Annie paused and said, "Thank you for inviting me to dinner. I'm going to enjoy spending Christmas with you."

Amanda laughed. "You don't want to answer, do you? Probably wise."

When the twenty guests took their places at the long table a few minutes later, Annie found herself between Mr. Tripp and Mr. Norton. Amanda sat at one end of the table, facing her father with John on her right. Elizabeth sat with the other children at a table in another room.

As she took a sip of water, Annie glanced toward John. He looked so handsome in formal wear, his black coat a perfect fit on his solid shoulders, highlighting the darkness of his hair and the blue of his eyes. He'd nodded at her earlier in the evening but they'd not spoken.

After Mr. Hanson prayed, the servants began serving. The table almost shook with the weight of ham, mashed potatoes, sweet potatoes, corn, squash and many other treats that covered it.

Games followed the delicious meal, the last being the cobweb game. Ribbons of different colors hung from the ceiling, making a brilliant design. The end of each ribbon disappeared into the other parlor or down the hallway. Some went upstairs while others wound under furniture and doors.

"Take that one," Amanda whispered. "The red one with the white lace."

Startled, Annie did as she was told, taking the ribbon and attempting to untangle it — not easy with everyone else concentrating on the same task. A few minutes later, she found herself following her ribbon up the stairs and down the hall. It led to a closed door. She knocked, received no response and she stepped inside. The ribbon went under the bed so she knelt down and reached under the ruffles of the bed skirt where, after much searching, she felt a small box. Inside, she found a pair of earrings, each a graceful spiral of dark gold.

"What do you think?" Annie looked up to see Amanda at the door.

"They are lovely, but I can't accept them."

Amanda waved her hand. "Of course you can. You found them in the game."

"But you told me which ribbon —"

"Can you imagine how Mr. Johnson would look in those earrings?"

Annie laughed. When Amanda had her mind made up, no one could change it.

"Let me put them on you." Amanda assisted her and said, "Now, look in the mirror. Don't they look nice?"

Annie examined her reflection. Who was the woman who stared back at her? She was much prettier than she remembered, with her hair so full and shiny, set off by the dangling earrings and the warm golden color of her basque. "Thank you." With a laugh, she turned toward her friend. "I have a present for you." Annie pulled Amanda to the parlor and opened her purse. "Not nearly as grand."

Amanda pulled the paper off to reveal a handkerchief that Annie had embroidered with her friend's initials. She'd sewed lace around the edges using the tiniest stitches she could.

"You made this for me." Amanda hugged Annie. "It means so much to me. Thank you."

After all the guests had found their gifts, they gathered in the parlor to show them off. Annie glanced at her watch. Almost five o'clock. It would be dark before six. She started toward Amanda to tell her she needed to leave when Mr. Hanson said, "Let's sing some Christmas songs. Miss Cunningham," he said, bowing toward her, "would you play for us?"

Annie sat at the beautiful square piano with intricately carved legs. "I don't know very many."

"I'll stand right here and sing," Amanda said.

After singing "Jingle Bells" and attempting to remember the words of "The Twelve Days of Christmas," Annie pushed the bench back and stood.

"I have to leave," she whispered to Amanda. "I walked."

"Matilda, you cannot walk home now." Amanda looked out the window. "It's too dark and too cold. John," she said, turning to the group of guests, "would you drive Matilda back to the schoolhouse? She walked and it's far too late for her to walk back."

Everyone in the parlor looked up at John, who showed no reaction to the request. "Of course." He inclined his head a bit. "I wouldn't want our schoolteacher to get lost or ill." He turned toward his daughter. "Elizabeth?"

"May I stay here?" Elizabeth waved toward a girl of the same age. "Agatha is visiting for a few days. She wants me to spend the night with her."

John blinked. Annie guessed he was considering the discomfort of driving alone with the woman who had been so unenthusiastic about his request to court her. No one else seemed to realize his reluctance.

"I'll be fine. I walked here. It isn't far. Please don't leave early. Stay and enjoy the party." Annie hastened to the hall and took her cape from the servant there, scrambling toward the door. Not a very ladylike action, but she wanted to leave quickly. She did not want to be alone with John, not when her attraction for him warred with reality, leaving her so nervous and bewildered.

"Matilda, I must insist," he said from the hall. He wore his solemn expression and his eyes — although not icy — were certainly not warm. "It has become much colder over the hours we spent inside."

Annie opened the door. A gust of icy wind hit her, tugging at her hat and swirling her cape around her. Immediately, her eyes began to water and she shivered. She pulled her hood over her head in an attempt to keep her new hat in place and tried to hold the cape closed with her other hand.

"Amanda has already sent someone to the stable for my carriage. It will be around shortly. Why don't we wait inside in the warmth?"

Annie couldn't see to the end of the drive in the dark, and the cold wind cut to the bone. As much as she hated to do it, she said, "Yes, thank you, John."

Once inside the house again, Annie settled on a bench beside a window while John stood in the entry area and, after taking his coat from the maid, watched for the carriage.

"Why didn't you ask me for a ride to the party?" he said. "Certainly you knew I'd have been happy to stop for you."

"I didn't know if . . . if it would be comfortable."

"Certainly more comfortable than attempting to walk home on such a cold, windy evening."

"Sometimes I don't plan well." She realized she probably shouldn't have said that. His idea of a teacher probably included the ability to plan well.

"Aah. Exactly the kind of person I like. People who make plans often end up boring, but people who run off in the cold and dark often end up . . . frozen."

She glanced at him. Had he made a joke? She rather thought he had. She smiled.

For a few seconds, he watched her with

the gaze he had turned on her before —
warm, but showing as much puzzlement as
she felt.

"I believe our transportation has arrived."
He opened the door, followed her out and
held out his arm to hand her into a covered
carriage. Although open in the front, the
roof and sides kept the wind off. Once she
had settled on the seat, she discovered a
warm brick under her feet. What luxury.

After he got in on the other side and accepted the reins from the stable boy, they
rode in silence.

"John." She paused in an effort to gather
her thoughts. He deserved an explanation
for her odd behavior. "John, I'm sorry for
my ungracious answer when you asked
what . . . what you asked. You see, I have no
experience with this sort of thing." She
paused. "I've never received a request to be
courted."

"The men from Houston must be very
slow."

She heard a note of laughter in his voice.

"Nor have I ever met a man like you."

"What does that mean?" He turned to
look at her intently.

"So very upright at times, but so different, so considerate with your daughter, and
with animals . . . and very often with me."

The carriage had reached the road. He didn't say anything while he turned into the drive to the schoolhouse. As they drove again in silence, the carriage felt warm and cozy with just the two of them inside.

"I don't know why you would ask to court me," she said to finally break the silence. "Your question surprised me."

"Did I frighten you again?"

"I wasn't frightened."

"Does it scare you to be alone with me in this carriage?"

She paused to consider that. "Not at all."

No longer was the problem between them fear of him, but fear of what might be between them. How would she react to a deeper relationship with a man — one as good as John? How would she handle the damage from her past? How would he?

He smiled. "I'm glad because I need to ask you something, and this seems like the perfect time." Instead of taking the road to the schoolhouse, he headed toward the ranch. "It's an issue of trust."

"You missed the turn to the schoolhouse," Annie said.

"No, I meant to go this way. As I said, I have a request, a favor to ask you."

Within a few minutes, he pulled up to the stable, handed the reins to Duffy and swung out of the carriage.

"Good evenin', teacher." Duffy nodded at her.

"Good evening, Duffy."

"You going to help that pretty filly out of the carriage or do you want me to?" he asked John.

"I can do this, *viejo.* You just take care of the horses and keep them ready to go. I'll be back to take Matilda home in a few minutes."

When John put his arm out, Annie placed her hand on it and stepped carefully from the carriage.

"My favor isn't difficult," he said as they walked to the house. Once there, they entered the hallway where Lucia took his coat, gloves and hat, and Annie's cape.

"Please sit down." He waved at a chair as he sat behind the desk. "I believe Elizabeth has told you we'll be leaving Trail's End in mid-January, a few days before the end of the term. We're going to St. Louis to visit my wife's parents, Elizabeth's grandparents."

"A long trip."

"We'll be gone for nearly two weeks." He looked down at his desk, then back at Annie, as if judging her in some way. "Matilda, I don't have an accountant or manager for

239

my ranch. It's not a large spread. I employ only Ramon, Lucia, Miguel and Duffy for the house, and have fifteen cowboys and their foreman in the bunkhouse to take care of the land and cattle."

It sounded like a huge place to her.

"Usually when I go out of town, Farley Hanson takes care of emergencies, especially if they involve money, but Farley plans to spend time in Fredericksburg." He smiled at her. "I wonder if I could prevail upon you to handle any emergency financial issues that come up."

"John, I don't have that much money."

He laughed, a deep, rich sound that pulled her into its warm embrace. "No, I don't expect you to pay. I need to be able to entrust the key to my safe drawer to someone in case there is a need for more money than I'm leaving with Lucia."

"Couldn't Lucia handle this?"

He shook his head. "I wish she could, but I need someone who can write down the withdrawal. None of the people here have that ability." He smiled at her. "I don't believe there's an urgent need for this precaution, but I'll feel better if someone I trust is here to take care of any money required for an emergency."

Someone he could trust? Not a word that

had been used to describe Annie often.

"Of course."

He stood and turned to the bookshelves behind him. "I keep one key with me at all times, but the other key is here, in this book." He pulled a massive tome from the shelf, put it on the desk and opened it. "I glued an envelope in the front."

She watched him take the key out and noted the place on the shelf the book had come from. The name of the book was Moby-Dick; or the Whale — an odd title. She hadn't realized people wrote entire books on whales, but then she'd read so little.

He closed the book and handed her the key. "Come around to this side of the desk and let me show you the drawer."

As Annie moved around the desk, he took a few steps back to allow her room. "Put the key in."

When Annie did as requested, the drawer opened. She pulled it out and flipped open a lid to find stacks of money inside. "Oh, my. I've never seen so much. How much is here?"

"More than a thousand. The exact amount is in the account book there." He picked up a book on the corner of his desk. "Precisely two-thousand fifty-three dollars. If you need to withdraw any, please write it here," he said, placing his finger on a column. "And give the reason."

"Why do you need so much money?"

"A rancher can have large, unexpected expenditures. If the boys needed to move the cattle, they have to have expense money. Or if they need to purchase cattle, or if Lucia runs out of food or Ramon needs more feed." He closed the drawer and locked it. "I don't expect any of that. We have an account at the general store and the cattle should be fine. But if there were an emergency, I'd feel better knowing you'd take care of it."

She nodded. "Thank you for trusting me."

He slipped the key back into the book and put it on the shelf. "Now, shall I take you home?"

When he turned, they stood only inches from each other, so close together in that small space behind his desk. For a moment, his gaze tenderly stroked her face. He took her hand.

"You look very lovely tonight," he said in a warm, soft voice. "Are your earrings new?"

She nodded. "Amanda gave them to me."

As she smiled a little self-consciously, he studied her face. "Very pretty." He looked as if he wanted to say more, but then he lifted his eyes and glanced toward the door.

Aah, yes. It was open. She stepped back and broke the connection that had entranced them for a few seconds.

"It's time for me to take you home." He held her hand for a few more seconds before he dropped it. "Lucia," he called. "We'll need our wraps again."

By the time they'd reached the hall, Lucia held up Annie's cape for her to slip inside. Once swathed in their winter garments, he led her toward the stable where Duffy stood with the horses.

"Here they are, boss. I stuck a new hot brick in there, Miss Cunningham."

"Thank you, Duffy."

After carefully assisting Annie into the carriage, John got in on his side and took the reins from the older man. Without a word, he flicked the reins and the horses took off.

They approached the schoolhouse in a comfortable silence. Once there, he pulled the vehicle next to a stand of trees, which sheltered it from the wind and the road. The moonlight shining through the leaves of the live oak trees covered them with lacy shadows. She breathed in the pungency of evergreens, the smell of the leather of the carriage and John's scent of bay rum. An owl called from a tree on the other side of the schoolhouse. Only a second later, an answering hoot came from the meadow.

Warmth radiated from where her arm touched his — only a small area, but the slight heat filled her. It was a perfect moment.

She looked up at him, surprised to see his head bent toward her, so close while they sat in this secluded haven of peace and security.

When he placed his hand over hers, she didn't pull away. They were alone, just the two of them, with the rest of the world far away. Her past, her fear held at bay by the kindness and strength of the man who bent toward her as if all he wanted was to keep her safe, to protect her, to be with her.

"Matilda, it can be no secret how I feel about you. I believe I'm falling in love with you. I would like to know what you think about the two of us together. If you truly don't welcome my attentions, I'll leave you alone, but I've felt this evening a change in you, as if my attention may be appreciated."

She could tell by the ragged edge of his voice, in the yearning she heard, that he didn't want to leave her alone. She said, "I have so little to offer."

He took her hand. "You are beautiful."

"Oh, no. Amanda is. I'm not." She held

her hand up when he started to interrupt. "Your wife came from St. Louis, from a good family, I've heard. The Hansons are a good family, and Amanda's rich and beautiful. She's perfect for you." She shook her head. "I'm a mere schoolteacher."

"You should not disagree with a man who tells you you're beautiful." Laughter echoed in his voice. "Besides being beautiful, you're intelligent and a fine teacher. You care about the children, you sing wonderfully, you play the organ and share your gifts with everyone. You're good and innocent and generous." He stopped and studied her face. "Have I left anything out?"

She wanted to move away from him, to escape his compliments, but she couldn't create any space between them in the tiny enclosure. "Oh, no. I'm not all that. I'm not good, not a bit."

"That's what I see, and you *are* beautiful."

For another minute, they sat next to each other. He slid his arm across her shoulders and kept his hand on hers while the shadow of the moonlight played across his features. Then he lifted her chin with the other hand and whispered, "Now I'm going to kiss you."

Fear stopped up her throat while tears

gathered in her eyes.

"I've done it again, haven't I? I've moved too fast." He withdrew his hand from hers. "You're such an innocent. I promise to remember that."

He sounded so sad. "Perhaps a kiss on the cheek?" she whispered. She would like that, she believed. She hoped.

"That would be nice." She heard a smile in his voice. He leaned his head closer to hers until she felt his breath feather across her cheek. Then he placed his lips there for a few seconds.

When he pulled away from her, she placed the palm of her hand over the place that he had kissed.

"Now," he said briskly, "if you don't want another kiss, let me escort you inside before you freeze out here."

She paused for a moment, wondering if another kiss might not be exactly what she'd like, but John had already turned and opened his door. "I can —"

"Of course you can get out of the carriage and walk to the door by yourself, but I enjoy playing the part of a gentleman." He leaped down from the seat and strode to her side, assisting her down, his touch filling her with a glow on this cold evening. He kept hold of her hand and ambled slowly toward the schoolhouse. He stopped at the bottom step and leaned toward her so she could feel his cheek close to hers. "Good night," he whispered in her ear, his words tickling a little.

Dazed, she climbed the steps and let herself inside. As she turned to close the door, she saw him get in the carriage. In a few seconds, it disappeared. Again Annie put her hand against her cheek as if she could feel his kiss there.

The wonder of it all — she had not been frightened by his nearness or his kiss, not a bit. And he trusted her, enough to show her where he kept that money, all that money, more than she'd ever seen before. He trusted her, which made her want to trust him in return.

After a minute, the world rushed back. No matter what he said or felt, she was not good and beautiful. And she hadn't been an innocent for years. No, she was only Annie. No amount of moonlight or sweet words or kisses would change that, no matter how much she wanted it to. No matter how much she yearned to be good enough for John, she had to remember who she was and what she'd been. Otherwise, she could lose absolutely everything she'd come to love so dearly in Trail's End.

CHAPTER THIRTEEN

On January eighth of the new year, Annie watched the students leave on the last day of fall-term classes. She had ten days to study before the spring term began.

Elizabeth and John had left a few days earlier to visit her mother's family in St. Louis. They'd taken a train to Corsicana, then changed to another headed for St. Louis. The trip, Elizabeth had explained, would take over three days each way. "Which," she had added, "leaves us less than a week to visit with my grandparents but my father says that is more than enough time to spend with people he doesn't like anyway."

Probably one of those bits of information John wished his daughter hadn't shared.

Over two weeks had passed since John had brought her home from the Christmas party. Other than the few times he'd come by to collect Elizabeth, she hadn't seen him.

With a sigh, she picked up Minnie, who was meowing at her feet for attention. "You are such good company," she said to the cat. Minnie had grown so much in the months since Annie had found her on the doorstep — she was no longer a little ball of fur.

She settled at the desk with Minnie purring in her lap and turned to the geometry section of the math book. Wilber would be ready to start on it soon. He ate up lessons as if he were starved and, indeed, she believed he was. Staying ahead of him taxed her, but she would use this section when Ida and Martha came back next term.

If Annie were still here next term.

A few hours later, she heard a vehicle stop in the yard. Moments later, Amanda called out to her.

"What do you have planned for this week?" Amanda said as she closed the door behind her. "Anything fun?"

"Studying, as usual." She pushed the book away.

"How do you plan to celebrate Valentine's Day with the students?"

"Valentine's Day? What is that? When is it?" Annie frowned.

"February fourteenth. How could you not know?"

"We didn't celebrate it where I'm from. I

don't even know what it is."

"It's the day when we tell people how much we love them. I always give my father a present."

"Like Christmas?"

"Not as grand and not at all religious. It's really just for fun. Let me show you something." Amanda reached in her purse and handed a piece of paper to Annie.

On the front of a folded page were two layers of paper lace with flowers around the edges. "This is lovely," Annie said. "What is it?" She turned the page over. "Where did you get it?"

"It's a Valentine's Day card. They're very popular in the East. A friend sent it to me." She opened it up. "She wrote a verse inside."

"Friends are life's greatest gift," Annie read. "That's so true."

"Do you want me to come and help the students make cards with you?"

"They'd really enjoy that. You made decorating so much fun at Christmas." Annie studied the card and ran her hand over the lace. "Do you have plans for this Valentine's Day?"

"I'll make my last attempt on the sheriff."

"Your *last* attempt? You're giving up?"

"I can't tell you what I'm going to do, but if my plan doesn't win the man, I *am* going to give up." She looked at an unconvinced Annie. "Really, I am. Truly. The spectacle of my chasing the sheriff while he runs the other direction has become entirely too mortifying. My failures have completely destroyed my confidence."

"Miss Cunningham, you have a letter."

Annie was in the mercantile, her work for the day finished. After completing a few purchases, she was admiring a piece of fabric.

A letter? Probably from Miss Palfrey, which was not good news. She hated deceiving Miss Cunningham's friend.

"I recognize the handwriting. It's from John Sullivan," Mr. Johnson said.

The grocer's words made her heart beat faster. She took the letter from his hand and noted John's clear handwriting. Why would he do such an improper thing as to write her a letter? "Must be something about school," Annie said.

"Must be."

Even if Mr. Johnson didn't seem the least bit concerned about the scandal of a single man writing an unmarried woman, Annie was. But she had to read the letter. It came from John, after all.

Once outside the store, Annie tore the

envelope open and scanned the words.

My Dear Matilda,
Although I know it is not proper to write
you, I can't stop myself. I have not been
able to talk to you since Christmas and
have missed you. Please know that I hold
you in my deepest affection and will see
you when we return home.
Yours, John

When she reached the schoolhouse, Annie
settled on a chair and read the epistle again
and again, touching the thick strokes of the
pen, running her finger over his signature.
"I hold you in my deepest affection," she
read aloud, and smiled.

"What do you hear from your friend Miss
Hanson?" The sheriff sat on the bench
outside the schoolhouse and watched the
children playing with battledores and
shuttlecocks on a sunny and unusually
warm afternoon in late January.

Annie pulled her gaze away from the
students to glance at him. "Why do you ask,
Sheriff?"

He studied the children more intently. "I
haven't seen her in a few weeks. That
concerns me.

"Who knows what she might get into that pretty head?" He stretched his legs. "She hasn't approached me lately. I don't sleep at night, wondering what she might be planning."

"Why, Sheriff Bennett. I believe you pine for Miss Hanson's attention."

He didn't look at her, but a muscle in his cheek tensed.

"You do find her attractive."

He shook his head. "Doesn't matter if I do. Her father wouldn't allow me to court her. Some things in life you just have to accept."

"But you do find her attractive."

He leaned forward on the bench and smiled at her. "Miss Cunningham, if there's a man in Texas who doesn't find Miss Hanson beautiful, he must either be dead, blind or too stupid to survive out here. She's one of nature's finest works." He stood. "And you'd better not tell your pretty friend anything I said because I'll deny it and that would make her unhappy."

Annie grinned as he stood and ambled toward his horse. She'd love to see the final showdown between Amanda and Sheriff Bennett. No doubt existed in her mind who would win — Amanda was determined and the sheriff wasn't dead, blind or stupid.

He turned back to Annie and shook his head. "I'm too old to play games like this. That's what you can tell her."

"You can tell her yourself, but I don't think you will. It seems she's finally breaking down your resistance."

"I'm hardly any young woman's dream man. I'm old and used up and ugly." He touched the scar for an instant.

"Sheriff, you are far from ugly. Clearly Amanda thinks you are the handsomest man in Trail's End."

He grinned for a second at her reply. "Certainly you have to admit I'm hardly the stuff a young woman's dreams are made of."

"One young woman seems to believe you are, Sheriff."

He stared at Annie for a moment, and then mounted his horse and left without a reply. Annie could hardly wait for Valentine's Day.

Annie awakened to knocking on the door of the schoolhouse and shook her head. She must have fallen asleep at her desk. It was late at night and the sound startled her. Who on earth could it be?

"Matilda?"

It sounded like Mr. Sullivan. Why would he be here? She stood and started toward the door in the flickering light of the oil lamp.

"It's John Sullivan."

She opened the door. "Hello, John." She smiled at the sight of him. "Welcome back. Is everything all right? Is there an emergency?"

"I'm sorry to bother you." He looked at her, taking in her hair, which she knew must be standing up at odd angles, and her face, which probably had deep marks on her cheek from the edges of her books.

She put her hands up in an effort to tidy the mess, but he took them in his grasp and held them.

"I shouldn't be here, but I've missed you." He smiled.

She couldn't help but smile back. Then she yawned.

"Were you studying?"

"Until I fell asleep. Where have you been? Elizabeth has been back in school for days."

"I've been away on business. When we returned from St. Louis, I received a telegram that I was needed in Austin to deal with a legal matter about the boundaries of the ranch." He stopped and studied her face. After half a minute, he continued. "I brought Elizabeth home, then took a coach that was leaving for the capital immediately.

It all happened so quickly, I didn't have a chance to tell you. I feared writing another letter would cause gossip and speculation."

"Boss, you ready to go?" Duffy called from the shadows. "I'm an old man and getting cold."

"Duffy picked me up in town. The stage arrived late."

She nodded. "Are you all right? Is someone sick?"

"No." He continued to scrutinize her. "I wanted to see you. That's all. It's been so long."

She could hear the affection in his voice. As usual, she didn't know how to respond.

"I'm attempting to guard your reputation, although it would be done better if I hadn't come by." He laughed softly. "*El viejo* has never been a chaperone before. But if anyone finds out I've visited you this late, he can say that nothing improper happened."

"But he might tell —"

"No, Duffy knows better than that." He gazed at her for a few moments more without speaking. "I just wanted to see you," he whispered. "Only for a minute, but I had to see you. I've missed you." He touched her cheek softly. "Good night, my dear."

"Good night, John."

"Boss, I'm really . . ."

He reluctantly dropped her hand before he headed down the steps and toward the surrey on the other side of the grove of trees.

What had just happened? And where had the usually solemn, upright John Matthew Sullivan gone? She smiled. She liked the lighthearted John she'd met before. Perhaps, she'd find away to spend more time with him.

On Thursday afternoon, both Miguel and Wilber worked in the schoolroom.

"Very well done," Annie told Miguel as he copied his spelling words. Lucia smiled. She was learning a great deal while she watched her son.

"Miss Cunningham." Wilber closed his science book and put it on the desk. "I'm going to have to leave now. My brothers and I won't be back the rest of the week." He stood, carried the book to the shelf and paused by her desk, his large frame towering over her.

"Why not, Wilber?" She got to her feet.

Wilber shrugged. "We have to dig a new well for the livestock. The old one dried up." He shook his head. "If we don't get some rain soon, we're going to lose crops and livestock. But what really scares us is the possibility of prairie fires."

"But it's only February, Wilber. Surely we'll have some rain soon."

"The drought started in May, ma'am. It's going to take a lot of rain to make any difference." He turned and headed toward the back door.

"Do you want to take a book with you?" she asked.

"No, but thank you. I won't have time. I'll miss being here."

"We'll miss you, too, Wilber." After Wilber left, Lucia rose. "We need to go, *mi hijo,* my son."

"Please, no, *Mamá.* I'm in the middle of answering questions about a story." He kept his eyes on the book.

"This drought," Annie said. "It's really bad?"

Lucia nodded. "We had another like it six years ago. Mr. Sullivan worries. Up north, they're getting some rain so the streams are running fairly well. As long as that keeps up, the cattle will be fine. But the crops suffer, and the grass and shrubs that feed the cattle, and the dry trees — all that could go up in flames any minute."

"Hello?" John stood in the door of the school. "A word, please?" His gaze settled on Miguel and Lucia.

"Mr. Sullivan," Lucia said, curtsying. "Come along, Miguel." She took her son's hand and hurried him away.

With the exception of church and evening meetings, Annie hadn't seen John since he'd come by that late evening in January. She didn't understand his inconsistent courting — was this how it was done?

Annie stood next to her desk. "Hello, John." He had obviously assumed his identity as member of the school board, serious and solemn. His expression worried her.

He frowned and said, "I have something serious I need to talk to you about."

She nodded.

"I'd heard something but I didn't know if it were true. But now . . . you're teaching Miguel?"

"Yes. Lucia comes to chaperone while Wilber is getting his extra lessons. Miguel comes with her."

"Matilda, you were not hired by the school board to give Wilber extra work or to teach Miguel."

"I don't mind. Wilber's making up lessons he's missed because he helps his father. He's so smart. I wish he could go to high school. He'd be a wonderful teacher."

"As you know, such a future is not pos-

259

sible, but Wilber is not the problem we need to discuss."

"What is the problem?" She thought for a moment. "Certainly you can't mean Miguel? You believe I shouldn't teach Miguel?"

"Not at all. I wish every child in the county could afford to come to school. I'd like to have to build a bigger school and hire another teacher. My dream is to have this school overrun with the children of the community — all the children."

"John, that's wonderful. That's my dream, too."

"Farley and I are concerned about the children who can't afford tuition, or who have to work to help their families. We're discussing solutions."

"I should have known you would do all that," she said.

"I support your teaching Miguel, but I have to pass on some concerns of the community. There are those who believe Miguel should not be in school."

"Why not? Because he's Mexican?"

"A few people have complained."

"I'm paid to teach from seven-thirty to two-thirty for two terms of three months each. Isn't that correct?"

He nodded.

"Who I teach the other hours of the day

is nobody else's business."

"You don't have to argue with me." He held his hand up as if deflecting her barely concealed anger. "But some members of the community would argue that you teach in a building owned by the board. As such it *is* the concern of the school board."

She sat down, so sickened by the reminder of the prejudice she'd fought all her life that her stomach churned. She did not want Miguel to go through that. "Does the school board want me to stop teaching Miguel?" she asked calmly, wanting to avoid a confrontation if possible. "Do *you* expect me to stop teaching Miguel?" she asked, her voice soft as she reminded herself that she needed John's support to keep her position.

"No. I'm just telling you what a few people have told me."

She stood, leaning on the desk to steady herself. "John, I'm a teacher. I'm supposed to teach. It's very much like a call from God." She stopped, amazed at her words. She'd never considered that before, but it felt right and true. "It truly is a call from God. If I continue to teach Miguel, will I be fired?"

"No, I just felt you needed to know that there has been discussion."

"Will the school board support me?"

"I'm not sure. But I do, after all, have some influence."

"I must teach him, even if the school board threatens to fire me." Those were the hardest words she'd ever spoken.

"Matilda, I will try to make sure the school board supports you. If there are consequences, I'll do my best to shield you."

"Thank you." She put her hand on her chest and felt her heart beating. "I was so frightened," she whispered.

"And yet you fought for Miguel."

Yes, she had, and the fact astonished her. She'd never stood up for herself before, but she'd found the strength to stand up for Miguel. Where had it come from?

But she knew. The courage came from God, who wanted her to teach. How she'd arrived here at this school, she didn't understand. She didn't believe God killed one woman so another would become a teacher. She just knew that she'd found God and been able to use the twists and turns of life to discover where she could and should serve.

She sat down, her legs no longer able to support her after the confrontation.

"Matilda, are you ill?" John knelt next to her chair.

Although she felt cold all over, when she

put her hand on her cheek, it was hot. The physical reaction overwhelmed her because conflict scared her, and yet she had done it. *Thank You, God.* After several deep breaths, her head had stopped spinning and her heart had calmed down.

"I'm fine." And she was. "Discussing this with you wasn't easy for me."

"May I tell you how much I respect you for taking that stand?" He took her hand. "I can see that it was not easy for you."

For a moment, his eyes caressed her face. "May I also explain why I have not come to see you?" He settled on a bench. "An emergency came up, one I thought I'd settled before. I had to go out of town again." He shook his head. "There's something strange going on with that parcel of land. A question of ownership. That's why I had to go to Austin again."

"Did it turn out as you wanted?"

"It took longer than I would have expected, but I hope this time it has been resolved." He smiled. "And now I'm home."

His voice and his words suggested she was an important part of his pleasure in being home.

"When I'm away, I miss you." He shook his head. "I've never understood men who could not control their emotions, but now I do. I didn't mean to care for you, Matilda — in fact, I fought it." He gave an odd little laugh. "Now I find myself in an uncomfortable situation by wishing to spend time with you but not wanting to place your reputation in peril."

She tilted her head in an effort to understand where his thoughts had taken him.

"If I come down to the schoolhouse too often, even as isolated as it is, people will notice and talk." He shook his head. "I need to consider your circumstances, both how to court you and how to protect you."

"Can that be done?"

"I don't know, but I'll think about it. Please be assured that your reputation is safe with me, that I'll do nothing — like that foolish visit the other evening when I could not stay away from you — without due consideration."

He strode toward the door but turned when he got there. For a moment, he gazed at her as if he held her face tenderly in his hands and caressed it, as if he kissed her gently, as if he softly touched her lips with his finger.

And then he left, closing the door behind him. She heard him descend the steps, mount his horse and ride off, but even when she no longer heard the sound of hoofbeats, she still felt the phantom touch of his hand lightly stroking her face and the whisper of his breath against her cheek.

CHAPTER FOURTEEN

Amanda stood outside the door to the sheriff's office feeling a little foolish.

If the sheriff did not fall at her feet, if he didn't swear undying love — although she couldn't imagine in a hundred years that he would — she'd stop chasing him. Taking a deep breath, Amanda opened the door and walked inside. The sheriff sat at his desk working on some papers. Although he barely even glanced up at her, his scowl showed he wasn't pleased to see her.

Nevertheless, she squared her shoulders. "Good morning, Sheriff Bennett."

"Mornin', Miss Hanson." He nodded.

Why was she doing this when she knew he'd reject her? For a moment, she considered turning around, going home and giving up. But he looked up at her and that rugged face and level stare made her heart flutter.

"How can I help you, Miss Hanson?" His

voice was polite but disinterested.

"Happy Valentine's Day." She took off her cape to reveal a lacy white dress trimmed in pink feather hearts.

For a moment, his grim expression softened as he drank in the sight before him. His eyes moved from the pink roses twined in her hair all the way down the frilly dress to her white shoes tied with pink ribbons.

"Very, very pretty, Miss Hanson. I guess you're looking to flirt with some handsome young man. Don't have any here."

"No, Sheriff, I'm here to charm you."

He laughed and went back to reading the papers on the desk.

That's exactly what she'd predicted he'd do, but if the man thought he could get away from her so easily, he didn't know Amanda Hanson at all. As fast as dry lightning could start a blaze on the prairie, Amanda opened his desk drawer and pulled out his keys. Once she had her prize, she ran into a cell and slammed the door behind her. She put her hand through the bars and locked the door before she pranced to the hard bench next to the wall and sat down. Victory!

Stunned, the sheriff didn't move at first. Then he stood and ambled toward the cell. "What do you think you're doing, Miss

Hanson?"

"Sheriff Bennett, you have ignored me since you came here a year ago." She stood and walked to the cell door. "I have tried every flirtatious trick I know to get you to notice me. You refused."

"You're wrong. I noticed every one. I just didn't fall for any of them."

She stamped her foot. "Oh, you're such a difficult man." She threw herself on the bench again. "I decided to lock myself up in your jail until you give in and court me."

"Is this the most romantic scheme you could come up with?" A smile tickled his lips.

"I've used up all the romantic schemes. I'm desperate now."

"Because you have found the one man in Texas who refuses to fall in love with you."

"You make me sound silly."

He raised an eyebrow in response.

"I . . ." She turned away. "I'm not playing now. This started as a game, but I discover I like you, very much."

"Why? Because I'm such a handsome man? Valiant and courageous."

She stood, closed the space between them and placed each hand on a bar. "As sheriff, of course you are valiant and courageous, as well as tough and rugged, which I find —

much to my surprise, I must tell you — very attractive."

"I'm older than you, Miss Hanson, years older. I've lived a hard life and have nothing to offer a spoiled little girl."

"Now, see, if you didn't care about me, you wouldn't call me a spoiled little girl. You use that to discourage me." She smiled. "I don't discourage easily, and, although my father has given me everything I want, that does not make me spoiled."

"I'm forty years old. Double your age. More than twenty years of my life were spent as a hired gun. Not the kind of background a loving father would choose for his darling daughter's husband."

"Sheriff." She held his glance in hers. "Your attempts to reason your way out of this tête-à-tête convince me even more that you do care about me."

With that, he reached into his pocket and pulled out his key ring.

She blinked. "What is that?"

"This would be a pretty poor jail if we had only one set of keys, wouldn't it?" He stuck the key in the lock and opened the door. "Miss Hanson, why don't you go home so I can work?"

"No." Haughtily, she sat down on the bench. "I don't need to lock myself up. I'll stay in here even with the door wide-open."

"No, you cannot. This is my jail." The sheriff strode into the cell, picked her up and attempted to carry her out. He had not considered the vast petticoats under her dress or her strength. Every time he started through the cell door, she used her hands or her legs to stay inside while her ruffles covered his face so he couldn't see where he was going.

After a few minutes, sweat rolled down his body and pink feathers stuck to his neck and face. "You are harder to rope than an angry heifer and more trouble than an unbroken colt."

He tried a few more times before admitting defeat. "All right," he finally said. "You can stay here." He dumped her on the bench, picked up both sets of keys, left the cell and locked it behind him.

"You're locking me in?"

"Just until you father gets here."

"My father." She closed her eyes and leaned against the wall. "Why do you have to bring my father into this?"

"Isn't speaking to your father the proper action?" He wiped his face and hands with a towel.

With that, he left the office, leaving her locked inside the cell in her Valentine's Day dress, feathers floating around and roses tumbling from her rumpled locks.

She sincerely hoped no hardened criminals wandered in.

Half an hour later, she heard horses pull up in front of the jail, followed by the opening of the door.

"You have a dangerous felon in your cell?" her father said. "What do you want me to do?"

"I believe when you see who that felon is, you'll understand."

She buried her face in the froth of white lace.

"Amanda, is that you?"

She looked up.

"My daughter is a felon?"

"Well, Mr. Hanson, one definition of a felony is breaking and entering. I don't know if that covers stealing a set of keys from the sheriff's desk and locking herself in a cell."

Amanda's father looked at the sheriff. "My daughter took your keys and locked herself in a cell?" He slowly turned to study Amanda, shaking his head. "I spoiled you. I gave you too much. Bennett," he said, and turned back toward the sheriff, "on her deathbed, her mother made me promise to take care of Amanda." He shook his head again. "I tried. I cannot account for this."

"Father," Amanda began, "I can explain." But the more she thought about it, the more she decided she really couldn't. She buried her head in her dress again.

"Sounds as if she may need another man to take over, one who is not daunted by the difficulties and dangers that life with her seems to promise."

Amanda stood up and marched to the bars. "Another man to take over?"

"Miss Hanson has stated that she'd like to marry me."

Her father fell onto a chair. "I never thought she'd be so forward. I do apologize."

"What would your response be if I were to ask you permission to marry your daughter?"

Her father clutched his chest and seemed to be having a heart attack.

"Father, are you all right?"

After he took a few deep, shuddering breaths, he said, "You'd do that? You'd take my daughter off my hands? I warn you, as much as I love her, she's a bothersome filly. She gets something in her mind and no one can change it."

"Father!"

"Yes, sir. I'm aware she's a bothersome,

stubborn filly."

"Sheriff!"

"But, Mr. Hanson, I have become one of those ideas that she won't change her mind about." He shrugged. "She's made my life hard, but if she's determined to marry me, we should probably just go ahead."

Fanning himself with his handkerchief, her father stood and walked to the cell. "Is the sheriff right? Do you want to marry him?"

She flounced toward the bench and threw herself on it. "I don't have the least desire to marry someone who says I am bothersome and stubborn." Tears began to seep from her eyes.

"Mr. Hanson, before I attempt to persuade your daughter to marry me, would you be agreeable to such a match?" the sheriff asked.

"Sheriff, I've waited years to find a man to marry her. She's turned down every single one. My daughter is my only family. There's no one to inherit the ranch. As long as I've known you, I've been impressed by your hard work and honesty. I'd be very happy if you would marry her and take over the ranch when I'm gone. Hold it in trust for your children."

She reached her hand through the bars.

273

"Father, you're not dying soon."

"No, but it's going to happen someday." He extended his hand to the sheriff and glanced at his daughter. "She doesn't look happy with you now, but if you can persuade her, she's yours and so is the ranch."

Amanda watched in amazement as they sealed the deal. A handshake between men, that's what she'd become. She wiped the tears from her cheeks with the hem of her dress, only to discover lace did not absorb tears well at all.

"Good day and good luck, Sheriff Bennett." Her father closed the door behind him, leaving her in the cell while the sheriff watched from a few feet away.

"Please let me out," she said in a small voice. "I'm sorry I've bothered you. I'll never bother you again. I promise."

"Does that mean we won't be getting married?"

"That's exactly what it means." Suddenly angry at his teasing, she leaped to her feet, took two steps to the door and grasped the bars. "Let me out of here now," she shouted.

He unlocked the door but pushed her back inside and then locked the cell behind him, and tossed both sets of keys out between the bars.

"Why did you do that?" Her head snapped

up to study his face.

"I thought you might need a few minutes to cool off, and I didn't want you getting away before we came to an agreement."

She took a few steps back until she ran into the bars on the other side of the cell. "An agreement about what?"

"Our wedding."

"But you don't want to marry me."

"I've wanted to marry you ever since the first time we met, but I told myself I didn't have the right." He took a step closer to her.

"I never . . ." She couldn't move any farther.

He took another step.

"What changed your mind?" she asked in a breathy voice.

"Well, you seem absolutely determined to marry me, and I would hate to disappoint you."

She wanted to argue with him, but she couldn't. Instead, she allowed him to lean closer, dizzy with the nearness of him.

"That kind of determination deserves a reward. Besides, I've always had a weakness for a forward little flirt. I just never thought your father would agree to my courting you. When you locked yourself in my jail, I decided that would show him the peril my life was in and he'd agree, if only to avoid the scandal." He put his arms around her and searched her face. "Do you truly love me or has this all been a game?"

"I love you," she whispered. "I've never said that before, to any man."

He nodded. "Will you marry me?"

She narrowed her eyes. "So that you can have the ranch?"

"Now that you mention it —"

She kicked him in the shin. He smiled at her.

"Because I love you more than I thought possible," he whispered.

"Oh."

"I don't want the ranch for myself. Your father wants it held in trust for our —" he paused to clear his throat "— for *our* children, Amanda." He studied her face for a moment, his eyes full of yearning. "Will you please marry me?"

She nodded and he finally kissed her. Kissing was something the sheriff did very well, which didn't surprise her one bit.

Then he pulled out another key ring and opened the door.

"Where did you get that?"

"You don't think I'd enter a cell with a very angry woman and not have a means of escape, did you?"

"Well." She took his arm and held it

firmly. "I'd hoped, perhaps, we could spend a little more time here." She gave him the smile she'd learned he could not resist. "To discuss the wedding, you know."

"Hello, hello!" Amanda shouted from outside. Annie heard her phaeton stop and the jingle of the harness as her friend tossed the reins onto the seat.

It was Saturday morning. Did Amanda have more to tell her about her campaign to win the sheriff?

"Matilda?" Amanda called from the door.

"I'm right here." Annie stacked the slates and stood, wondering what had sparked such excitement in her friend's eyes. Indeed, Amanda almost flew around the classroom with the grace and splendor of a butterfly.

"Tell me. What is it?"

Amanda stopped and put her hands to her mouth for a moment as tears came to her eyes. "I'm getting married."

"What?" Annie stared. "The sheriff?" Annie nodded her head. "But I can't imagine he'd ask you to marry him or that your father would approve."

"He did and he did. In fact, they both did." Amanda threw her arms in the air and laughed.

"Isn't it wonderful?"

Annie gave her friend a hug. "Tell me everything!"

Amanda settled on a bench and regaled Annie with one of the funniest tales she'd ever heard. She was amazed by Amanda's boldness and wished she could have seen the sheriff's reaction.

"Oh, my." Annie shook her head in disbelief. "How is the sheriff? Has he recovered?"

"He's very happy." Amanda laughed.

"You're exactly the right woman for him. I'm glad he finally figured that out." As she'd predicted, the man had never stood a chance against a force of nature like Amanda.

"I'm not sure he even realizes what happened, but I don't care." Amanda wiggled on the bench. "Now let me tell you all the plans. We'll be getting married the next time Reverend Thompson is here."

"So soon?"

Amanda sighed and squeezed her friend's hand. "Oh, yes. That soon."

CHAPTER FIFTEEN

Annie brushed down the new gray skirt Lucia had made her and tugged the collar of the white basque. The earrings Amanda had given her swung merrily. With a twist, she wound her thick hair into a bun on top of her head, stuck in several hairpins and smoothed the sides back. Her hair had grown in the nearly five months she'd been in Trail's End, as had her wardrobe. Now the owner of four skirts and seven tops, she felt very stylish. With stockings to go with her two pairs of shoes, a new petticoat, two plain cotton nightgowns and a pretty shawl, she had nearly filled her dresser. And she had a nice amount of money in the bank.

She hadn't seen John in a week, not since Amanda's wedding. But he'd sent a note with Ramon telling her he'd be by early this evening.

But she was ready early, had planned that because she needed some time in prayer.

She patted her hair once again, then entered the schoolroom and sat on the bench next to the large window overlooking the grove of trees behind the building.

"Loving and forgiving God," she began. She paused, studying the scene outside. The trees were beginning to bud with that pale, sweet greenness that announced the coming of spring and birds flitted through the branches. "Dear God, You have give me so much. Please help me find one more thing — the wisdom to know what to do next." She dropped her face in her hands to listen. If she'd learned anything besides what she'd picked up from all the books she'd studied, it was how little patience she possessed, how difficult she found it to listen for the leading of her Lord and her Savior. She slowed her breathing and bowed her head, waiting.

"Matilda?"

Feeling quieted and filled, she turned toward John.

"I knocked and called but no one answered so I came in." He looked down at her for a moment with a hint of a frown.

"I'm sorry." Should she explain? She hated to discuss her faith. Of course, she couldn't discuss it with most people. They wouldn't understand how God had changed her. With John, she worried that saying she'd been praying might sound . . . well, pretentious, but how else could she account for her behavior? "I didn't hear you because I was praying."

He sat on the bench in front of her and looked into her eyes. "You were praying? Do you pray a lot?"

She smiled. "I don't know what *a lot* means. I pray when I feel the need, when I am overwhelmed or happy or worried or . . . I don't know. I pray whenever I need to."

John considered that. "Does God always answer you?"

"I don't know yet."

"Well, if you don't know if God answers you," he said, "why do it?"

"I've learned God's response may not be immediate. And because God has given me courage and strength and hope and forgiveness every time I pray." She looked into his eyes. "Doesn't that happen when you pray?"

"I don't pray a lot."

"But you go to church every Sunday."

"Yes, but I go to be an example. Faith," he said, "hasn't been that important to me."

"I'm sorry," she said, surprised by his admission.

"But I'm not here to discuss faith," John said decisively as he took her hand and stood. "Why don't we go outside?" He led her to the spot where she often watched the children at play.

Once he sat down next to her, his voice and his expression became serious. "Matilda, do you know how much I care about you?"

She nodded.

"When I can work in a few minutes to see you, I feel as if I'm sneaking around."

That would be hard on a man as principled as John.

"I can think of only one way to be together." He stood and walked a few feet away before turning back, his hands behind his back and his expression even more solemn. "Farley tells me Amanda and the sheriff will be having an 'at home' on Saturday. I'd like to escort you."

"What?" The idea astonished her. "But, if you do that, if we go together, people will think we're courting. They'll know how we feel."

He laughed. "Yes, that's what I hope."

"But this is so . . . so personal." Could she express this more clearly without hurting his feelings? How could she explain the fact that she did want him to court her and her reluctance to tell the world? "I've always been a private person."

He sat beside her and seemed to think

about his words before he spoke. "I'm tired of seeing you only now and then. I want to be with you more, and I want everyone to know that we're together."

She'd both feared and hoped this would happen. Because John had such strong principles, hiding their relationship would eat away at him, deception would wound him.

She'd been through so much. After such a life, didn't she deserve happiness finally? After going through such horror and turmoil, didn't she finally deserve to be loved and cared for?

Looking into John's eyes, she saw that his solemn facade only disguised his vulnerability and yearning. She couldn't turn him down. She'd deal with the problems her response might bring later, but not now.

"I'd like that."

The joy on John's face convinced her she'd made the right decision. He let out a deep breath, smiling broadly.

"You've made me a happy man." He leaned forward and put his cheek next to hers. "I'll be by tomorrow evening at eight." As he spoke, his words tickled her ear. Reluctantly, he stood and looked at her, love shining in his eyes. "Goodbye, my love," he said.

She watched him leave, noticing a light-heartedness in his step as he ran toward Orion and mounted. After she could no longer see him, she closed the door.

She smiled again. She now understood what love meant, and she realized that she had been in love with him for some time. Why John cared for her she couldn't guess, but he did and she wouldn't argue with him about that.

The sheriff never stopped smiling. He looked like a different man during the visit he and Amanda made on Friday, the day after their return from their wedding trip.

"I don't intimidate anyone anymore," he said as he sat beside his wife outside the schoolhouse. "This town's going to be overrun by thieves and killers, vicious men, heartless criminals and the dregs of humanity, all cheering because Sheriff Cole Bennett has fallen in love."

"And you don't mind at all." After patting the sheriff on the arm, Amanda turned to speak to Annie. "Cole bought the sweetest little house for us. Daddy had moved us in while we were gone."

"*Little* is the important word. There's barely enough room for two — not much space for her huge wardrobe or all those shoes and wraps and hats and gewgaws."

"Who needs all that when I have you?" Amanda teased. He smiled at her. "We stopped by to make sure you know about the at home we're having at my father's house tomorrow."

"Yes, I do." It was, Annie realized with not a little trepidation, time to tell Amanda. "John will take me."

"John?" Amanda tilted her head. "John Sullivan?" Her eyes brows shot up. "John will take you?" When Annie nodded, then she leaned forward. "Are you and John courting?"

Annie nodded.

"Well, my, my, my." Amanda leaned back against her husband's arm. "When did this happen?"

"Little by little, over a few weeks. I'm not sure I realized it."

"I swan! Are you happy? Well, of course you are." She turned toward her husband. "Cole, would you please go check on the horses? I need to talk to Annie."

"Bossiest woman in Texas," he said with a grin as he moved toward the carriage.

"Tell me everything," Amanda said.

"John and I felt an attraction for each other, and he asked to court me." She leaned closer to Amanda. "Now, you tell me all about marriage. Is it marvelous?"

"Oh, Annie." Amanda sighed. "It's the most magnificent thing in the world. I'm so happy and so in love and Cole is amazing and he loves me." A giddy smile covered her face. "There's a lot it wouldn't be proper for me to tell an unmarried woman, but being married is wonderful if you're married to a man who really loves you."

With that Amanda leaped to her feet, pulled Annie up and gave her a quick hug. "We'll see you — and John — tomorrow," she said as she ran to join her husband.

Annie watched her friends drive off. She'd never known two people who truly loved each other and made each other happy. She'd thought her parents had been happy once, but she didn't remember exactly. Could a happy marriage have disappeared so quickly and left behind a person as miserable as her father?

Annie believed it was possible for a marriage to work. Perhaps love could be enough to bring two different people together. Maybe love could build a bridge between them.

She could only hope it did.

Saturday night when Annie and John arrived at the Hanson home, luminarias lined the drive crowded with carriages and horses. Candles sparkled in every window and guests ambled around the front porch and the side garden, the sound of their voices mingling with the music coming through the open windows.

She put her hand on her skirt to smooth out wrinkles that she knew were not there. Although Lucia had made sure her white cashmere basque and blue skirt looked perfect, Annie knew the other women were dressed much more formally and grandly in satin and lace with bustles and jewelry and other fashionable accessories.

"You're the most beautiful woman in the county," John whispered to her as he helped her from the surrey, seemingly reading her thoughts.

Annie put her hand to the top of the high-necked basque. Out of place, that was how she would look, the schoolteacher on the arm of John Matthew Sullivan. If a groom hadn't already taken the carriage away, she would've climbed right back on it and gone home.

Perhaps she could escape before anyone noticed she was there.

He took her hand and placed it on his arm. "Shall we?"

Clinging to him, Annie realized it was very

good to be courted by a man so strong, a man whose arm felt sturdy and protective and comforting beneath her hand.

"John and Matilda," Amanda said as they approached the receiving line. "It's my good friend, Matilda Cunningham, the school-teacher." Amanda spoke the words clearly and in a voice loud enough for guests in the farthest garden to hear.

When her friend leaned down and whispered, "You'll be fine," Annie realized she must have looked as frightened as she felt. She lifted her chin, straightened her back and vowed not to embarrass John, although she'd much prefer to run or hide. After all, hadn't Amanda just told everyone there that they were friends? That she belonged at the party?

"Miss Cunningham, how nice to see you and John." A very courtly Farley Hanson bowed over her hand. "I don't believe you have met my friend Sara Harper from Fredericksburg."

John continued to escort her around the room, greeting people and keeping her hand on his arm to show everyone that Annie was with him. Little by little, she relaxed and chatted with friends. When they returned from a walk in the gardens, a small orchestra had begun to play again in the large parlor and couples were beginning to gather.

"If you would join me for the first dance," Mr. Hanson said with another bow.

"I don't know how to dance," Annie whispered. The girls in the brothel had had to learn dances to entertain the gentlemen, but she was quite sure those were not the dances polite society performed.

"The first dance will be a turning waltz. I'll show you exactly what to do." He took her hand and led her into the parlor. "We'll allow the happy couple to start the dance. When you and I join them, that will signal for the others to follow."

"Mr. Hanson, you do me such an honor. Thank you."

"Nonsense," he said. "John is my friend."

Mr. Hanson did exactly as he'd said he would. With his hand resting on her back, he lightly guided her. Mistakes were not obvious in the crowd of dancers, fortunately.

When they finished the waltz, John claimed her for a schottische. Although she realized she knew this dance, she allowed him to show her the slides, hops and turns because she enjoyed his attention. After that, Mr. Johnson invited her to polka, and she joined a visiting Hanson relative from San Antonio in a reel. By then, Annie had lost her reticence and enjoyed every dance.

John appeared next to her and offered his arm. "I'm a fortunate man," he whispered to her. "Every man here is jealous that I arrived with the loveliest woman on my arm."

Annie grabbed his arm and held on to it, grateful he'd found her.

"May I suggest a cooling walk in the garden?" John asked. "You've been dancing for hours."

"Thank you, John. I've had the most wonderful time."

Many of the guests had begun to leave and the garden was nearly deserted. As they walked past a trellis in the far corner, John pulled Annie behind it.

"Now that I have you alone," he said, "I'd like to kiss you."

Annie closed her eyes. She didn't want to kiss him. She'd be crushed if she discovered she didn't like it. But surely she could do it to make him happy. It was so little to ask.

"Matilda, may I kiss you?"

Taking a deep breath, she nodded. John lifted her chin gently and rested his lips on hers for only a few seconds. His kiss was sweet and loving. It warmed her and she melted against him.

When he lifted his head, she whispered, "That was the first time." The first time she'd enjoyed a kiss and wanted another.

The first time a man hadn't frightened her with his touch.

They left the party soon after. She fell asleep with her head on John's shoulder and laughed when he woke her by carrying her to the door.

"Matilda, I have something more I would like to ask you," he said, his voice sounding rough and uncertain. He cleared his throat as they stood in the doorway.

Reaching up to touch his face, she could feel tension in his jaw.

"Would you marry me?" He held his hand up. "I know I should ask a male relative for permission first, but I don't believe you have any. Is that correct?"

She nodded, not that she'd have wanted John to meet her father even if he had still been alive.

Marry him? Being close to him filled her with breathless joy and made her feel sparkly inside, as if she'd swallowed a star. She opened her mouth to answer but had no idea what to say. She wanted to say yes. Didn't she have a right to be happy? Didn't John? She'd make him happy — she'd do everything in her power to make him happy. He was her rock, her strength. The answer seemed very simple.

"Yes, I'll marry you." She beamed at him.

He leaned down and kissed her again, which made her shiver with pleasure. There could be no happier person in the entire world than Annie.

"I have something for you." He reached in his pocket and took out something small. "It's a claddagh ring that's been in my family for a hundred years."

She rubbed her finger along the gold and felt a heart and a crown.

"My great-great grandfather gave it to his intended." He slipped it on her finger. "The message of the ring is, 'Let love reign.' "

"Thank you, John," she whispered. "It's lovely."

"I have one more request." He paused. "I haven't talked to Elizabeth about this yet. If you don't mind, would you wait until Monday to wear the ring? I know she'll be happy, but I need to . . . well, let her know."

"Of course." What did one more day matter? She and John would be together forever.

On Monday morning, Annie gazed at her ring, studying the symbol John had slipped on her finger and smiling at the promise they'd made. The engraving was so worn she could barely make out the heart after years and years of wear. With this ring, she joined the line of women who'd become part of the Sullivan family.

As soon as Annie entered the classroom, she saw Elizabeth waiting at her desk. The child hurried to Annie and reached up to hug her.

"Are you going to be my new mother?" she asked.

Annie took her hand and led her to a bench where they both settled. "I'm going to marry your father, Elizabeth. Do you want me to be your mother?"

Without a pause, Elizabeth said, "Oh, yes, Miss Cunningham, I'd really like you to be my mother." She hugged Annie again. "What should I call you?"

"You could call me Matilda or Mother. What do you think?"

"Mother." Elizabeth nodded. "That's what I want to call you, but not at school when other children are around. Here in school, you're still Miss Cunningham, at least until you marry my father, when you'll be Mrs. Sullivan." She nodded confidently after she reasoned this out.

When they heard more children crossing the lawn, Elizabeth stood. "I'm very happy." She paused before she smiled and added, "Mother."

The spring term passed quickly. Annie

learned geometry but that forbidding calculus would take more time than she had to master.

She and John had set the date for their wedding for June sixth, when the preacher came through. This gave her time to complete the spring term in mid-April and prepare for the ceremony.

Easter had come and gone, but she was still filled with the joy of what she'd learned: in the midst of darkness, resurrection lies ahead.

Annie had never felt so loved, so cared for, so pampered. Wherever they went, John introduced her proudly as his bride-to-be. They'd taken Elizabeth to shop in Austin and gone to Fredericksburg for dinner. She'd never believed she would have a fiancé — certainly not a fiancé like John Sullivan.

Only the continuation of the drought dampened their happiness. As the weather warmed, and February and March passed, every morning Annie looked out the window for clouds or signs of moisture. There were none. The usually glorious wildflowers bloomed in tattered patches and dried up quickly in the blazing sun.

Even the rain in areas north of Trail's End had ended and the creeks and streams had narrowed to trickles of water and barren arroyos. The Bryan boys came to school more often because there was nothing to do on the rain-starved farm. No cattle had died yet, but if this drought went on longer, they would — herds of them that none of the ranchers could afford to lose. Annie noticed Wilber's troubled expression. Of the three boys, he knew best what was at stake.

John worried, too. The level in the stock ponds had become so low the cattle crowded to share the small amount of water remaining. Duffy had taken crews out to dig for underground water but whenever they found a well, it lasted only a few days.

Prayers were lifted in church, but still the sun shone in the cloudless sky and temperatures soared. No rain came. A hot wind blew unrelentingly across the parched, baked land.

They heard reports of dry lightning starting fires in neighboring towns and watched the sky, praying that would not happen here, not in Trail's End.

Late one afternoon, Annie headed out across the meadows surrounding the Sullivan ranch for a walk. The grass was pale tan and high, scorched by the sun and scoured by the wind. On the broad, open plain, the meadow looked like a field of dry wheat waving in the strong gusts. For a moment, she stood watching the sunset while dust billowed around her. Then she settled under a tree to watch the orange and yellow and scarlet rays of the setting sun play across the rustling grass.

She gasped — for a moment, the colors of the sky and the rays of the sun shimmered on the grass as if the prairie had caught fire. Flames of gold and crimson seem to surround her while the wind blew flickering waves of heat over her.

Remembering the stories about fires destroying neighboring towns, the illusion terrified her. She leaped to her feet and dashed toward the schoolhouse. After running forty yards, she turned around. Her imagination was acting up — all she saw now was tall, dry grass and the last glow of the sunset.

Her vision of the fire was the scariest thing to happen to Annie that spring — at least until she saw Willie Preston in town again on a warm, clear morning in early May.

Chapter Sixteen

Rocking back and forth on scuffed boots, Willie Preston stood in the middle of the road and watched Annie with a smile that showed a missing front tooth. An ugly, scruffy man with a patchy beard and mean eyes, he was her past personified.

He took a step toward her. "Well, if it ain't Annie MacAllister, and lookin' real pretty." He shook his head. "Me and the boys missed you when you left Weaver City."

Afraid of what he might say or do, she longed to turn toward the schoolhouse and run, but what good would come of that? He'd catch her easily. She lifted her head and continued to walk. With calm determination, she strode around him toward town, which was only around the next bend in the road. Certainly he wouldn't hurt her with people around.

"Don't act so high and mighty, Annie," he shouted as he swaggered next to her. "You ain't nothing but a common prostitute. Your father was a drunk and murderer."

"I'm not like that anymore. I'm respectable."

He grabbed her arm and stopped her. "Don't care." He snorted. "More like you changed names. Didn't know you was a schoolteacher, Matilda," he said, spitting out her new name with disgust.

She felt as if icy water was trickling down her neck. How could he know? Forcing herself not to shake, she turned toward him. "What do you mean?"

He laughed. "I saw you the other time I was through. Didn't think I did, did you? I come back and asked about you. They told me there wasn't no Annie MacAllister around, but the woman I described sure sounded like the new schoolteacher."

She took a deep breath and held it, forcing herself to remain on her feet, but she couldn't say a word.

"Yeah, you look pretty. Nice clothes." He grinned. "Hear you're getting married. To a rich man."

She nodded. Foolish to deny what anyone in town could tell him, what he already knew.

"Well, well. Seems like you wouldn't want that man, Mr. John Matthew Sullivan —"

he drew the syllables of the name out "— to know who you really are." He nodded his head, as if he were thinking. "Seems like you'd do anything to make sure he didn't find out who his sweet little bride really was."

What did he want? She looked around and considered running again, but she wouldn't get far, only a few feet before he'd catch up and knock her into the dust covering the hard, dry road.

"Money, that's what I want."

He dropped her arm and took a step closer to her. She forced herself to stay in place, to look straight into his eyes.

"I don't have money. I'm a schoolteacher."

"Let me see your hands."

When she reluctantly held them out, he said, "That ring ain't worth a thing, but I know Sullivan has money." She could feel his spittle on her face and smell his putrid breath. "If you don't want him to know, you'll give me five hundred dollars."

She gasped. "I don't have that much."

"Bet your fancy fiancé has more than that just lying around his house. Get it for me tomorrow or I tell him everything." He stepped back. "Meet me in the meadow behind the schoolhouse at nine in the morning. Bring the money." He swaggered past her and toward town.

How much money did she have? She'd worked for six months for thirty-two dollars a month. Even if she hadn't spent a penny, that made only one hundred ninety-two dollars. A grand sum for her, but nowhere near what Preston wanted. Subtract the cost of her expenses and purchases, and she probably had one hundred fifty left, at the most. Would he settle for that amount?

John had thousands of dollars. She knew exactly where he kept the money and how to get to it. He wouldn't miss five hundred dollars — not right away. She could go to the house, slip into the study and borrow what she needed. Somehow she'd pay it back, little by little, after they were married.

She'd gone into town this morning to buy some ribbons, happy in the thought that her wedding was less than three weeks away. Now dread filled her and uncertainty about where she'd be in three weeks. As she considered this, she found herself walking in the direction of the schoolhouse. But she knew one thing. She wouldn't steal the money from John. No matter what, she couldn't rob him. He loved and trusted her.

So how could she get so much money? She suddenly stopped and stood absolutely still with the dust billowing around her and filling her shoes. What was she thinking? She'd known — always known — that she had to tell John about her past. She'd made excuses not to: the time wasn't right, she was tired from a day of teaching, there were people around, she didn't have enough time and on and on.

The real reason? She didn't want to. As much as John said he loved her, he hated liars. He was moral and upright. No matter how much she'd changed, she knew John. Her former life would shock and disgust him. He would not be able to accept her if he knew she was a soiled dove. And he'd never forgive the fact that she'd deceived him.

Tears slid down her face. When she took her handkerchief out and wiped her cheeks, the white cloth came away filthy. But still the tears came and streaked her face with grime.

Not wanting anyone to see her, Annie hurried down the road and turned toward the schoolhouse, taking a shorter way through brambles, which tore at her dress. She didn't care. She had to be alone to think, to reason this out, to decide.

Loving Savior, please give me strength and guidance.

Once at the schoolhouse, she ran up the

steps, tore the door open and slammed it behind her. She dashed into the bedroom and threw herself on the bed and sobbed. Worried, Minnie rubbed against her and patted Annie's cheek with her paw.

When the initial storm had passed, Annie lay there hurting so much inside she could hardly breathe. She prayed again but heard no answer.

Because, she realized as she sat up, the answer lay within her. She'd always known that. She should have told John long ago, before she'd fallen so deeply in love with him, back when she'd thought and hoped no one would ever find out about her past.

But if she had confessed, not only would she have lost the man she loved and the daughter she'd found, she'd never be able to teach again. With Minnie behind her, Annie stood and entered the schoolroom. She ran her hand along the desktops and thought of the sounds of the children learning and playing. She loved this place and this life and these people. These had been the most wonderful months of her entire existence.

She forced her thoughts back to the past, back to the day she'd assumed the identity of Miss Matilda Cunningham. At that time, she'd prayed for a few days, then for a week

302

and finally for a month of warmth and food. She'd been given over six months filled with joy and love. That should be enough to last her forever, but she was greedy, so greedy she wanted more. She wanted a life like everyone else's, happiness like Amanda's. She didn't care about the money or the big house, she only wanted what she could no longer have: John, Elizabeth, her students and her friend.

She'd built her new life on a lie. She had to face that and accept the consequences. She had to tell John. Turning back to the bedroom, she picked up Matilda's valise and packed it so she could collect it and leave after she told John. She had no idea what she'd do or where she'd go, but she knew she had to leave.

On the bed, she left what didn't fit inside the suitcase: the clothes she'd worn when she first became Matilda. She no longer was Matilda, but neither was she suddenly Annie MacAllister again. In fact, she had no idea who she was.

But she knew who she wasn't. She could no longer pretend to be Matilda. She sat down and wrote a letter to Miss Palfrey, to tell her what had happened to Matilda and beg forgiveness for her lies. Finished, she folded it, slipped it inside an envelope she'd addressed and left it on the desk.

Now, she had to go tell John. She couldn't put it off any longer.

She pushed herself to her feet and stood, drawing herself as straight as possible. After a deep breath, she left the building and headed toward the ranch with steps as reluctant as a woman making her way to the guillotine during the French Revolution.

John studied numbers on the balance sheet in front of him and made a few corrections. From the front hall, he heard Lucia's voice, followed by a knock on the door.

"Come in," he called.

When Matilda entered, he stood. "What a nice surprise."

Then he saw that her beautiful eyes were red and swollen. Her hands clenched her purse so tightly that her knuckles were white.

"What is it?" He started around the desk, but she held up a hand.

"Please sit down."

He wanted to hold her as she swayed in front of the desk, but the clear determination on her face convinced him to obey her request. What was the matter? Why did she look so ill?

"Lucia," he shouted, "bring —"

"No," she said, shaking her head.

"Sit down, my love."

She squeezed her eyes shut and continued to shake her head. "I need to stand." She placed her purse on the desk and said what sounded like, "I'm not Matilda Susan Cunningham."

She couldn't have said that.

"I am not Matilda Susan Cunningham," she repeated, each word clearly enunciated.

He frowned. "What? Of course you are."

"No." She fell onto a chair as if her legs would no longer hold her. "You have to listen to me. Be patient. This is hard to tell and hard to understand." She took a deep breath. "My name is Annie MacAllister. Matilda Cunningham died in the accident. I assumed her identity."

"What?" John leaned back in his chair and shook his head, attempting to make sense of her words. "Why?"

She took a deep breath and swallowed hard. "Because I'm not a person you'd want to know."

He shook his head. "Matilda —"

"My name is Annie MacAllister. I'm not a schoolteacher. I've never even been to school." She swallowed hard and closed her eyes before speaking. "I wasn't a moral woman."

"What are you saying?"

"John." She looked at him, her face pale. "I used to be a prostitute in Weaver City. I got on the stagecoach that day in October to escape that life."

It took a few seconds for her words to sink in. When he finally understood what she'd said, he felt as if he were being squeezed by a giant fist. His head hurt and his stomach clenched. Before he realized what he was doing, he stood and asked in tones of shock and bewilderment, "You're a prostitute?"

She continued to look at him. "I was."

He walked around the desk and glared down at her. "I brought a prostitute here to teach the children?" Then he whispered, "I fell in love with a prostitute?"

He crossed to the fireplace and leaned against the mantel, his head on his hand. He couldn't think, couldn't take in what she'd told him. After almost a minute, he heard her stand.

He turned around and studied her, not sure if he was angry or wounded, or which hurt more, the deception or the facts. Her lovely face suddenly appeared mottled to him, and her lips curved down in what looked like a death mask. Pity stabbed at him, but he forced it away, thinking of her past and her lies. She stood.

She put the ring on his desk, then turned and ran from the room. When he heard the front door slam after her, he lurched heavily into the desk chair. He put his face in his hands and felt tears, except that John Matthew Sullivan would never cry over a woman like . . .

He didn't even remember what she called herself — Annie something — but he knew he'd never cry over whoever she said she was. He couldn't allow himself to grieve for a prostitute.

When she ran out of the house, Duffy waited for her outside the front door. "Miss Cunningham," he said as he took off his hat. "Let me take you home."

"I don't have a home," she whispered, stunned to realize that truth.

He took a step toward her and reached to support her but she pulled away.

"I'll have the wagon hitched up in a few minutes. Come down to the stable and wait. I'll give you a ride back to the schoolhouse."

"Did you hear what happened? What he said?" she asked.

He nodded. "I was workin' next to the window. I'm real sorry. You've had a rough time. Now you come down here and sit down while I get the wagon ready," he said, attempting to take her arm again. "Mr. Sullivan doesn't mean those things. He's upset now."

She pushed his hand away. "Thank you, Duffy, but you know he does. And you'll get in trouble if you help me."

"You think I care about that?"

"But I do, Duffy. I don't want anyone to get in trouble because of me." She attempted to smile at him but couldn't. "I have to . . ." She stopped. She really had no idea what she had to do because a tiny part of her had hoped John would forgive her, accept her. What now?

"Thank you," she said, and started to walk back toward the schoolhouse.

Halfway there, Annie heard a vehicle coming up the road. She looked around, ready to run toward the trees and hide. She didn't want to see anyone. But before she could move, Amanda called out to her. Oh, she didn't want to see Amanda. Annie could only guess how she would recoil when she heard the story.

"Matilda, where are you going? Do you want to go to town with me?" The phaeton stopped. After a pause, Amanda said, "What's wrong?" She jumped from the carriage and took her friend's shoulders. "What happened? Are you hurt?" Amanda took out her handkerchief and wiped Annie's face.

"No." Annie shook her head. "Go away. Leave me alone. You don't want to be near me," she croaked. "You don't want to know me."

"Of course I do." Amanda embraced Annie. "You're my dear friend."

"No." Annie took a deep breath and pushed her away. Telling Amanda would be nearly as difficult as telling John. "I'm not Matilda Cunningham."

"Of course you are, dear." Amanda took Annie's hand and helped her into the phaeton. "Let's get you home." Before Annie could protest, Amanda had cracked the reins and the horse took off.

"Matilda Cunningham died in the stagecoach accident. Annie MacAllister survived."

Amanda frowned as if trying to understand.

"I'm not Matilda. I'm Annie MacAllister." She looked at Amanda and could tell her friend still didn't understand. Gently, she put her hand on Amanda's. "Please listen to me." When her friend pulled the phaeton to a stop in front of the schoolhouse, Annie said, "Before I came here, when I lived in Weaver City, I was a prostitute."

Her eyes round, Amanda titled her head to study her friend. Annie had known she'd be upset. Blinking tears back, she turned in her seat to get down from the carriage.

"You poor dear." Amanda hugged her again. "That must have been terrible."

Annie sat back and gazed at her friend. Tears ran down Amanda's face. Where was the condemnation she'd expected? "Did you hear what I said?"

"Yes. Life must have been very difficult for you. You must have suffered and hated every minute of it. Let's go inside and you can tell me about it, if you want to."

"I can't go back to the schoolhouse."

"Did you tell John?" At Annie's nod, she said, "He didn't take it at all well, did he?" She sighed. "John is a proud man, too proud of his family and reputation. I'd hoped you'd soften that." She shook her head. "This would be hard for him to accept."

Annie didn't know how to respond. "I need to pick up my valise and Minnie, and I have a letter to mail." She looked down at her clenched hands. "I don't know where I'll go after that. Probably to the hotel so I can wait for the stage."

"No, you won't. You'll come live with Cole and me until you decide what to do."

"The sheriff won't want me there."

"Of course he will. Matilda, you're our friend."

"And there's no room." Annie knew the small house well from her many visits. "The other bedroom is filled with your —" she paused to try to remember what the sheriff had called them "— with your gewgaws."

"My friend, you are much more important to me than all the gewgaws in the world. Don't you know that?"

Once they had picked up her belongings, Amanda drove Annie to the tiny white cottage with dark blue trim. In front was a trellis, which Amanda planned to fill with roses in a few weeks, whenever it finally rained.

Amanda helped Annie from the phaeton and supported her up the steps as if she were an invalid. Once inside, Amanda settled her in the sheriff's comfortable chair. "I have to take the horse to the stable boy," she said. "I'll be right back. We'll talk when Cole gets home," Amanda said. Before she left, she fixed Annie a cup of tea.

Annie didn't know how long it would be before Amanda came back and the sheriff arrived home. While the tea cooled on the table, she sat quietly with Minnie curled on her lap and looked out the window. A few clouds drifted in the sky, more than she'd seen for months. As she watched, the sun sank lower and lower. She reminded herself about the message of Easter. It didn't help with the pain much now, but it would eventually.

When the sheriff walked into the house, Amanda took him aside for a few minutes. Then she served dinner, but Annie only pushed the food around on her plate and nibbled on a biscuit. After dinner, they settled around the cleared table.

"Annie, if you can, will you please tell us what happened?" Amanda put her hand on Annie's.

She looked at her friends. Concern showed on both faces. She swallowed and began her story. "My father was a weak man. He married my mother and changed because he loved her." Annie looked down at her hands. "She died when I was five, and he couldn't handle her death. He started drinking and gambling. In the end, he lost everything. I started working when I was seven, cleaning houses to support us."

"Did he ever hurt you?" Amanda asked gently.

Annie nodded. "When I didn't bring enough money home, he'd beat me. Finally I started sleeping outside, when the weather was good enough." She stopped to calm herself. She'd wished for years she could forget the terror of those days but never had. "The drinking and the fighting got worse. When I was fourteen, he killed a man in the bar and was strung up right there."

"Hung?" the sheriff asked.

Annie nodded. "After that, the good women of the community didn't want the daughter of a killer in their houses." She shrugged. "I couldn't read or write. No one would hire me. I didn't have any money. I couldn't even leave town. So I became a prostitute." She shivered and couldn't look at her friends. "I hated every minute of it. I saved my money for five years and finally bought a ticket to Trail's End. You know everything else except that my real name is Annie MacAllister. The woman who died on the stagecoach was the real teacher, Matilda Susan Cunningham. I took her place because . . . because I knew that was the only way to escape my past." She gave a forced laugh. "All that effort, and it didn't work. Didn't make a bit of difference."

"You couldn't read or write?" the sheriff asked.

She shook her head. "I taught myself to. I studied every night and taught myself what I needed to know to teach the students the next day."

"You are an amazing woman." Amanda shook her head. "You are courageous and remarkable. I can't believe you taught yourself all that."

She shrugged. "I had to."

"Why did you decide to tell John?" the sheriff asked. "You didn't have to."

"I did. I always knew I had to, but I couldn't find the courage to do it until yesterday. A man from Weaver City saw me and threatened to tell John if I didn't pay him five hundred dollars."

"What's his name?" The sheriff leaned forward.

"Willie Preston."

"Preston knew you from Weaver City?"

"Yes, he works for one of the ranchers there, Roy Martin."

The sheriff nodded. "I know Roy Martin. Mean as a snake and greedy."

Suddenly she began to shiver. She'd stayed calm for hours, but the hopelessness of her future and the loss of John hit her again, hard. And what would people think when they found out who she was? She had to leave town before that happened. She couldn't face the Johnsons or her students once they found out what she'd been.

Where would she go?

Amanda held her. "Matilda or Annie, I

don't care who you are. We're your friends."

The sheriff took her hand. "Stay here until you know what's ahead for you and where you want to go."

Overwhelmed by their kindness and unable to speak, Annie nodded and allowed Amanda to take her to the spare bedroom. All of Amanda's gewgaws had been shoved in a corner and a small bed had been made up for her. Annie knew she'd never fit.

Not that it mattered. She doubted if she would sleep anyway. She sat next to Minnie on the side of the bed and clasped her hands. From the parlor, she heard voices, then the sound of the sheriff walking across the room and out the door. From outside on the prairie came the howling of a coyote who sounded as lonely as she felt.

She tried to sleep but couldn't stop thinking about how happy she'd been here, and how much she'd loved her students. And then John's angry face appeared, his furious shouts ringing in her ears over and over.

"Dear Lord. . . ." She didn't know what more to say. He knew her sorrow. He shared her grief.

And He had forgiven her. When she turned her life over to Him, He'd given her a second chance. She clung to that as sleep finally claimed her.

CHAPTER SEVENTEEN

"Father?" Elizabeth knocked on the door. "May I come in?"

John turned to look out the window of his study. Dark already. How much time had he spent pacing from one side of the room to the other? Rubbing his hand across his eyes, he moved slowly to the door, feeling as if he'd been very sick, as stiff as if he'd grown old. "What is it?"

Elizabeth stood before him, her hair braided neatly and wearing her long cotton nightgown. "My prayers. It's bedtime but you haven't heard my prayers."

"Not tonight." He didn't think he could bear to listen to prayers tonight, not when God had deserted him. "Go on to bed. I'll be up later." He started to close the door but Elizabeth put her hand up to stop it.

"Lucia told me Miss Cunningham was here earlier." She paused. "I didn't get to see her."

What should he tell his daughter? Probably at least part of the truth. "Miss Cunningham had to leave. She came to say goodbye."

"Why didn't she tell me in person? Why is she leaving?"

"An emergency." Not a complete lie. "Of course, she wanted to see you, but she didn't have time."

Elizabeth came into the study and sat in one of the chairs. As he watched, he realized how tiny she was, so little she took up less than half of the chair. How could he tell his daughter exactly what had happened? Of course he couldn't. She'd never understand. He barely did.

"When will she be back?"

"She won't come back."

She looked at him in surprise before her chin trembled. "She won't come back? She won't be my mother?"

He shook his head.

Elizabeth leaned forward and pointed at the desk. "It's the ring. She left the ring. She won't be back." Her body trembled and tears began. "Doesn't she love me?"

"Of course she does." He kneeled before her. "Sometimes things happen. She didn't *want* to leave, but she had to."

"Why? If she loved us, she wouldn't leave

us." She gazed at him, her eyes filled with grief. "Did I do something to make her leave?"

"No, no. You didn't do anything wrong." He took her hand but didn't know how to comfort her. "She . . . she just had to go away."

"Where did she go? Can I visit her?" she sobbed.

John stood. He couldn't answer. He couldn't talk about this anymore. Selfish, he knew, but it hurt too much to respond to the child's questions. He picked Elizabeth up and cradled her in his arms, holding and rocking her until she fell asleep, worn out from crying.

"Lucia," he called. When the woman appeared at the door, he said, "Please take Elizabeth to her room and put her to bed." He handed his tiny, sleeping daughter to Lucia, then fell back into his chair. If he were a drinking man, he'd probably attempt to lose himself in a bottle, but he wasn't and knew that indulgence wouldn't solve the problem or alleviate the pain.

"How could she have lied to me?" he whispered.

He would have been happier never knowing, to live with Matilda — or whatever her name was — in happiness and ignorance.

He wished she hadn't told him. But she had. If only he hadn't been brought up in a family that expected so much from him. Perhaps then he could've married a former prostitute without feeling as if he'd betrayed his name.

For a moment he clasped his hands, closed his eyes and attempted to pray, but he and God had never been all that close. His God was a moral being, not one John could go to in sorrow. In fact, he and God were barely on speaking terms. How could he confess or feel close to a distant God? He'd never been the type of man who told God about his problems and expected God to listen or solve them.

And yet *she* had.

Reaching out his hand, he picked up the ring and clenched it until the crown cut into his finger.

"I'd like to see Mr. Sullivan, please," a man's voice came from the front hall.

Who would come by so late? Before he could move, the study door was thrown open and the sheriff entered.

"Sullivan," he said, and settled in a chair in front of the desk as if he'd been invited.

"Sheriff." John nodded politely. "How are you and your wife?"

"Very well."

But the smile that usually covered the sheriff's face when he thought of his new wife didn't appear. "I came to talk to you about something. Actually, two things. First, I hear someone has shown interest in that parcel of land over northwest."

"Yes, I've been in and out of Austin because a lien was placed on it and questions have been raised about its ownership. How did you know that, Sheriff?"

He answered that query with another question. "Do you know a rancher up in Weaver City named Roy Martin?"

"Only by name. He's the man who's challenging my right to the title."

"Seems there's a man named Willie Preston in town, a man who works for Martin. Preston's come to Trail's End a couple of times for his boss. Don't know much more than that, but thought I should drop by and mention it."

"I don't know a Willie Preston, either." He glanced up at the sheriff, wondering. "Again, how do you know this?"

"Preston knew Matilda — or rather, Annie — in Weaver City. He recognized her in town and attempted to blackmail her. Said if she gave him five hundred dollars, he wouldn't tell you who she was." The sheriff nodded. "Guess you know the rest of that story."

The fact that Annie — he must think of her that way from now on — had come forward herself made no difference. She was who she was, and he didn't want to talk about her. "I still don't understand. Why is Preston here?"

"Might be that Martin sent him down to see if he could do a little mischief, figure out a way to get that piece of land cheap. Don't know. I'm going to talk to the man tomorrow."

"You think my land is safe?"

"Don't know." He sat in silence for a moment before he looked into John's eyes and said, in a soft voice with an edge of anger, "I hear you tossed her out."

"Men like Roy Martin and his man Preston are what a sheriff should deal with." John stood. "But this woman? She's none of your business, Bennett."

"Yes, she is. You see, she's a friend of mine and a friend of my wife, and that makes it my business. They're both over at my place, crying. A man can take only so much of that."

John leaned his palms on the desk and glared at the other man. "Your wife shouldn't be around that woman."

"I guess you mean Annie when you call her 'that woman.' Well, Sullivan, if you wouldn't mind sitting down, I'd like to tell you something about her." When John continued to stand, the sheriff said, "Have it your way. I'm going to tell you no matter what."

As the sheriff talked, John had to sit down to listen. The details of her life horrified him.

"Just seven years old," the sheriff said. "Younger than your daughter, beaten every day, sleeping outside and working to support her drunken father."

John's stomach churned. He stood and went to the open window to take a deep breath and gain control of himself. "She didn't need to become a prostitute."

"Not many choices for an illiterate fourteen-year-old out here that don't include a man."

John turned. "Illiterate?"

"Amazing, isn't she? She couldn't read or write when she got here. She taught herself and worked hard to stay ahead of the students."

"Sheriff, I appreciate your coming by, but —"

"Lucia told me that your daughter is upset and crying." The sheriff stood. "Think about what you're doing, Sullivan. Your daughter already lost one mother. Now she's lost another because you can't accept the love of a good woman." He turned toward the door. "Doesn't make sense to me."

"What you said sickens me, Sheriff, but what kind of man could forgive and accept that woman's lies and her past?"

The sheriff looked back at him. "Only a good Christian could, John."

He watched the sheriff leave and soon heard the front door shut behind him. For a moment, he considered what Bennett had said about Annie. It didn't change the fact that he'd had fallen in love with a prostitute. He'd been deceived and he couldn't forgive that. Guess he wasn't that much of a Christian. The idea of forgiveness had never sat well with him.

When Annie heard Amanda in the kitchen the next morning, relief filled her. Now she could stop pretending to be asleep.

She'd barely been able to sleep, all night, she'd looked out the window. She'd sat on the edge of the bed, thinking and praying. She knew God had heard, and felt the comfort of His presence holding her in love.

Whatever happened, she wouldn't face it alone.

She rolled out of the tiny bed, washed up and straightened her clothing before she went out to the kitchen. In the early light, she checked her watch. Only six-thirty.

"Breakfast?" Amanda asked, then she gasped when she saw Annie. "Didn't you get any sleep?"

"A bit. Do I look that bad?" Annie tried to smile. "I'll sleep later, after I see Willie Preston. I'm not hungry, but thank you." She looked at her friend. "You're really becoming a homemaker, aren't you? Cooking and cleaning house?"

Amanda nodded, refusing to be distracted. "Coffee?"

Annie shook her head and walked to the window. Dark clouds roiled across the sky and the wind blew so hard the trees bent before its strength. "Do you think it will rain?"

"Probably not." The sheriff entered the room and sat at the table. "Looks like perfect conditions for dry lightning. Hope we don't get any."

After Amanda made a few attempts at conversation, they all finished breakfast in silence. Then the sheriff took a gulp of coffee and pulled Amanda to him.

"Goodbye." He kissed her, then turned toward the door. "Annie, don't you forget we're your friends."

Annie watched him ride out, holding onto his hat as the wind tried to tear it from his fingers. Once he'd left, she turned to Amanda. "I'm going out now."

"You can't." Amanda dipped a plate in the dishpan and picked up a towel. "The weather is terrible." She gestured toward the window. "You can't go out there."

"I have to meet Willie Preston. I want to know why he came to Trail's End, and I have to stand up to him." She hugged her friend. "I'll be fine. I'll be back as soon as I talk to him."

"But you're almost ninety minutes early."

"I'll be fine," Annie repeated.

When she opened the door, the blast of wind hit her, almost pushing her back into the house. Leaning forward, she forced her way through the gusts that tore at her hair and clothing. Above her, dark storm clouds scuttled across the sky.

With the struggle against the searing, dusky blast, the walk took over an hour, nearly three times longer than usual. Upon her arrival, she looked around the plain but saw only the blowing grass that looked like a dry ocean.

Almost nine o'clock. He would be here soon.

After a few minutes of being buffeted by the wind, she sought shelter under a live oak, sitting against the rough bark of its trunk. Time passed, but there was still no sign of Preston. With an exhausted sigh, she rested her head on the tree trunk and closed her eyes, just for a moment.

Annie awoke with a start. How long had she slept? She blinked and covered her eyes as dust blew into her face. The clouds churned, dark and ugly, but no rain fell from them. In the distance she saw a flash of lightning.

Dry lightning, the plague of a parched prairie.

It took a moment for her to wake up enough to become aware of her surroundings. She leaned forward and took a deep breath. Thick smoke filled her lungs. Annie took a deeper breath. Yes, smoke. A roar reverberated across the meadow. She leaped to her feet and looked around her.

The fire must have started from a stroke of dry lightning while she slept. Or perhaps Willie Preston had started it. Not that it mattered.

From the east she saw smoke and flames,

blown by the storm and headed directly toward her and the Sullivan ranch. With no thought for her own safety, she began to run. She had to get there before the fire did. She had to warn them.

As she sprinted across the rapidly closing space, she realized how quickly the wind raced and swirled across the plain. Flames leapt and spun and sowed more fires all over the prairie. The new conflagrations were fed by the maelstrom and moving much faster than Annie could. In no time, the blaze surrounded her, a huge roaring circle closing in.

To the south, she saw an opening. Could she reach it before it closed?

Hot air scorched her lungs and she gasped for air in short pants as she ran. She pushed herself, coming nearer and nearer to the quickly disappearing space.

Intent on reaching the gap, she almost didn't hear the distant call for help. Stopping, she turned west. When she'd run twenty yards and could see the top of the ranch house, she heard people yelling on the other side of the blaze, their words indistinguishable but their panic unmistakable.

After a few more feet, she saw the reason. Elizabeth stood perhaps fifty feet from her, and a glowing, crackling wall of fire separated the child from the house.

With a burst of speed, she dashed toward her and shouted, "Elizabeth!"

"Miss Cunningham!" Elizabeth ran toward Annie and launched herself into her teacher's arms. "My father said you were gone," she sobbed.

"I'm here now." Annie clenched the child to her chest. "We have to get out of here." She put the child down and tore off part of her own skirt. "Put this over your nose and breathe through it." She placed another piece over her own mouth and nose, picked Elizabeth up and ran toward the narrowing passage on the south end of the blaze. "Hold on tight."

"I was just playing next to the stock tank. I didn't notice the fire until I couldn't get out."

"I'm here. You'll be fine." But Annie knew she couldn't run fast enough holding Elizabeth, even as tiny as she was.

"I'm going to put you down now," Annie said, and pointed. "See that opening down there? We're going to run to it together. Hold my hand. I know you can run really fast."

Elizabeth clung more tightly to Annie's neck. "No, don't put me down," she sobbed.

"I'm scared. Don't leave me."

Annie looked up in time to see the gap to the south close as two fires met in an astounding blaze. She had to find a way to save the terrified child. "Let's go back to where you were."

"But there's fire, Miss Cunningham. Father and Duffy tried to save me, but they couldn't get through."

"I'll think of something." *Dear Lord, please help me think of something.*

As they ran toward the stock tank, Annie studied the fire. Six-feet high and collapsing in on them. She looked around her. She could put Elizabeth in the tank until the blaze passed but thought there wasn't nearly enough water to cover her, and the child would be so frightened alone.

"Look, Miss Cunningham! The fire's almost as high as the roof!" Elizabeth began to sob.

"Elizabeth!" someone called from the other side of the fire.

"I'm here with her!" Annie shouted.

Of course being together only meant that she and Elizabeth would both die in the blaze if she didn't think of something. If the flames didn't kill them, the smoke would.

"Elizabeth, get in the water." She took her to the stock tank. Obediently, the child followed her direction. "Throw me a blanket!" she shouted to the group on the other side.

She waited for the blanket as the flames raced closer. It finally arrived, tied in a ball and soaring over the fire.

"What now, Miss Cunningham?" Elizabeth was coughing so much Annie could barely understand her words.

"Stand up and wring your skirt to get as much of the water out as you can. I'm going to dip the blanket in there."

"Won't the water make me safer?"

"Yes, but I'm going to wrap you in the blanket and throw you over the flame. You'll be too heavy with too much water in your clothing."

"Throw me?" Tears mixed with soot on Elizabeth's face.

Annie knelt beside the child. "Pretend you're the alle-over ball. I'm going to toss you over the flame and into your father's arms."

A smile glimmered. "Pretend I'm the alle-over ball? I can do that."

Annie nodded and grabbed the wet blanket, wrung it out and wrapped Elizabeth in it. She closed the blanket tightly, took the four corners and tied them together, then shouted as she approached the narrowest section of flames. "I'm going to toss Elizabeth to you! Get ready! You'll have to catch her!"

Elizabeth was a lot heavier than the ball they used for alle-over but Annie hoped she'd be able to do it. It was her only idea, her only option. If this didn't work, if she tossed the child into the flames, it meant death. But if she could gather all her strength to make this throw, at least the child would survive.

"Hold still, Elizabeth." She stood sideways, held the knot on the blanket tightly with both hands. Using every bit of muscle she could muster, she swung the blanket back, then forward and let it go at the highest arc.

"Here she comes!" she shouted as the blanket cleared the flames. Within a second she heard a cheer. "We got her!"

"Thank You, God," she whispered.

The flame crackled, close and hot. She had only a few more seconds to breathe. Hurrying to the tank, she stood in it to dampen her skirt and then ripped her wet petticoat off and wound it around her hands and covered her head. Could she make it through? If she didn't try, death was certain.

"Annie!" she heard John cry.

"I'm coming." Taking a breath through the wet cotton, she located a place in the flame that looked narrow and began to run through the fire, her sodden skirt ensnaring her legs.

Flames licked at her, catching her sleeves on fire and swirling around her body. It felt as if the heat were melting her bones and flesh. Finally, she couldn't move any farther, couldn't stand up any longer. As she began to sink into the inferno, hands caught her and pulled her out while someone poured water on her.

She didn't remember anything after that for a long time.

When she awoke in a dark room, Lucia was kneeling on the floor beside her, praying. Annie's lips were parched and her throat and lungs hurt when she attempted to speak.

"Water," she croaked.

"Oh, Miss Cunningham, you woke up!" Lucia held the glass out and slowly trickled the liquid down Annie's throat and on her dry lips.

Waves of pain swept over Annie's body. Her arms were wrapped in something, as were her feet and legs. Her hands were slathered with balm.

"How long?" she whispered, after painfully swallowing the water.

"Two days. The doctor gave you medicine for the pain, to help you sleep."

"The fire?" she whispered.

"It rained. Only minutes after you came through the blaze, the clouds opened and it rained and put the fire out."

Rain. That was good. She fell asleep again.

The fifth day after the fire, she awakened to see John and Elizabeth by her side. Elizabeth leaned over, careful not to touch Annie. "I'm fine, Miss Cunningham. Only a few burns. Thank you."

Annie tried to smile.

"Thank you for saving my daughter," John said.

Were there tears on his cheek? Probably tears of joy for his daughter. Then she noticed his hands, both heavily bandaged.

"That was you?" she asked. "You pulled me through the fire?"

"Yes."

"Thank you." Of course. He was a good man. He'd have helped anyone caught in the fire. She closed her eyes and fell back to sleep.

The next day, Annie examined her injuries as Amanda changed the wrappings.

"I trimmed a little of your hair that was burned, but the petticoat protected your head and hands well." She moved down to unwind the bandages on Annie's legs. "The doctor said we can leave these off today. Your legs weren't burned too badly and the shoes protected your feet. But your ankles." She shook her head.

Then Amanda leaned back. "The worst burns are on your arms and your lungs."

Annie bit her lip as Amanda attempted to remove the wrappings slowly and gently. "I'll have scars."

Amanda nodded.

"Will I be able to write?" She looked at her hands, which were puffy and blackened.

"The doctor believes you'll heal completely, except for the scars." Amanda attempted to blink back tears. "You were so brave. You saved Elizabeth."

"When can I leave here?"

"John says you may stay for as long as you wish."

"How long does the doctor say?" she whispered, having trouble catching her breath.

"No one knows. You have to heal."

She nodded and closed her eyes again, remembering the hands that had reached out to save her.

A week later, Annie stood at the window. The rain had lasted two days, she'd been told. She could see the scarred section of the prairie where the fire had raged, but the rest was thick and green. Pink flox and orange-red standing cypress poked their heads up through the luxurious grass. Here and there she saw the fragile purple petals of the wine cup.

"Annie."

She turned to see John in the doorway. It was strange to hear him use her real name.

"You're leaving now?" No affection showed in his eyes.

"Yes. Amanda has asked me to spend a few days with her before I decide where to go."

He nodded again. "I'd like you to know that I've reconsidered my earlier words and actions."

"Oh?"

"Yes, I'd like for you to stay here. Because my daughter loves you and you saved her life, I'm grateful and willing to forgive you. Therefore, I'm asking you again to marry me."

Her gaze flew to his face but still no emotion showed there. He stood stiffly, his weight balanced on both feet, his healing hands at his sides. Annie didn't feel a proposal that started with *therefore* came with a promise of eternal love.

"Why would you do that?"

"It's what a Christian would do."

She blinked. He'd asked her because it was his duty.

"No, thank you." She picked up her purse and headed toward the door. Although her legs still hurt, she refused to allow him to see that.

He started to take her arm, but she pulled away. She refused to lean on him again. He dropped his hand.

"But you must marry me. Certainly you know you cannot go back into the world alone again. Here you'll be cared for."

"Thank you, John, but no." She moved past him and, holding on to the rail, slowly descended the stairs.

"You're not well enough," he said. "You still need to rest."

Even though she heard the pleading in his voice, his words didn't stop her. "Thank you for your hospitality and care." And she walked out the door without a backward glance.

Once outside the house, she refused Duffy's hand and pulled herself into the phaeton. The ride was not comfortable, but she sat up proudly.

For the first time in many years, she'd stood up for herself. She'd said "no" to a man. Although John may not realize it, she was a blessed and beloved child of God, a person of value, worthy of love and deserving of forgiveness.

CHAPTER EIGHTEEN

Out of all the choices that had been forced on him, John knew he'd made one correct decision. He just wasn't sure which one it was.

At first, he'd believed he was right to break the engagement. After all, he'd spent his whole life as a moral leader of the community, an elder of the church, an example to all of the decent, ethical ways to live. He'd asked a fallen woman to marry him not once but twice. Showing no gratitude at all, she'd refused the second time, an action he now admired greatly considering the manner in which he'd presented it.

But the more time that passed, the less certain he became about his decisions, about which was the right one.

When he thought about her, he had to remind himself of the grievous sin she'd committed so he wouldn't soften his opinion of her. But now he wondered, why didn't judging immoral behavior feel right to him anymore? Why wasn't it enough to be both right and righteous?

Three days after Annie's departure from his home, he spent the evening with Farley Hanson and several bankers and cattlemen from Llano County, discussing the rumors about the railroad. If it came through, what route would it take? What land would be bought? Who'd make money and who wouldn't?

Once the men left, John felt alone, very much alone. Because he hadn't convinced Annie to stay, Elizabeth was angry with him. He hoped she would forgive him but for now she was in her bedroom, refusing to talk to him. Lucia and Ramon were polite to him as usual, but not warm.

Duffy told him right out to his face that he was a fool. Duffy pretty much described the whole problem only he didn't go far enough. A stiff-necked fool who didn't know how to change. Oh, he bet Duffy could add even more to that picture, but John preferred not to give him another chance.

He didn't like who he was and apparently no one else did, either.

Before he headed upstairs, John looked out across the scorched strip of land between the ranch and the schoolhouse. For a moment he remembered Annie, how she looked playing alle-over with the children, her hair spilling down, her face flushed and happy. She had glowed with pride for her students at the Christmas program. He thought of the sheriff's words, of her terrible childhood and her remarkable transformation after she arrived in Trail's End.

No wonder he'd detected a little panic when he first met her, after he'd told her she was the schoolteacher. How desperate she must have felt. She'd looked as if she wanted to turn and run, but she hadn't. Instead, she'd taught herself to read and write. She'd found a way to survive and had lived a moral life since her arrival. Annie MacAllister was a survivor and a remarkable woman. He admired her greatly.

In fact, he still loved her, but he had no idea what to do about it. At the moment, his high standards were of very little comfort and wouldn't bring him warmth and love, not like Annie would.

A few hours after midnight, he climbed the stairs but didn't go to the bed. He knew he wouldn't sleep because he didn't sleep at all anymore. He looked again at the charred swatch in the land and at the graveyard where Celeste and his parents lay. Finally, he allowed his eyes to move toward the schoolhouse.

The building was dark. Not a flicker of light shone through the windows. Of course not. She wasn't there. The longer he stood looking out at the dark, empty schoolhouse, the more obvious it was that Annie would never return to his life again.

In spite of her deception, in spite of her past, he couldn't forget her warmth and her love and her laughter and all the things that had made her the woman he cherished, in spite of everything.

Or maybe, because of all that. The woman who escaped from her terrible past and had built a respectful life and gave back to the community was a far stronger, braver woman than he'd realized — far more courageous than he.

What would she do if he went to her? If he were a different man, he could do that, but he was the upstanding son of Joshua Matthew Sullivan, heir to over sixty years of Texas history.

As he thought of the rest of his life without her, his soul groaned in anguish, a torment that continued to grow worse with each passing day.

What was he going to do?

A sob escaped his lips. Almost before he knew it, his legs collapsed beneath him, and he fell to the floor on his knees with his hands clenched in prayer. It was like nothing he'd ever done before, but never had his soul been in such agony. In fact, he'd never quite realized he had a soul until the pain began.

"Dear God, what should I do?" Tears ran down his face. He couldn't think of anything else to say. "What should I do?"

As he knelt, he felt a presence around him and within. The assurance of God's closeness filled him. It was as if God knelt beside him and shared his agony. Overwhelmed by the knowledge that he couldn't face the shambles of his life alone, he attempted to accept his utter dependence on God, to place his life in God's hands.

Giving up his self-reliance was not comfortable for John. For nearly an hour he struggled, until he realized the peace that flooded him felt so much better than his constant resistance and his efforts to control his life. Finally he whispered, "I turn my life over to You, Lord. Please help me."

He was not a man who poured out his feelings to anyone, but he'd never felt such serenity, comfort and understanding before. Letting down the last barrier, he prayed, "I still love her, Lord. What should I do?"

The answer came to him — so clear, so

easy — as he remembered the words of the Scripture he himself had read at church. "Jesus said unto her, 'Neither do I condemn thee: go, and sin no more.' " He repeated the words aloud. "Neither do I condemn thee: go, and sin no more."

From what she'd said, Annie knew Jesus had forgiven her. Wasn't he incredibly presumptuous not to?

Filled with peace and assured of God's leading, he stood and looked out the window again. The darkness didn't seem as bleak to him. He fell into bed and slept immediately, finally certain of God's guidance and the calm acceptance that had eluded him for so long.

"I wish you'd stay longer." Amanda folded Annie's blue basque and placed it in the valise. "I'm going to cook something new tonight, a pineapple upside-down cake. I'd love to have your help."

"Sounds good." Annie studied herself in the mirror. Amanda had arranged her hair so the burns on her neck were covered. Most of the redness on her face had disappeared in the weeks since the fire. Her hands showed only a few patches of red against the pink skin. The long sleeves of her basque covered the dressings on her arms. Although the pain hadn't disappeared completely and she still struggled to breathe occasionally, she'd regained most of her strength. "It's time for me to go."

"Everyone will miss you."

Over the weeks of Annie's recuperation, people had dropped by, bringing food and small gifts for her, asking her to stay. As far as she could tell, no one had heard about her past.

She'd decided to remain Matilda Susan Cunningham until she left because explanations seemed foolish and hurtful now. Let the students and their parents remember her as a fine teacher.

"You have the recommendation I wrote for you?"

Annie nodded.

"You know you don't have to worry about Willie Preston. Cole tossed him out of town and told him never to come back. He told Preston to tell Roy Martin the same."

"That's good to know."

"I hope you'll teach again." Amanda sat on the bed.

She shook her head. "I'm through with that. I'll go to a big city, use my new name, and be a shop girl." She smiled at Amanda to comfort her. "That was what I'd always dreamed of doing. I'll be fine."

"Why don't you lie down and rest? The stage doesn't leave for two hours."

Annie nodded. The preparation to leave had exhausted her. "Thank you for taking care of Minnie." She picked up the cat and scratched her ears. "I'll miss her."

"Mr. Sullivan?" Lucia tapped on the door. "Breakfast is ready."

He sat up. The sun streamed through his window. "What time is it?"

"It's nearly ten o'clock."

He never slept that late, but he couldn't be angry with Lucia. She had firm instructions never to wake him.

However, he had things to do this morning. Leaping out of bed and feeling better than he had in a long time, he got ready to start the day, a day he hoped would end far more happily than it had begun.

The first thing he did after he washed and dressed was to find Elizabeth, and apologize to her. Next he grabbed a bit of breakfast while Ramon hitched the horses to the surrey. By ten-thirty, he'd left the ranch and tooled along the road to the sheriff's new house where he'd heard she was staying.

No one was home.

He knocked on every door and window. He looked inside, going all the way around the house twice. Both times, Minnie sat in the parlor window and meowed. That was good, right? Annie wouldn't leave Minnie behind, would she?

John checked on the horses in the stable and found only the stable boy. All the boy knew was that everyone had left nearly an hour earlier, including the pretty schoolteacher with her suitcase.

John couldn't be too late. He couldn't.

It took only minutes to get to town. The stagecoach didn't leave until eleven. She couldn't be gone, not yet. Certainly he had time. Thoughts, worries and reproaches echoed through his brain.

When he reached town, he saw Amanda's phaeton next to the hotel. Annie was with her. Carefully, she swung out of the carriage. Once on the road, she picked up her valise and placed it next to her.

She was leaving town today.

He'd known she would at some point. She'd told him. The sheriff had told him. He'd just never considered that she really would, not until he could make some sense out of what had happened between them. Had he dithered too long? Had he left his apology until too late? Still he couldn't move as he drank in the sight of her.

Her hair was different, swooped low over

her ears and in a braid on the nape of her neck. She was thinner, almost willowy now. When she smiled at Amanda, he felt as if he'd been kicked in the stomach. She was so lovely.

And she was leaving.

What was he going to do? He knew what he *should* do. He knew what he and God had decided together only a few hours ago, but he couldn't move.

Then he heard the sound of the stagecoach coming into town. In a few minutes, Annie would get onto the stage and disappear from his life. He couldn't allow that.

"Annie."

Annie turned when she heard John's voice and saw him driving his carriage toward the hotel. She turned away to lift her valise off the street.

"John, what are you doing here?" Amanda said from the seat of the phaeton.

He ignored her, got out of his surrey, twisted the reins around a post and crossed to Annie. Taking the valise from her hands, he said, "Please don't go."

Annie attempted to wrestle the bag away from him. "Mr. Sullivan —"

"Please, you used to call me John."

"I called you *John* when I was Matilda

347

Susan Cunningham, your fiancée." Anger so consumed her that, with a strong tug, she pulled the satchel from his hand and turned away.

"I don't care who you are, Annie or Matilda or Miss Cunningham or Miss MacAllister. I only know I love you and want to marry you."

"John, there's quite a crowd gathering," Amanda said.

Annie looked around to see faces peering from all the stores while people spilled out of the buildings.

"I don't care," he repeated.

"You don't care?" Annie said.

"All I care about is you." He paused and cleared his throat. "I'm sorry for everything I said and did. I can't tell you how sorry I am."

"Mr. Sullivan," Annie whispered. "I'm Annie MacAllister. I always will be. You can't pretend I'm not. If you can't accept who I was and what I did, I can understand that." She turned away. "Please leave me alone. I'm getting on the stagecoach in a few minutes."

"Annie, I love you and accept everything you did to survive." When she didn't answer, he said loudly and clearly, "I love you."

The watching crowd murmured and

laughed.

"John, we're in the middle of town." She looked around. More people had joined the crowd. "There are dozens of people watching. You can't say that out here."

"I prayed about this. I asked God to forgive me for being so stiff-necked."

"You did?" Annie asked.

John took her hands. "I don't care about the past. I want us to be together. I want you to be my wife."

"Why? Because that's what a Christian does?"

"No." He shook his head. "No, because I love you. Please forgive me."

She looked at him, at the pleading in his eyes. "I can't," she whispered.

"I hurt you too much. Please forgive me." He gazed at her. "Will you marry me? I beg you."

He begged her to marry him? John Matthew Sullivan begged her to forgive him? "I can't," she whispered. "I have a past. Men like Willie Preston could appear at any time. They could hurt you and Elizabeth."

"I don't care who you are," he said in a low voice. "As Matilda or Annie, whichever you choose, you would be my wife. No one would dare to threaten my wife."

"I can't," she whispered again. "I'm afraid

of disappointing you again, of failing." With as much strength as she could muster, she took a step toward the stage but glanced back. She had to see John again before she left.

She could read both love and pain in his eyes. He wouldn't be easy to live with. He struggled for balance between his past and who he'd become, just as she did.

But he'd asked her forgiveness. As a Christian, how could she turn her back on him?

Seeing her indecision, he hurried toward her and took her hand, careful not to hurt her. "Please."

"I forgive you, but how can you forgive me? You know what I've done, you know how I lied to you."

"We'll work this out together, but God will be with us."

"God will be with us," she repeated. Did she have the courage to try?

"Will you please stay and marry me?"

She watched him and considered his expression, which looked stripped of all pride. In its place she found warmth and love. Warm blue eyes pleaded with her.

She nodded. "I'll stay." She dropped the valise.

"And marry me?" he persisted.

She nodded. "I love you, John."

"Thank you, God!" he shouted, then he put his hands around Annie's waist and lifted her in the air, turning round and round. Then, to the delight of the cheering crowd, he carried her to his surrey and gently settled her in the seat before he climbed in beside her.

"Let's go tell Elizabeth." He pulled her next to him and whispered, "I'll love you forever, Annie."

In that moment, surrounded by people who cared about them, with puffy clouds floating across a clear blue Texas sky and the cactus blossoms blooming yellow and purple, Annie knew she wasn't the only one blessed.

John Matthew Sullivan had received a second chance, as well.

Dear Reader,

When I started to research this book, I discovered that alle-over was a popular schoolyard game in central Texas in the nineteenth century. Imagine my amazement to remember my father and my brother playing the same game when I was a child. They would stand, one on each side of the garage. One would throw the ball across the roof and shout, "Alle-over." Then they would run around the garage. My father learned this as a child from his father.

The game Annie MacAllister and her students played is a link between my past and my present — the game Dad learned so long ago occurring in a book I've just written.

That's what Annie learned: her past was part of her present, no matter how she attempted to hide it. But she also learned that the God of the Bible and the Savior who died on the cross centuries ago are still with us, still active today, leading and guiding us in our present and toward our eternal future.

Jane Myers Perrine

QUESTIONS FOR DISCUSSION

1. Annie has lived a hard life. Even as she attempts to escape it, her past follows her. Has there been an event or action in your past you have tried to hide or get away from or forgive? How did your faith help you?

2. During church Annie hears a scripture that changes her. What scriptures have been important in your life? How?

3. John's faith has mostly been a matter of expectations: going to church was what a member of his family did. Have you ever felt this way? Do you know someone who has? How did your faith become deeper for you?

4. Because of his family background and his pride in his family's history, John feels he must live his life in a certain way. Do you

know people who allow their pride to divide them from God or from others? Would hearing the scripture that changes Annie help these people or would they still be likely to judge?

5. Because of her childhood, Annie finds it hard to trust people, to believe that people will accept her. Has there been an experience in your life that affected you in the same way? How did you overcome it or compensate for it?

6. During a time of sorrow, Annie's father changed. What words from the Scriptures might help a person who allows traumatic events in life to turn them away from God and those who love them? What words of healing could you use?

7. Have you had a friend who has gone through a time when his or her faith was tested? Did you find a way to support this friend? How?

8. Annie has to decide either to tell the truth and lose everything or to continue with a life she loves. How would you decide which to do? Do you believe Annie's

choice was correct? Why?

9. Has there been a moment in your life when you had to take a stand for something you believed? Have you ever faced a time when this stand cost you what you wanted most? How did you handle that?

10. Annie learns that she can overcome her difficult past through hard work. Do you believe this is possible, or do you believe people are constantly judged by their choices, even though they may have repented? Does God allow us a second chance? Can you give an example in your life of a second chance?

11. If we see problems in our friends' lives — broken personal relationships, addictions — how can we speak a word of healing?

12. How often should we forgive others? The title of the book suggests giving others a second chance, but in Matthew, Jesus tells us to forgive seventy times seven. What do you believe? Why? Could you have forgiven Annie for her lies and her past? Why and how?

13. John finally recognizes that he's judgmental and controlling. Do you believe we can overcome these traits? Do you know people like this? How can they change? Can faith help? How?

ABOUT THE AUTHOR

Jane Myers Perrine grew up in Kansas City, Missouri, has a B.A. from Kansas State University and an M.Ed. in Spanish from the University of Louisville. She has taught high school Spanish in five states. Presently she teaches in the beautiful hill country of Texas. Her husband is minister of a Christian church in Central Texas where Jane teaches an adult Sunday school class. Jane was a finalist in the Regency category of the Golden Heart Awards. Her short pieces have appeared in the *Houston Chronicle, Woman's World* magazine and other publications. The Perrines share their home with two spoiled cats and an arthritic cocker spaniel. Readers can visit her Web page, www.janemyersperrine.com.

The employees of Thorndike Press hope you have enjoyed this Large Print book. All our Thorndike, Wheeler, and Kennebec Large Print titles are designed for easy reading, and all our books are made to last. Other Thorndike Press Large Print books are available at your library, through selected bookstores, or directly from us.

For information about titles, please call:
(800) 223-1244

or visit our Web site at:
http://gale.cengage.com/thorndike

To share your comments, please write:
Publisher
Thorndike Press
295 Kennedy Memorial Drive
Waterville, ME 04901